Along Came a Cowboy

A Romantic Showdown
in Small-Town Arkansas

Christine Lynxwiler

BARBOUR
PUBLISHING

ISBN 978-1-59789-896-6

For more information about Christine Lynxwiler, please access the author's Web site at the following Internet address: www.christinelynxwiler.com

Cover design by The DesignWorks Group

Published by Barbour Publishing, Inc., P.O. Box 719, Uhrichsville, OH 44683, www.barbourbooks.com

Our mission is to publish and distribute inspirational products offering exceptional value and biblical encouragement to the masses.

ecpa Member of the
Evangelical Christian
Publishers Association

Printed in the United States of America

Dedication/Acknowledgments

Every chiropractor who loves, gives, and serves unselfishly,
striving to make the world a healthier place,
one patient at a time. God bless you all.

And to my favorite chiropractor and very own hero,
Dr. Kevin Lynxwiler, who constantly shows me
the true meaning of sacrificial giving,
both with his patients and with his family.

With special thanks to:
Susan May Warren, Annalisa Daughety, Sandy Gaskin,
Jan Reynolds, Vicky Daughety, Tracey Bateman,
Susan K. Downs, Rachel Hauck, Ellen Tarver,
Dean Miller, and Rebecca Germany.
This book took a village, and y'all are an amazing village!

In Him we have redemption through His blood,
the forgiveness of our trespasses,
according to the riches of His grace.
EPHESIANS 1:7 NASB

1	5	7	6	2			8	
		9		7	4		6	5
4	3	6	5			7	2	
			9	6	7	5	1	
9	1					6	4	7
7	6	5	4	1			9	
	7	2			6	1	5	
6			8				7	
5	9		7	4			3	6

67

GENTLE **MODERATE** TOUGH FIENDISH

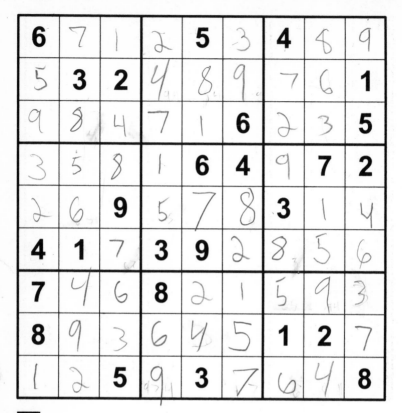

6	7	1	2	5	3	4	8	9
5	3	2	4	8	9	7	6	1
9	8	4	7	1	6	2	3	5
3	5	8	1	6	4	9	7	2
2	6	9	5	7	8	3	1	4
4	1	7	3	9	2	8	5	6
7	4	6	8	2	1	5	9	3
8	9	3	6	4	5	1	2	7
1	2	5	9	3	7	6	4	8

66

123456789

GENTLE   MODERATE   TOUGH   FIENDISH

Chapter 1

Babies complicate life, but the human race can't survive without them. Maybe I should write that on the dry erase board out in the waiting room—Dr. Rachel Donovan's Profound Thought for the Day.

Ever notice how some months are all about weddings? When you turn on the TV or pick up a magazine, everything is white tulle and old lace. Then there are what I think of as baby months. Unlike June and December for weddings, baby months can pop up anytime.

And here in Shady Grove, Arkansas—just in time for summer, when the irises are pushing up from the ground, the new leaves are green on the trees, and the crepe myrtles are starting to bloom—we're smack dab in the middle of a baby month.

I finger the latest birth announcement on my desk. One of my patients just had her fifth child. You'd think, at this point, she'd be sending out SOS messages instead of announcements, but the pink card proudly proclaims the arrival of her newest bundle of joy.

The front door chime signals the arrival of our first patient, so I send up a silent prayer for the baby. Then my eyes fall on the family picture on my desk.

Lord, please be with Tammy, too, in her pregnancy.

My thirty-eight-year-old sister was so thrilled when she called a couple of months ago to tell me she was pregnant and so scared yesterday when the doctor put her on temporary bed rest.

While I'm on the baby thread, I mention my friend Lark who is desperate to adopt. I say amen, steadfastly ignoring my own out-of-whack biological clock.

My receptionist, Norma, sidles into my office like a spy in an old movie, softly shuts the door and turns to face me, her brown eyes wide. "Whoever warned mamas not to let their babies grow up to be cowboys," she whispers, "never saw the man in our waiting room."

"What?" I absently flip through the small pile of files on my desk. Not long ago I remodeled my entire clinic—repainted the walls with calming blues and browns, added new chiropractic tables and new waiting room chairs, and even got solid oak office furniture with nifty little cubbies. For about a week I could find things.

And did she just say the word *babies*? What did I tell you? It's one of those months. "Do you know where Mrs. Faulkner's file is? I thought it was here, but I can't find it."

Norma raises her eyebrows. "You saw her after hours Tuesday night, didn't you? I think it's on my desk waiting for charges."

Now I remember. "No charge," I say automatically.

She puts her hands on her hips. "C'mon, Doc, you can't fall for every sob story you hear."

I grin. "We make it, don't we? If I can't help out a sixty-two-year-old woman who lifts and bathes and cares for her grown son around the clock, then I'd just as soon not be in practice."

She shrugs. "You're the one who has to worry about paying your bills. I get my paycheck regardless." Her round face lights up and she motions to me. "Now come look."

Norma's always slightly out of sync with reality, but today is shaping up to be odd even for her.

"At the man in the waiting room," she clarifies, as if I'm a little slow. "You have to see him."

"I usually do see everyone who's in the waiting room, don't I? Eventually?"

She blows out her breath and folds her arms. "It'll only take a second."

"Who is it?"

She shakes her head, her short brunette curls springing with the movement. "I'm not telling. You'll have to see for yourself."

I sigh. I know I'm the boss, but once Norma has something in her head, it's easier just to go along with her. She turns to lead the way out to her desk where a large window overlooks the main waiting room. I promise she's tiptoeing.

"Hey, Nancy Drew," I say quietly.

She jumps and spins around. "What?" she hisses.

I grin. "Let's try not to be so obvious."

She presses her back against the wall and motions for me to go ahead of her. I saunter to her desk. Right on top is the file I was looking for. At least this wasn't a wasted trip. I retrieve it while I give the waiting room a cursory glance. The cowboy chooses that moment to look up, of course. A slow grin spreads across his face.

I fumble with the file and almost drop it.

Jack Westwood.

I don't believe it. Alma Westwood could give the-little-engine-that-could lessons in persistence. I return his grin with a quick professional smile and—holding the file high enough that he can see I had a valid reason for being there—walk back to my office.

Norma is right on my heels. She closes the door. "So? What did I tell you? That's Alma Westwood's son. The rodeo star."

"I know who he is." I toss the file on my desk and plop down in my chair to look at it.

"You know him?"

I shake my head. "We were friends when we were kids, but I don't know him really. I've just seen his picture in the paper like everyone else." And since he moved back a few months ago, I've seen him around town enough to know that women fall all over themselves when he walks by. Definitely not my type. Which is *one* reason I've avoided him.

"Oh yeah. His hat was shading his face in that picture." Her brows draw together. "Which is a cryin' shame."

I look up at her cherub face. "Hey, remember old What's His Name? The handsome guy you're happily married to?" I grin.

She shrugs. "Doesn't mean I'm blind. Besides, *you* aren't married."

Thanks for the reminder.

"So when Alma signed in, she said she brought her son to see her new X-rays."

"How nice." Not that I'm falling for her flimsy excuse. Alma is just one in a long line of Mama Matchmakers. My patients with unmarried sons seem to take my singlehood as a personal affront. Ever since Rodeo Jack moved back to run his family ranch next door to my parents, Alma has upped her efforts to make me her daughter-in-law, or at least reintroduce me to him.

Don't ask me why Jack needs his mama to fix him up with someone in the first place. Norma is not exaggerating. He was passably cute back when we were kids, and he's one of those men who gets better-looking with age. If he's lost any teeth or broken his nose riding in the rodeo, he's covered it well. Not only is he a real cowboy, but he could play one on TV. Last week at the diner, I was two tables away from him when he smiled at the waitress. For a moment I was jealous that the smile wasn't for me. But only for a moment.

Then common sense kicked in. Me and Jack Westwood? Not likely. Which is just as well, because on a less personal note. . .a chiropractor and a rodeo star? What a combination. I'd spend the rest of my life trying to fix the mess he makes of his body. Besides, I can't imagine myself with someone whose belt buckle is bigger than his IQ. And even though he seemed smart when we were in school, as far as I'm concerned, anyone who'll willingly climb on a bucking bull over and over is a few calves short of a herd.

Still, it's my job to educate patients and their families about their health. I turn back to Norma. "After you put them in a room, pull Alma's X-rays for me, okay?"

Norma starts to leave then smacks her forehead with the palm of her hand. "Oh, I almost forgot. Lark Murray is on line one."

I glance at the phone. Sure enough, line one is blinking. "Thanks."

Never mind that we let Lark sit and wait while we sneaked a peek at Alma's cowboy son. Norma marches to her own drummer, and I run along behind her trying to stay in step.

I reach toward the phone, and for a split second, I consider having Norma take a message. Lark is one of my three closest friends. I'm a few years younger than the rest and came late to the Pinky Promise Sisterhood group they formed in childhood. But ever since the night they found me crying in the bowling alley bathroom, the Pinkies have been family to me. We share our deepest secrets and craziest dreams and—now that we all live in Shady Grove, Arkansas, again—regular face-to-face gabfests.

And any other day of the year, I'm happy to hear from any of them. But this particular anniversary day is always filled with awkward conversations. They never know what to say, and neither do I.

I snatch the handset up before I give in to my cowardice. I'll just make it short and sweet. "Hey, girl."

"Rach, I'm so glad I caught you. I was afraid you'd already started with patients."

"No. Sorry you had to wait." Here it comes. The gentle "You okay today?" Or the "Just called to say hi and wish you a good day for no particular reason."

"I can't take this anymore." Her voice is trembling.

Okay, I wasn't expecting that. "What?"

"The waiting. Why do they make us go through an inspection worthy of a Spanish Inquisition if they're not going to give us a baby?"

I release a breath I didn't know I was holding and sink back onto my chair. Lark is focused on one thing and one thing only these days, so thankfully this call isn't about me. "They're going to give you a baby. They'd be crazy not to. These things just take time."

"You sound like the caseworker." She sighs. "I called her last night even though Craig didn't think I should."

"Lark, honey, I know it's hard to wait now that you've finally decided to adopt. But you're going to have to. God has—" My throat constricts, but I push the words out. "God has the perfect baby for you."

"It doesn't feel like it." She must be upset, because that's definitely a bit of a whine, something she never does.

"Has He ever let you down?"

10

"No. But maybe I was right before. Maybe it's just not His will for me to be a mom."

I thought we'd settled all that a few months ago when she showed up on my doorstep late one night with a suitcase because her husband wanted to adopt. Still, I can totally relate to old insecurities sneaking back in when you least expect them. "You're going to have to think about something else for a while, Lark. Are you helping Allie today?"

"I'm supposed to. I was thinking about seeing if she can make it without me though."

"How are y'all coming along?" Our Pinky friend Allie Richards recently won the Shady Grove Pre-Centennial Beautiful Town Landscaping Contest and consequently landed the town landscaping maintenance contract for the year. She has some real employees now, but during the contest her crew consisted of Allie's brother, Adam, Lark, me, and our other Pinky, Victoria Worthington. So we all have a vested emotional interest in TLC Landscaping.

Lark sighs. "We're swamped trying to get everything in perfect shape before the centennial celebration really gets going. I guess I really should work today. I know Allie needs me."

Good girl. "You know what your granny always said—a busy mind doesn't have time to worry."

"You're right. I'm going to have to trust God to handle this and go get ready for work. Thanks for talking me down off the ledge."

"Anytime."

"See you tonight, Rach."

"I'll be there." When the connection is broken, I close my eyes.

Lord, please give me strength to face today.

I open my eyes and push to my feet. Time to cowgirl up.

~

As soon as I walk into the adjusting room, Alma stands. "Dr. Donovan, I'm sure you remember my son, Jack."

Jack holds his cowboy hat in his left hand and offers me the right. I promise I expect him to say, "Ma'am," and duck his head. "Dr. Donovan," he drawls, and from the boy who used to pull my braids, the title sounds a little mocking. "Nice to see you again." As we shake hands, he flashes that heartbeat-accelerating smile again.

"You, too." His hands are nice. Slightly calloused. Working hands, but not so tough that they're like leather.

I look up into his puzzled brown eyes and then back down at his hand, which I'm *still* holding. Behind him, his mother beams as if she has personally discovered the cure for every terminal illness known to humankind. I jerk my hand away. Should I tell him that I always notice hands, since my own hands are what I use most in my profession? Or would he think that was a pickup line? I'm sure he's heard some doozies.

Better to ignore it. I slap the X-rays up on the view box then focus my attention on Alma as I point out the key spots we're working on.

When I finish, Jack crosses the room in two steps and points to the X-ray. "This increased whiteness is arthritis, right?"

My eyebrows draw together. "You've had experience with X-rays?"

He shrugs and gives me a rueful grin. "Occupational hazard."

Of course. "In any case, you're right. It *is* arthritis, but no more than normal for someone your mother's age."

"Thankfully, Dr. Donovan keeps me going. Otherwise I'd be like the Tin Man in *The Wizard of Oz*," Alma pipes up from her chair in the corner.

"To hear Mom tell it, *you're* the Wizard of Oz," Jack mutters, still standing beside me. He turns to Alma. "Your X-rays are normal?"

Her eyes open wide. "Yes."

"Totally normal?"

She blinks at him. "Isn't that wonderful?"

"Yes, but—"

"I thought you'd be pleased to know your old mom was going to be getting around without a walker for a few more years." Alma's voice is soft and sweet.

He frowns. "You know I am. But since Dr. Donovan has apparently already explained these X-rays to you, you could have told me that on the ph—" He stops, apparently realizing that I'm like a reluctant spectator at a tennis game, watching their verbal volleying.

"But this way you can see for yourself," Alma says with a satisfied smile.

He opens his mouth then closes it and nods.

Game, set, match to Alma.

I turn back to her. "Any questions?"

She smiles. "Not a one. Thank you so much for taking the time to go over this with us."

"I'm always glad to help you understand your health better."

"I'm going to go freshen up before we head home," Alma says. And just like that, she's gone, leaving me with her son. No doubt the whole point.

"Jack," I say in what I hope is a coolly professional voice, "thank you for coming by."

He nods. "I'm sorry we wasted your time. I don't know why I'm surprised this was a setup. Our mothers have been singing your praises ever since I got back in town."

"*Our* mothers?" My mother and I barely speak, and I'm

certain she's never sung my praises a day in my life. At least not since I was a teenager.

"They make you sound like Mother Teresa and the Alberts all rolled into one."

I raise a brow. "The Alberts?"

"Einstein and Schweitzer."

I can't keep from laughing. "Now that's an appealing combination. And don't forget the Wizard of Oz."

"They're probably not far off, actually. It's just that—" He runs his hands around the brim of the hat he's still holding. "Thanks for being a good sport." He grins. "And at least now when we see each other at the diner, we can say hello."

A hot blush spreads across my face. The curse of being a redhead. I blush easily and at the oddest times. It's not like he knows I was admiring him the other day while I was waiting for my food. At least, I sure hope not. "True." I open the door and step back for him to go through.

"I guess I'd better go. I'll just wait for Mom out here," he says dryly and saunters down the hall.

"Not a moment too soon," I mutter under my breath and retreat to my office for a few minutes. The last thing I need is a blast from the past. Especially in the form of a rugged, sweet-smiling cowboy.

Chapter 2

I'm mulling over the things Jack said, particularly the part about my mother, when Norma sticks her head in the door. "Problem."

"What's up?"

"The mayor's fifteen minutes early. And Mrs. Tillman walked in a minute after him, but she's on time and her appointment is before his. If I take her back to a room first, he'll be mad, but if I take him back first, that's cheating, I guess?" Her tone goes up on the last two words.

I take a deep breath and smile. I'm actually glad to have normal office things to think about. Too many of my thoughts the last few minutes have been in a Western motif. "Tell Ron that Mrs. Tillman's appointment is first and we'll be with him in just a few minutes."

"But he's the mayor."

"In this office, he's a patient. And he's no more or no less important than anyone else."

She nods. Like she's never heard me say that before.

When I finally get to him, our esteemed mayor is perched on the long padded bench in the waiting cubicle, huffing and puffing like the big bad wolf.

"Good morning, Ron." I motion him into the adjusting room.

He grunts as he hobbles past me. "Easy for you to say."

Beneath his crusty exterior is another equally crusty interior. If life in Shady Grove were a sitcom, there'd be a heart of gold buried somewhere in the mix. But this is real life, and with our mayor, I'm not so sure.

He takes his glasses off and slips them in the eyeglass holder mounted on the wall. Then he turns back to me and squints. "A person doesn't get to be Citizen of the Year by keeping the mayor waiting."

I cough to cover a laugh. "I told you last time you brought that up that I have no desire to be Citizen of the Year."

"Ah, save your 'It's just an honor to be nominated' speech for someone who believes it. Everybody wants to be noticed," he grumbles.

Not everybody. I've spent my adult life blending in, trying to be all I can be while not being noticed. Unfortunately, I ended up with too many patients who are members of the Shady Grove Civic Club. So according to Ron's top-secret info, I've been nominated for Citizen of the Year. I'm not holding my breath.

"You mark my words: This centennial celebration is going to be the death of me." He slowly moves toward the table.

I bite back a smile. "You sounded so excited about it just awhile ago at the big kick-off."

"That was before Alma Westwood started driving me crazy." He limps the last few feet.

"Are you hurting this morning, Ron?" He's seventy, but he can normally outwalk most men half his age.

He ignores my question with a wave of his hand. "She even

cornered me out here in your waiting room just now and started yakking about it. Who has a yearlong celebration anyway? Why couldn't we settle for a week like normal towns?" He cuts his gaze to me as he steps up on the foot pedestal of my hi-lo table. "You know, you'd be the perfect person to get me out of this pickle and do your civic duty at the same time."

"You're still trying to get me to be on the committee?" I grin again and shake my head. "My answer is the same as last time you asked. You'll have to find another sucker." I put one hand on his shoulder and kick the pedal to lower the table. Back to business.

When he is facedown, I lift his feet for a leg check.

"Ow!" He kicks my hand.

Not a normal reaction to a simple leg check. I carefully lower his foot. "Where's the pain?"

"My knee. Bursitis, I guess." His voice is muffled against the face paper.

"Mind if I take a look?" I kick the lever to raise him back to standing.

"Be my guest." He lifts the leg of his loose-fitting khaki pants.

I feel my eyes grow wide, but I quickly put on a professional face. "That's a lot of swelling."

He shrugs. "It is a mite big, but I figure I'm old enough to be having a few aches and pains."

"Maybe, but I don't think this is bursitis." I squat down and touch the flesh lightly with my fingers; then something at the side of his knee catches my attention. "Ron, that looks like a bite."

"A bite? What kind of a bite?" He twists his upper body around to try to see but can't.

"I can't say for sure, but it could be a spider bite. Have you seen any brown recluse spiders around?" When his wife died a few years back, Ron moved out to a little log cabin by the river. Wonderful for peace and quiet. And perfect for spiders.

He grunts. "A few. But we have a deal. I don't bother them, and they don't bother me."

I shake my head. "I'm afraid one of them didn't keep that bargain. You have to get Dr. Jackson to check this out."

"I don't have time to go to two doctors today."

I look toward my phone. "Maybe I should call an ambulance to come take you." A totally empty bluff on my part, but it gets the desired result.

"The day I can't drive myself to the doctor will be the day—" He gives me an abashed grin. Which is quickly replaced by a worried frown. "What if he tells me I have to stay off my feet? What about the centennial celebration?"

"If there's anything pressing in the next day or two, I'll take care of it for you."

"You sure?"

I nod. "You get that knee looked at and don't worry about anything else."

"I'll stop by my office and send you a few notes for the meeting tonight."

"Tonight?"

He nods. "We're supposed to meet at Coffee Central Bookstore at six."

"How many people are on the committee besides you and Alma?"

"That's the problem, actually. Why do you think I was trying to recruit you?"

"You're kidding." I'm incredulous. The centennial celebration may not be much compared to Mardi Gras or New Year's Eve at Times Square, but around here it's a huge deal. And two people are handling it?

He snorts. "There *were* five of us. But Rupert passed away after the first meeting—"

"Now there's a real selling point. Where do I sign up?"

He laughs. "He was ninety and died with a fishing pole in his hand."

"Likely story." Of course I'd heard about Rupert's dying at his favorite fishing spot. But I still have to give Ron a hard time. "So what about the others?"

"When we started the committee, Retha Holland conveniently neglected to mention that she goes to Florida every summer."

"Ever heard of the Internet? Or even good old-fashioned Ma Bell? She can still help from down there."

He grimaces. "We tried that at first, but she was always running off to some senior citizen social. And finally she quit answering her phone."

"Okay, so short of calling in a bounty hunter who specializes in tracking down little old ladies, I guess you're stuck. But that should still leave one other person."

"Lucy Blount took a 'leave of absence' not long after Retha skipped town. I think she just wanted to get away from Alma."

Alma's and Ron's bickering is more like it.

"But she *said* she had to go to Alaska to be with her daughter."

"I remember that now." My patients love to share the latest news with me, so I've lost count of how many times I've heard that the optometrist's wife went to Fairbanks to take care of their daughter who is about to have her first child. Sometimes our town is almost too small.

I stare out my tiny window at the brick building next door. In my dream clinic, I'll have a floor-to-ceiling window overlooking a small stream and rolling green hills. And patients who are more concerned with their health than their neighbor's business. Okay, that last is pure fantasy, but a girl can dream.

Who picked this committee is what I want to know, but I don't ask. The mayor is known for being hard to get along with. And I love Alma to death, but this morning proves that when she wants something, she can be a bulldog. Still, I can handle anything for a couple of days. Most things can be postponed. Like tonight's meeting.

"So you want me to meet with Alma, and it has to be tonight?"

"Not just Alma. Jack will be there, too. Alma's son. He's producing the centennial rodeo, which is what we're planning right now."

I don't say a word.

"Real nice guy. Volunteers as a part-time sheriff's deputy." He peers at me. "Better be careful. Might give you a run for your money for Citizen of the Year."

Ron is still talking, something about Jack and me being close to the same age and how he was born and raised next door to my folks' ranch, wasn't he? But I've stopped listening. "You know what, Ron? I'm afraid I can't do this. I'll call Alma and explain the situation. She can contact Jack. I'm sure they'd rather wait until you're available to meet."

He frowns and rubs his knee. "Somebody said you were meeting your friends there tonight anyway. What's it going to hurt to go a little early and meet with the committee?"

If I lived anywhere else, the fact that he knows the Pinky routine might be construed as stalking, but around here, we just call it small-town life.

"Sorry. I just can't do it."

Ron steps off the table, winces, and grabs his knee. "If you can't go to the meeting, I'll have to go," he grunts. "It's too close to time for the rodeo for us to postpone."

"I'm sure Alma will manage."

He casts his gaze toward the ceiling. "Yeah, she'll manage all right. Manage to make this rodeo a disaster. Her son is running a ranch for wanna-be cowboys, and whaddaya bet one of them gets hurt in the ring? You were at the rodeo that night a few years ago when the Lancaster boy got busted up so bad, weren't you?"

I nod. Was I ever. I still remember the announcer's voice over the intercom asking if there was a doctor in the house. Unfortunately, the local vet and I were the only ones who even remotely fit the bill. It took both of us working together to keep the teenager stable until the EMTs got there. It was a rough night and a rough few weeks for the town while one of their favorite sons lay in intensive care. Thankfully he lived, but he still walks with a limp. That was the last rodeo I ever went to.

"And Alma—she thinks this town was built on a gold mine." He shakes his head. "Without me to hold them down. . . or you to do it in my place."

I groan inwardly. I'd do anything for my patients and Shady Grove. But this is asking too much.

He hobbles toward the door. "Thanks anyway. Maybe I can get a free minute to go see Doc Jackson in the next couple of weeks."

He wouldn't.

He would.

He has. He's pulled it out of his sleeve and quietly laid it on the table. The I'm-overworked-and-sacrificing-my-life-servant-of-Shady-Grove trump card.

I know there's nothing higher in my hand.

I fold.

"If I agree to go to the committee meeting tonight, will you go straight from here to the doctor?" I ask sternly.

He turns around slowly. "Right after I stop by the office to get a few papers you'll need for the meeting."

I sigh. "Great. Just fax them over."

Thirty minutes later, I'm between patients when Norma peeks in the adjusting room. "Mayor Kingsley on line one."

I groan. Norma's only lived in Shady Grove a couple of years and doesn't realize that having the mayor as a patient is really a pain in the neck, not a status symbol.

I step into my office and pick up the phone. "Hi, Ron. Did you call Dr. Jackson?"

"They said to come right in."

"Good. And you're going, right?" I say.

"That depends. Are you sure you'll be able to go tonight?"

I consider my commitment, because once I make it, I won't go back on it. I've been cautious and avoided Jack all I could since he got back to town several months ago, but maybe it's time for me to let the past be the past and look toward the future. "Ron, I promise I'll take care of the committee stuff until you're able to do it. Put that out of your mind."

"In that case, I'm having a courier drop some papers off at your office."

As if everyone didn't know that Mayor Kingsley's "courier" is old Sam Helms who sits out on the town-square bench all day just watching folks go by. I guess Ron thinks hand delivery is more prestigious than a fax. "Okay, thanks. I'll tell Norma to keep an eye out for Sam."

Chapter 3

The "papers" Sam brings by turn out to be a large white binder full of notes. I barely have time to tuck it under my arm and hurry to Coffee Central Bookstore after I see my last patient. I sit in the car and skim the short handwritten note Ron tucked in the front. My name is at the top, but it's more like a priority list than a note.

SAFETY FIRST. The words are underscored twice and followed by: "Keep liability in mind. Turn a profit. Publicity a must."

My pounding heart calms some as I walk into the bookstore-coffee shop combination. Daniel Montgomery, Allie's fiancé, has taken a building that used to house a junk store and turned it into a haven for book lovers and java nuts. And anyone else who just wants a peaceful place to get away with friends or be alone. Rich coffee-color leather sofas are scattered throughout the book sections, and jewel-toned aqua paint accents the walls. I especially love how the coffee shop is in the center of the store. The man got his priorities right. The whole place smells like the coffee of the day—vanilla spice. I think I'm in heaven.

Alma waves from a table, and I make my way toward

her. Beside the table, Jack stands, talking to two other men in cowboy hats. This has gone from baby month in Shady Grove to cowboy month with no warning. Maybe heaven is an understatement.

I nod. The men leave just as I reach the table. I try for my most professional tone. "Alma. Jack."

Alma smiles. "Dr. Donovan, glad you decided to join us. I'll go get us all a drink."

I fumble in my purse, but she holds up her hand. "It's on the city since this is official business." Jack and I tell her what we want, and she's gone faster than a weekend.

Jack pulls out my chair. "It's good to see you again so soon."

Since "You, too" would be a lie, I settle for "Thank you" and hope he doesn't notice. A grin splits his handsome face as if I'd welcomed him with open arms. Guilt nudges me hard. It's not his fault that he was a part of the past I'm trying to forget.

I sink into the seat.

He takes the chair beside me. "So Ron appointed you to take his place while he's out of commission?"

I cringe and nod. "Appointed" sounds so official. "I'm filling in for him temporarily, but I'm sure he'll be back soon."

"Let's pray you're right. Those spider bites can be nasty."

I nod, unnerved by his casual reference to prayer. Hard for me to picture the rough-riding rodeo star praying.

"You still ride quite a bit?"

I look up at him. "Yep. Quite a bit. You?"

He grins, his brows drawing together. "Yep."

Okay, obviously if I don't make small talk, he's going to. At least if I start it, I can choose the topic. "Don't you have some kind of cowboy school at your ranch, besides raising rodeo stock?"

"Cowboy school? Some people would say that's the school

of hard knocks. Literally." He laughs. "Seriously, I don't have an official 'school,' but a couple nights a week, I open up the arena to let local yokels practice bull riding, roping, whatever they need to work on."

"For free?"

He nods. "To be honest, I hope these boys learn a few things besides ridin' and ropin'."

"Like what?"

"Honor, integrity, faith. Cowboy values."

Yeah, right. I frown. "Cowboy values?"

He ducks his head and touches the hat lying beside him on the table. "I admit some men have forgotten them over the last few decades, but there are still a lot of good cowboys."

Alma appears at the table holding two black coffees. She sets one in front of Jack then turns to me. "Your latte's going to be a few minutes, so the waitress said she'd bring it over."

"No problem. Thanks."

Alma sinks into her chair. "We're glad to have you, Dr. Donovan," she says and pats my hand. "Are you familiar with our rodeo plans at all?"

"Ron sent a notebook by this afternoon, but I didn't really have time to look at it much between patients. Sorry."

"No problem. Jack, why don't you fill Dr. Donovan in on what we've done so far?"

I smile. "Alma, since we're temporarily working together, why don't you and Jack just call me Rachel?" A lot of my patients call me by my first name, but even though Alma has been my parents' closest neighbor for as long as I can remember, she's been calling me Dr. Donovan ever since I moved back to Shady Grove and opened my practice. I think she started that because she's proud of me, but for whatever the reason, I've let her. Certainly not because I'm hung up on the status of being a doctor. But considering I left this town and my parents' house rather suddenly as a teenager, I figure I need all the help I can get in the respect department.

Jack smiles, his eyes twinkling. "Okay, then. . .*Rachel.*"

On his lips, my name sounds like an endearment. I have a feeling a talent like that takes practice.

Lots of practice.

"Oh, thank you. That's really nice of you, Dr.—" Alma cuts her sentence off with a grimace. "Rachel. You don't know how much it means—you steppin' in for Ron." Suddenly she stands. "Speaking of Ron, I'm going to call and check on him. Just to see what he found out. I'm sure we all want to know."

I narrow my eyes. It didn't take long for her to get back into matchmaking mode, did it?

"Actually, why don't I go call—" I start to stand, but Alma's expression falls, and Jack shakes his head almost imperceptibly. I have no idea what's going on, but I sit back down. "Or maybe you should go ahead?"

Alma grabs her phone and walks outside. Daniel had just instituted an ironclad rule about using cell phones inside. He got tired of having the shop's tranquil atmosphere being disrupted by loud ringtones and one-sided conversations, so he put up a few tasteful signs, and for the most part, people are appreciative of the new peacefulness.

"Thanks," Jack says as soon as his mother is gone.

"For what?"

Before he can answer, a blond wearing a Coffee Central apron approaches. We both look up at her, and she smiles at Jack then ever so slowly sets the latte on the table.

"Thanks," I murmur.

She nods but keeps her eyes on Jack as she turns to walk away. And bumps squarely into a customer in a business suit, sloshing his coffee down the front of his jacket.

As she hastens to clean up the mess, I glance back at Jack, who ducks his head.

"Another occupational hazard?" I say wryly, remembering what he said about being familiar with X-rays.

He shrugs. "Some people want to romanticize the cowboy life."

The woman's reaction had nothing to do with "the cowboy life" and everything to do with his good looks, but I'm not about to point that out, so I drop it. "What did you thank me for earlier when your mom left?"

To his credit, he keeps his attention on me. "For letting her make the call." He leans forward, and I can see the gold flecks in his brown eyes. "She has a real soft spot for Ron."

I raise my eyebrows, remembering Ron's exasperation about working with Alma. "Does he know it?"

Jack laughs. "I don't think so. But I have a feeling he will. I've not seen her really interested in anyone since my dad died."

Mr. Westwood passed on while I was still in Georgia, I'm pretty sure. "How long ago was that?"

"Ten years."

"Wow. Only a decade? I hope she's not rushing things."

He grins. "She's like me. We wait for what we want."

Funny. I would have taken him for more of a charge-in-and-take-it kind of guy.

He takes a sip of his coffee. "You don't see me that way?"

Okay, if he's going to read minds, I'm going to have to stop thinking.

"So tell me about the rodeo. How much is still left to do?"

"Not a lot. My company handles pretty much everything. We provide the stock, the announcer, and all the hands to actually work the rodeo. The town just needs to be sure that the liability insurance is paid up and stay out of the way."

I remember Ron's list and frown. "Surely there are things we can do to make it less dangerous."

He laughs. "I was kidding. The audience isn't in any danger. Those fences may look flimsy, but these guys are professionals. They know better than to let the bulls run amok."

"What about the bull *riders?*"

"The riders? You want to make it safer for the bull riders?" He takes a sip of his coffee.

Why does he have to make that sound like such a stupid idea? "Nothing big. Just a thicker padded vest and maybe require a helmet."

He snorts. "Require helmets?" he finally chokes out.

I ignore his dramatics and shrug. "It seems like I remember seeing guys wearing those when I was a kid."

"Anybody that wants to wears them. Especially the younger guys."

"Then why can't everyone?"

"Why not just make them wear suits of armor? You can't require thicker vests and helmets."

"It would be a lot safer. The town could pick up the tab. Or maybe my office could sponsor that part. What do you think the cost would be?"

"Cost?" He frowns.

"Is that something you could find out?"

"I could if I wanted to, but I don't want to."

"Why not? All we'd have to do is make wearing safety equipment a requirement to enter. And if we provided the helmets—"

"You know what? You can choose what you want to sell in the concession stand, but why don't you let me handle the rodeo?"

I open my eyes wide. "Sounds like a little bit of nepotism. Your mama is on the committee, so you get to produce the rodeo. . ."

" 'Get to?' I 'get to' produce the rodeo?" His brown eyes darken. "The committee took bids." He draws a deep breath. "Sealed bids."

"I see. Still sounds like a conflict of interest to me with your mother on the committee."

"I got the bid because I cut the town a deal. After all, it's my hometown."

"Such a good deal that you just decide things willy-nilly?" I can't believe it. I've never used the term *willy-nilly* in my life. This man makes me crazy. "You don't have to answer to the committee?"

He pushes to his feet. "I do. And I'm glad to. But last time I checked, that committee consisted of Ron Kingsley and my mother."

I stand. "Well, for now I'm filling in for Ron."

He gathers up his folder and gives me a hard look. "Mighty nice of you, but I'll just make my report at the next meeting. When Ron is back." He nods toward me. "I'm sorry if I offended you, Dr. Donovan." His words are clipped.

"Not a problem, Mr. Westwood."

"Ron's in the hospital."

I spin around to see Alma looking ten years older than she did when she went out to call.

Jack quickly crosses over to stand beside her.

"What's going on with Ron?" I ask quietly.

"It's definitely a spider bite. Brown recluse. But he let it go too long." She puts her hand to her chest. "They've tried lancing his knee, but the infection is too deep. He's got to be on IV antibiotics, and if he's not better right away, he'll have to have surgery."

"Oh no," I murmur.

"He sounded tired. And a little worried," she says, her own voice full of concern. "I'm sorry about the committee meeting, but I'm going to run to Batesville right now and see if there's anything I can do for him."

"I'll take you," Jack says.

"I have my car." She takes a few steps then turns back. "Oh, and Dr.— Rachel. . .Ron said to tell you something."

"What?"

"He feels so much better knowing you've taken his place on the committee." She hurries away.

Chapter 4

Jack and I stand in silence for a second after his mother's parting comment; then he gives me a wry grin. "I guess we'll have to figure out a way to work together, huh?"

For some reason, his easygoing attitude irritates me. "We'll have to figure something out all right."

He throws back his head and laughs. "You might as well give it up, Rachel Donovan. I have a contract. I think you're stuck with me."

"We'll see."

From behind me, a throat clears. Allie, Lark, and Victoria are standing there looking at Jack expectantly. Waiting for an introduction. And an explanation for what I'm doing at Coffee Central at the time of our monthly Pinky get-together with an excruciatingly handsome cowboy, I'm sure.

I oblige. With the introductions anyway. The explanation can wait. "I'll see you at the next meeting if Ron's not out by then," I say pointedly.

"I'll pass that info along," he drawls and nods to my friends before he disappears into the night. I'll say this for him, he can take a hint.

Which is more than I can say for Victoria. We order our drinks, and she still won't let the subject of Jack drop. When I finally explain the situation, she gapes at me. "You'll be spending a lot of time with that gorgeous man."

"You did get that he's the boy next door? The man I've spent months avoiding, right? Not to mention that he's a cowboy."

"Maybe it's time you moved past that particular prejudice," Lark says. Just to get her to shut up, I tell them about the rodeo disagreement I had with Jack. But when I reach the part about extra protective gear for the bull riders, they all laugh. Lark and Allie rather hysterically. But even Victoria is holding her sides.

"You actually suggested helmets be required for all the riders?" Lark says, wiping tears away. "Oh, Rachel. Thanks. I needed this laugh so badly."

I shrug. "Why wouldn't they want to be as safe as possible?"

"Maybe because that would defeat the whole purpose of riding the bull?" Allie takes a sip of her latte. "Don't you know those guys are all about the danger? They live for the action, the thrill of staying on the crazy bull for eight seconds."

"Well, Jack's in for a surprise then. I've seen too many spinal injuries because of unnecessary recklessness. So, as of today, I'm all about safety."

"Sounds like a match made in heaven," Lark says with a grin.

I shake my head. "Don't even go there. I may have no choice but to get along with him until Ron's back on his feet, but that's the end of my association with him."

"You're a true-blue Shady Grove citizen, Rach," Victoria drawls. "Working with that man must be a real sacrifice."

I run my finger around the rim of my latte mug. "Just because he's cute..."

Victoria winks. "Shugah, that's like saying the Grand Canyon dips down a bit."

"I know you don't want to be around Jack, but he seems really nice," Allie offers.

She's right. But it's imperative that I keep reality in focus. "He has a way with women, but I don't know how much is cowboy manners and how much is really him."

"Only time will tell," Lark says. "And since you're on the committee, you'll have plenty of time together to find out."

I clear my throat and look for a subject change. "So Allie, where's Daniel tonight?"

She blushes. "He's watching the kids."

"Well, aren't you just an old married couple?" I ask. "Did we miss the wedding?"

"Yeah, you promised we could be bridesmaids." Victoria fakes a whine.

"Now that you mention it"—Allie's eyes twinkle—"we have set the date. Assuming y'all can make it, we're going to have a small wedding in about a month—the last Saturday in June."

When the squeals die down and everyone is still chattering, I look around the table at my friends. Lark, happily married to her plumber prince charming. All they need is a little prince or princess to complete the picture. And Allie, already a doting mom to two daughters, now a beaming bride-to-be. Victoria, wealthy and confident, seemingly satisfied to raise her son, Dylan, alone and with plenty of resources to make it easier. And me. I have my dogs and my small house in town. Do I want more? Some days I'm fine with the life God has blessed me with. Then there are days like today when I dread going home to the empty—well, empty if you don't count four-footed creatures—house.

"Rach, sweetie, you okay?" Victoria's voice breaks through my reverie.

I look up to see them all watching me. I smile. "Yeah, fine. Why?"

Victoria frowns at my hands. "I know you think it's poison and we shouldn't use it, but is that any reason to mutilate that poor sugar packet?"

I drop the pieces of paper left in my hand and dust the white granules toward the middle of the table. "Sorry."

Lark puts her hand to her mouth. "I forgot what day it is. And me going on and on this morning about. . ."

So it begins.

"Rough day?" Allie asks softly.

I shake my head. "Just busy. Like any other." I slap the table lightly. "And long. I'm going to call it a night." Before they can protest, I push to my feet. When I realized our monthly get-together was going to fall on this date, I'd almost asked to reschedule but figured that would draw more attention than just leaving it. I probably should have gone with my first instinct.

"Sure you don't want to stay and talk?" Lark asks.

"Sorry we forgot." Victoria reaches over and touches my hand.

I sit back down. Because our number one Pinky Rule has always been honesty above all. And thanks to my hesitation to confront situations head-on, this talk is years overdue. "Actually, I'm glad you forgot. Y'all have remembered this date for long enough." I squeeze Victoria's hand. "I appreciate your support. But let's try something new and forget from now on, okay?"

"We will if you will," Allie says.

I chuckle. "I kind of have to remember, but y'all have my permission"—I raise an eyebrow—"my encouragement, actually. . .to forget."

"Duly noted," Lark says. "So if we do, will you stay for a while?"

Since there's no one to rush home to, it would be silly not to, wouldn't it? "Sure."

~

By ten thirty, I'm home and settled in bed with the dogs and a good book. My two labs are the perfect companions. Really. Satisfied to just rest at the foot of the bed and snore softly. No demands for bedtime stories or back rubs. I reach out to scratch Cocoa's head, and the doorbell chimes loudly. I jump, and Cocoa and Shadow come awake instantly, bounding off the bed in a chocolate and ebony blur before I can even register what the noise is. They run down the hall, barking loud and fast.

I follow, more cautiously. I've always enjoyed living alone—and my cute little bungalow is perfect for my bachelorette life. Small kitchen, a master bedroom, and two tiny guest bedrooms—one which I turned into an office with a sofa hide-a-bed—a bath and a half, and expansive windows that overlook my groomed lawn—thanks to Allie and her landscaping service.

The dogs are good security, but I can't remember ever having a visitor so late, which is probably a sad commentary on my humdrum life. When I get to the front door, I call out, "Who is it?"

"Rachel, it's Jack Westwood."

I peek out the side window. There are two figures standing on my doorstep. I can't see the second one in the shadows, but the one nearest me is indeed Jack. I cinch up my floor-length, hot pink fleece robe and swing the door open a crack, nudging the dogs back with my foot. "What's wrong?"

"I'm on duty tonight, and I picked up a hitchhiker coming from the bus station. She says she's your niece." The person in the shadows is still hanging back, but Jack reaches and pulls her forward.

I gasp and yank open the door. "Jennifer?"

35

"Hey, Aunt Rachel," she says softly. Cocoa and Shadow descend on her, wagging all over and sniffing.

"What are you doing here?"

Jennifer casts a sideways glance at Jack and purses her lips.

He frowns. "So you really are her aunt?"

Cocoa sits and barks once, as if chastising him for such a silly question.

I force a choked laugh and reach out to draw Jennifer into the house. "Yes. Remember my older sister, Tammy? This is her daughter, Jennifer. Thanks so much for bringing her by."

He nods. "Sure, I remember Tammy. So she's not a runaway?"

"Apparently she wanted to surprise me by visiting earlier than planned. And it worked." I give him a little wave. "Thanks again for getting her here safely."

"No problem," he says, sounding unconvinced. He glances back at me. "Nice robe."

I close the door behind him and lean my back against it, then stare at my niece, her long strawberry-blond hair disheveled and her face pale. "Jenn, honey, what are you doing here?"

Tears pool in her big green eyes, and she throws her arms around me. "I had nowhere else to go."

I stare over her shoulder at the dogs standing motionless now in the doorway to the living room. They appear as puzzled as I am by this sudden arrival. "Nowhere to go? What about Lissa's? When I called your mom earlier tonight, she said you were spending the night there."

Her answer is muffled against my robe.

I gently push her away from me a little. "What?"

"She's not really my mom."

My heart stops beating in my chest and moves to my ears where it pounds so loudly I can't hear myself think. "What do you mean?"

Jennifer throws herself down on my entryway bench. "I'm adopted."

I sink down beside her because my legs won't hold me up another second. "How did you find out?"

"Lissa told me yesterday. She overheard Aunt Jo and Uncle Kevin talking about this being Mom's first pregnancy."

I nod. My brother-in-law's sister, Jo, and her husband, Kevin, are two of the few people in Georgia who know that Jennifer's adopted, so I'm not surprised the news came from their daughter. "What did your mom say about it?"

"I didn't ask her."

"Why not?"

"The doctor put her on bed rest to keep her from losing the baby. I didn't want to upset her."

I push her long curls back away from her face. *So you ran away instead? I'm sure that won't upset her.*

She shrugs as if in answer to my unspoken thought. "Besides, I needed to talk to you."

"Me?"

"Aunt Rach, you have to help me find my biological mom."

I stare into the earnest green eyes of the child I gave birth to fifteen years ago today.

Babies aren't the only ones who can complicate your life.

Chapter 5

"Tammy?" I whisper into the phone and take a step backward to peer at the bathroom door where I can hear the water running. I hope Jennifer takes long showers like Tammy always did when she was that age.

"Rachel?" Tammy's voice is groggy. "What's wrong?"

Where do I start? "Is Russ with you?"

"Yes. He's right here. Do you need to talk to him?" Her puzzlement is obvious.

"No, no. Listen, don't panic. She's perfectly fine, but Jennifer's here."

"What? How?"

"The bus." I hold the phone away from my ear until her hysterical tone calms down. "Tammy, I'm so sorry, but she found out she's adopted."

Silence.

"Tammy?"

"Let me talk to her."

"Wait. She's in the shower. I volunteered to call you because I thought we needed to talk before you two do."

"Is she crying? I know she's devastated. Oh, I can't believe

I let this happen." My sister is blubbering, and I can hear Russ in the background trying to figure out what's going on.

"She's got a good head on her shoulders, and she's processing this. She's had a long bus ride to get over the initial shock."

"Does she hate me?" Tammy's voice sounds small and frightened.

"No! Her first concern was for you. She didn't confront you because she was worried about your pregnancy."

"How did she find out about the adoption?"

"Well, Lissa apparently overheard her parents talking about this being your first pregnancy."

"Oh no, Rach. How did this happen?"

"I guess Lissa thought that Jennifer should—"

"No, that's not what I mean. I mean how did we get here? To this point? I always meant to tell her she was adopted."

I rake my fingers through my hair, wishing my sister were here so we could figure this out in person instead of long distance.

"I should have explained that she was adopted, that we chose her. I knew she'd find out someday. She grew up faster than I thought she would." She gasps. "I can't breathe."

"Tam, calm down. Maybe you were afraid that if you told her she was adopted, she'd find out all of it. This is my fault, really."

"No, it's not. It's mine. Time just got away from me."

Suddenly Russ's deep voice breaks in. "Okay, enough kicking yourselves, girls. There's plenty of blame to go around. Including to Jennifer who shouldn't have run away. How are we going to handle this?"

"I'm going out there," Tammy squeaks.

"No, you're not," Russ replies, and for a minute I envision them standing in the same bedroom speaking into different phones, their gazes locked. His voice gentles. "The doctor said bed rest, and we both know that doesn't include a five-hundred-mile round-trip to Arkansas. I'll leave now and be there in the morning."

One of the things I love about my brother-in-law is that he's levelheaded and filled to the brim with common sense.

"Wait. You need to stay with Tammy. I can bring her home. I have a half day tomorrow and then the weekend. We'll leave right after I finish seeing patients."

They confer for a minute in muffled voices, so apparently they both have their hands over the mouthpieces of their respective phones. Then Tammy comes back. "Rachel, we have a favor to ask."

"Anything."

"Can Jennifer stay with you awhile?"

My stomach churns. "Why? Don't you think she needs to see y'all?"

"I want her home right now more than anything, but we have to think about what's best for her. She was going to visit this summer anyway. She's been talking about coming for years, remember?"

I remember. But even then the thought had made me nervous. What if she figured it all out? And now, as a precocious fifteen-year-old, hot on the trail of her birth mother, how much bigger is the chance? I brush my hair back from my clammy forehead. I can't think.

Shadow nuzzles my arm, and I look down into her worried face. Cocoa sits on the other side of me and presses her head against my leg. I know they can tell something's wrong.

"We'll talk to her, of course, but we think maybe she needs some time to accept this without having to actually face us. If we bring her back right now, she might just run away again." Her voice breaks. "Maybe to somewhere we can't find her."

My heart pounds in my throat at the thought. "She can stay here."

"Are you sure?"

"Definitely," I squeak, then take a deep breath and will myself to sound calm. "Why wouldn't I want my favorite niece to stay with me a few weeks?" Other than the fact I'm terrified she won't love me anymore if she finds out the truth.

Tammy sighs. "If you're sure and she wants to stay, I really think it's the best thing."

"You might not when you hear what she said to me tonight."

"What?"

"She wants me to help her look for her birth mother." I give Tammy a second to absorb that bombshell. Which is more than I had. I don't even remember how I responded to Jennifer earlier, but shortly after her request, I do know I suggested a long, hot shower to wash off the bus grime.

"Oh boy. Just stall. Do whatever it takes to distract her. Introduce her to Allie's daughters. Take her out to see the horses. And to visit Mama and Daddy. I'll call them in the morning and explain the situation so they don't give anything away."

"Okay." In spite of tonight's drama, I feel the same twinge I always feel when she talks so easily about "Mama and Daddy" and her communications with them. When I left home all those years ago, I left Mama and Daddy behind. From then on they became Mom and Dad in my mind. I even considered Alton and Daphine, but my Southern upbringing wouldn't let me go that far.

So now I live in the same zip code as they do, but Tammy, five hundred miles away, talks to them more often. My choice, I know.

She hesitates. "You're going to have to try harder with them if Jenn's going to stay for a while. They're her grandparents."

"I know."

"Adopted *and* biological." Her tone is gentle, but she couldn't have said it plainer if she'd just said, "They're your parents, too."

"I know." *As if I could ever forget.*

"Okay, it's settled then. We'll send her clothes and some money first thing tomorrow. But, Rachel?"

"Yeah?"

"I made you a promise fifteen years ago that I wouldn't tell her you were her biological mother unless you agreed. I've kept that promise, and now I need you to make me one." My normally flighty sister's voice is strained with earnestness.

"Anything, Tam."

"Well, obviously I can't deny she's adopted, but don't tell her the whole truth until I can come out there."

A humorless laugh escapes my lips. "I don't plan on ever telling her that. Not in a million years." Memories of Jennifer growing up, looking at me with adoring eyes, flash through my mind. I can't imagine how she'd look at me if she knew the truth.

Tammy stammers for a second then finally speaks. "Rach, I think we have to tell her—"

"No." I'm shaking my head in the empty room. "No, we don't have to tell her. You can admit she's adopted, but I have to have more time. When you tell her I'm the one who gave her up, I'll lose her completely." Panic constricts my throat. "I can't do it."

"Okay, we don't have to decide this tonight. Calm down." Tammy has shifted into big sister mode, and now our roles have reversed—she's soothing me.

Shame, hot and nauseating, trickles through my veins. I'm a coward. But I can't seem to help it.

I turn off the main highway toward my parents' ranch. Beside me, Jennifer sits, slouched down in the seat. Her hair is stuffed up under a Braves cap; one renegade curl sloops across her shoulder. "So, you looking forward to seeing the Grands?"

As the only grandchild, she could call them anything she wants and they'd be happy, but this term she coined when she was tiny makes both my parents beam.

She nods.

I'm relieved that she doesn't say anything about them not "really" being her grandparents, like she did about Tammy last night. As a matter of fact, she hasn't mentioned the adoption issue since she talked to her parents on the phone last night.

I turn the car down the lane leading to Mom and Dad's ranch.

"Maybe they know who my birth mother is."

So much for not mentioning it. My gut clenches. I look over at her. "I know you're upset, but it might be good if you just spend a little time visiting before you start questioning them, kiddo."

She mumbles something then closes her eyes, cranks up her iPod, and pretends to be completely absorbed in the music coming from the tiny earbuds in her ears.

Switch the iPod for a Sony Walkman and you have me the day my dad drove me the opposite direction down this lane. We didn't stop, other than a restroom break, until we got to Russ and Tammy's house in Georgia. I remember sitting in the passenger seat, much like Jennifer is now, trying to pretend the headphones blocked out the silent disapproval coming from my dad.

Only then, Jennifer was in my womb.

Even though I've been back many times since then, something about driving here with her beside me feels as if I've come full circle.

My parents are waiting on their wide porch looking as if they stepped right out of a lemonade commercial. Indeed, everything about my parents' ranch would fall in the "idyllic" category. Two-story white house with a red barn rising up behind it. A row of pines that flank the yard, planted when they were saplings, now towering above the house. A massive oak tree, perfect for climbing, in the front yard. Such perfection should have come with perfect daughters.

Unfortunately, I messed that up.

They wave broadly as I pull up in front and park. In an instant, they descend on my vehicle. And go straight to the passenger side.

Jenn slips off her earbuds.

Mom bends down to hug Jennifer as she's getting out of the car. "You look exhausted, honey."

I'd sent out an emergency e-mail to Lark, Allie, and Victoria while Jennifer was on the phone with Tammy last night, and my friends insisted on meeting me for breakfast so they could pray with me. I slipped out early and left Jennifer asleep, ate breakfast, and worked at the office until noon. She was still asleep when I got home. I doubt she's terribly exhausted, but Mom is overprotective. If she cares about you.

"Hey, girl," Dad says and pulls her into a bear hug. "You've grown up since Christmas." He nods to me over her shoulder. "Rachel."

I nod back. "Dad."

"Lunch is ready," Mom offers. "Come on in and eat before it gets cold."

They escort Jennifer up the steps while I follow behind.

I'm one of those corny people whose childhood home is her dream house. Maybe because I had a happy childhood. Until I ruined it with one impulsive act. I wasn't a troubled kid. Not even as an adolescent. I was just gullible and stupid.

But I don't think anyone in our family remembers much about my growing up except for that one gullible, stupid moment. Not Mom, not Dad, and certainly not me. It's mostly a haze before that point.

Chapter 6

Mom ushers us directly to the big oak table. As I pull out my chair, I glance out the dining room windows at the rolling green pasture. "It's beautiful out here this time of year."

"Maybe you'll get out here more often since Jenn's here," Mom says under her breath. "To the house and not just to the barn."

"Maybe."

"Let's pray," Dad says. He thanks God for allowing Jennifer to be with us then thanks Him for the food and asks Him to bless the hands that prepared it. When he says "Amen," I remember how special I always felt when I helped fix supper and Dad would say that in the prayer. The thought of God blessing my hands. . .

Suddenly I realize that God *has* blessed my hands, by allowing me to help so many people with them. I wonder if my being a chiropractor is partly an answer to my dad's prayers.

Mom has cooked a full spread. She's a once-a-month grocery shopper. Hard to believe she threw all this together after Tammy called her this morning.

"I ran into Alma Westwood in Price-Chopper this morning."

So either today's grocery day or she made a special trip. "You did?"

"She said she made Jack go with her to your office yesterday."

With the new privacy laws, I can't acknowledge that Alma comes in to the clinic, but like most of my patients, she doesn't hesitate to tell the world. Which is good for business but puts me in a bad spot sometimes when someone wants to discuss a patient with me. I concentrate on my green beans, unsure how to answer.

"He was very impressed with your presentation of Alma's X-rays."

I almost choke on a bean. Is my mother really joining Alma in her matchmaking? Why would she bother?

My dad clears his throat.

I look up from my plate.

"Your mother's talking to you."

I feel like a sullen teenager myself. "Sorry. Thanks to the privacy laws, I can't discuss patients."

"Well, Alma tells me all about her treatments." Mom stabs a piece of pork chop with her fork. "I wasn't asking for her medical history."

"Sorry."

"She said you'd taken Ron Kingsley's place on the centennial committee."

Thanks to Jennifer's unexpected arrival, I'd almost forgotten the committee. "Temporarily."

We eat in silence for a while.

Mom looks over at Jennifer, who is sneaking glances at us as if we're from another planet. "So, honey, are you glad school's out?" Leave it to Mom not to acknowledge the fact that Jennifer ran away. You'd think this was a regularly scheduled visit.

Jennifer shrugs. "I guess." She stares back at her own plate.

"Dad, what have you been working on lately?" I ask, because let's face it, right now, in terms of comfortable and easy, our dinner conversation is one notch above an IRS audit and one notch below a blind date.

"That fence along the lower half of the Strausand forty has been in bad shape for a while. I'm repairing it this week." My folks bought their ranch forty acres at a time, and they still call each piece of ground by its original owner's last name.

"Cool." I pick up my knife to cut my pork chop. "Sounds like fun."

Jenn looks at me. "You like to work on the ranch?"

This time I shrug. "I used to help Dad with fence repair every summer. It wasn't too bad."

Dad smiles at me, and his eyes crinkle at the corners. I've seen that smile directed to me so rarely in the last decade and a half that I've almost forgotten how good it makes me feel. "You were a big help from the time you were old enough to hold a pair of pliers. Tammy never did like to get her hands dirty, but I could always count on you to dive in, no matter how messy the job."

I return his smile. Maybe I remember more of my childhood than I thought.

"Yep. Even after you got older, you were always there to help, on up until you were. . ." His voice drifts off, and he lowers his gaze.

"Time for dessert," Mom says as she jumps up from the table. She hurries from the room.

"What did she make?" The way my stomach is churning, I ask more to fill the awkwardness than because I care about dessert.

Dad glances at Jennifer. "You two will just have to wait and see."

"Sorry," I say, because now I have a pretty good idea of what the dessert is.

Sure enough, Mom reaches back and flips the light switch off then steps into the dining room with a two-layer chocolate cake, complete with flaming candles.

"Happy birthday to you," Dad begins in his rich baritone, and Mom and I quickly join in.

Jennifer's face lights up, and I relax a little. When we finish singing, Mom and Dad lean together and harmonize: "And many mooore." Their signature closing. Even though I haven't celebrated a birthday around them in years, when anyone sings "Happy Birthday," no matter where I am, I always add that "and many mooore" in my head at the end.

Dad disappears and comes back with Yarnell's homemade vanilla ice cream. My mouth waters. I don't eat much sugar, but everyone knows I make an exception for this ice cream.

He scoops generous helpings on the four pieces of cake Mom has cut.

"Let's take our dessert into the den," Mom says. She leads the way and motions Jennifer and me to the loveseat. She and Dad sit in their chairs across from us.

Once we're seated with our bowls, Mom hands Jennifer an envelope. "Sorry it's a day late. There's one already waiting for you in Georgia, but your mom said you didn't get it yet."

"I can wait—," Jenn starts.

Mom holds up her hand and smiles. "Actually, we thought we'd just give you two this year."

Jennifer opens her card and squeals at the check amount.

"Not like we have any other grandkids to get their feelings hurt that you get double," Dad says gruffly.

"Yet," Mom says.

I assume she means Tammy's pregnancy, but the look she

gives me is really pointed, so I'm not so sure.

I glance away in time to see an expression flit across Jenn's face that I can't define. But if she's anything but happy, she covers with a remarkably gracious smile. "Thanks, Granddaddy. Grandmom." She stands to give them both a quick hug then sits back down.

"So, Rachel, business is good?" Dad asks.

I nod and take a bite of my cake and ice cream.

"Alma said she saw some drawings—plans for a new clinic—on your wall," Mom says.

I nod again, motioning toward my full mouth.

Dad frowns. "I don't remember you telling us about that."

I swallow. And stall. "I'm sorry. Right now, it's just a dream." *One that will involve buying some—if not all—of your land.* I actually got the idea a few years ago when my dad mentioned something one Christmas about their intention to sell the ranch and buy a smaller place sometime in the not-too-distant future.

The conversation stalls until Jennifer finishes and sets her bowl on the table beside her. She points toward something. "I forgot that you barrel raced, Aunt Rachel."

I lean forward to see what she's looking at. A trophy. Puzzled, I turn to Mom. "Where'd you find that?"

"In a box in the attic. I got that one out to remind me to have you take the box the next time you came by."

I cringe as Jennifer reaches over and wipes a layer of dust off the trophy with her finger. It's been a while since I stopped by, hasn't it?

"Your grandmother was quite the barrel racer in her time, too," Dad says, his green eyes sparkling with pride as he looks at my mom.

Jennifer picks up the trophy and examines it from all angles.

"Awesome. I've always wanted to be in a rodeo." For the first time since her arrival, excitement twinkles in her eyes.

"Well, why not? You can do anything you put your mind to," Dad says. There's no telling how many times he said that to me and Tammy when we were growing up. And even after I disappointed him beyond redemption, I clung to those words. They got me through the grueling schedule of chiropractic college and every tough time since.

"What about Mom?" Jenn asks. "Did she barrel race?" A shadow crosses her face again, and I know she's remembering that she's adopted.

Mom stares at the trophy as memories flit across her face. She smiles. "Tammy was more interested in being Miss Rodeo Queen than barrel racing. She liked horses, but only if they didn't wrinkle her outfit."

"Or clash with it," I add. Mom's eyes widen in surprise at my joke, but we laugh together, and Dad's soft chuckle rumbles underneath.

Jennifer clunks the trophy down onto the table and sits up straight. "I want to ride bulls."

My mom chokes, and my dad leans up to beat her on the back. "Sorry. Cake went down the"—she gasps—"wrong way."

I can totally sympathize.

"Girls don't ride bulls," I say quietly.

Jennifer looks at me, her mouth set. "I saw a really cool article about girl bull riders on Yahoo. Some associations don't let them ride, but there are plenty that do."

I stare at her. She knows how to shake things up, doesn't she? I can sit this one out, though. My parents will never stand for their precious and only granddaughter climbing on a twisting, snorting, stomping bull.

"I really want to ride bulls," she says, her big green eyes trained on Dad. "You said I could do anything I put my mind to."

Dad looks at Mom then back to Jennifer. "Have you ever seen anyone ride a bull? Other than on TV?"

She shakes her head.

"Then that's your first step."

She smirks. "You think if I do I'll chicken out, but I won't."

"Chicken out?" Dad says, disbelief in his voice. "No grand-daughter of mine is going to chicken out of anything."

Mom leans forward in her chair. "Of course, if you decided you didn't want to do it, no one would—"

Dad reaches over and puts his hand gently on Mom's arm, and she stops in midsentence. "You'll need a padded vest and a helmet," he says to Jennifer.

"And a spare brain," I mutter. I cannot believe he's seriously considering letting her do this. Even in the best of situations, she could break a bone.

"I know just the person to help you," Dad finishes as he walks over to the desk, picks up the cordless phone, and dials a number. Then he holds up a finger as he apparently waits for an answer on the other end. "Jack?" he booms. "Alton Donovan here. My fifteen-year-old granddaughter is visiting this summer, and she wants to learn to ride bulls."

Jack? As in Jack Westwood? Great.

"Yes, she's here with me now, and she rides horses, but she thinks riding bulls sounds like fun."

Jennifer is watching Dad, who is apparently listening intently to Jack, but I catch Mom's eye and lower my eyebrows. Has he lost his mind?

She shrugs.

That's comforting.

"Mm hm, mm hm. You will? I sure appreciate it."

He hangs up the phone and beams at Jennifer. "My neighbor

will be glad to show you a few things about bull riding."

"But I—" I stop. I don't even know what to say.

He looks at Jennifer in her shorts and sandals and then looks at me. "You mind running her home to get some jeans on? Maybe she can fit into a pair of your boots. Jack said if you'll bring her by this afternoon, he'll introduce her to a bull and see what she thinks."

Jennifer is already heading toward the door.

"But what will Tammy. . ." I stand.

He puts a hand at my back and gives me a very gentle push toward the door. "You girls go on. I'll call Tammy and explain."

I nod. When my dad makes up his mind, there's no room for argument. I'm sure he sees himself as a master of psychology. I just hope it doesn't backfire on him.

Chapter 7

"What's the deal with you and the Grands?" Jennifer asks on our way to the Lazy W.

"What do you mean?" I play dumb, like adults always seem to do when they're uncomfortable with a question. Something I never thought I'd do. But it beats handing her the iPod that's lying on the console between us and suggesting she find some good music to listen to. Which appears to be my other option.

"You kept apologizing. And when y'all talked"—she picks up the iPod herself, apparently growing tired of the conversation already, thankfully—"it was just weird. Nothing like when we're here for Christmas."

She's right. It's amazing what a buffer two extra adults can be. But without Russ and Tammy there, the awkwardness is palpable. Which is why, even though I drive out to the barn and ride several mornings a week, I don't go up to the house often.

Oh, I drop by on their birthdays. . .Mother's Day and Father's Day. . .and stay long enough to give them a generic-sounding card and equally generic gift. They mail me a card with a check in August for my birthday. And Mom usually calls. One time a few years ago, she got my machine and she and dad sang "Happy Birthday" complete with "and many mooore." I didn't delete that message until Christmas.

I open my mouth to try to explain, but the earbuds are in place, and her eyes are closed. One could quickly learn to love technology.

When we turn into the Lazy W driveway, I glance over at Jennifer, whose eyes are still closed, and slip my lip gloss from my purse. It's a light pink, barely noticeable really, but maybe it will help me not to feel so frazzled. I slow to a crawl and keep one eye on the road and one on the mirror as I quickly trace my lips with the wand.

"You know this guy?"

I jerk and make a shiny line on my cheek, then fumble for a napkin. I wipe it off and meet her level green gaze. She's not a little girl anymore.

"We were neighbors growing up, so of course I knew him back then. Not so much anymore."

"What's he like?"

"He's. . ." Smooth. A tad arrogant. Sometimes infuriating. Unbelievably good-looking. "Nice."

"Really?" Her brows draw together. "You don't sound very sure."

"Jenn, why do you want to ride a bull?"

She shrugs. "I just do."

"To prove that you're as opposite your mom as you can be?"

A shadow crosses over her face, and I know I nailed her motivation.

She folds her arms in front of her. "I really want to ride a bull. Do you think Granddaddy is just messin' with me?"

I shrug with my hands still on the steering wheel. "I quit trying to read his mind years ago."

"Do you still barrel race?"

"Not competitively."

"Why?"

I struggle to phrase an answer. I slip out to the ranch several times a week in the early morning hours and ride, but anything more than that would require days like today. And I'm sure not up for that. There are other, deeper reasons, but that one is enough. "I'm pretty busy with my practice."

She may not be a little girl anymore, but today she's asking as many questions as a five-year-old.

When we get out of the car, Jack and Dad are standing out near the barn talking. Dad waves us over. "Jack, this is my granddaughter, Jennifer."

Jack makes no indication that he picked Jenn up hitchhiking last night. Instead, he doffs his hat and smiles, his dimples deepening. "Jennifer."

She blushes.

Maybe she's embarrassed because he's the one who picked her up when she was on her way to my house, but it could just as easily be his good looks. It doesn't matter what age females are, he apparently has the same effect on them.

He smiles at me, and I pray I don't blush. "Rachel. Good to see you again."

I nod. "Small world."

Dad laughs and looks at Jack. "Remember what I told you the other day when we were fixing that stretch of fence that runs by the main road?"

Jack nods. "When we're working by the road and hear a car coming, I should just give a quick wave over my shoulder and keep on working. It's most likely either someone I know or someone who knows me."

"Or both," they finish together with a laugh.

Jennifer has wandered over to the horse stalls while Dad

and Jack are male-bonding. Dad excuses himself and goes over to introduce her to Jack's horses.

I'm amazed that I feel a flare of jealousy that Dad is so at home here, and with Jack, in general. Before I got pregnant, I did everything I could to be the son Dad never had. Is Jack filling that bill now?

When I look back at Jack, he's watching me, his eyes scrutinizing my expression.

I raise an eyebrow. "So do you have a plan?"

"Excuse me?" he asks as if he didn't hear me.

"A plan. To keep Jennifer from actually riding a wild bull."

He shrugs. "Your dad has a plan. We'll see how it goes."

I figure I might as well cut to the chase. I square my shoulders and look him straight in the eye. "Don't let her get on a bull."

"Don't worry." He flashes me a grin. "She won't be the one getting on the bull."

"You still ride bulls? I heard you retired."

"You heard right. But I'm doing this as a favor. And Alton rarely asks for those."

"You spend a lot of time with my dad?" I ask, hoping for a casual tone.

He shrugs. "Define 'a lot.' He's a good friend."

Call me suspicious, but he's also a man with "a lot" of premium property. And he makes no secret of the fact that he and Mom are planning on selling in a few years to get something smaller. What better way to get the prize than to bump the estranged daughter out of line and take her place. Okay, now you can call me paranoid. "I guess I was surprised because he's never mentioned you."

He lowers his eyebrows. "He mentions you often, but I don't get the impression he sees you much."

Maybe I started it, but we've crossed over into way-too-personal territory, and I'm not willing to go there. Since his words feel like a reprimand, though, I can't resist one little retort before I walk over to join Jennifer and Dad. "That must be why he forgot that this same psychological ploy backfired on him when I was fourteen and determined to tame a wild filly. Against Mom's protests, Dad let me try. Instead of breaking the horse, I broke my collarbone."

"Actually," he calls softly enough for my ears only, "I remember that was the summer you ended up barrel racing with your arm in a sling."

I pause. He remembers that? Unfortunately, it's in the past. One more place I can't go with him. I just keep walking.

"But you riding that wild filly is also one of the first things your dad reminded me about when I moved back here."

I spin around. "Really?"

He nods.

Curiosity draws me the two steps back toward him. I want to ask what else Dad "reminded" him about me. Instead I say, "I know he and your dad were friends, but how did you two get to be. . .close?"

He shrugs. "We're neighbors. We go to church together."

I knew Alma attended with Mom and Dad at the little congregation I grew up in, but I didn't realize Jack did. That explains part of the closeness. With fewer than fifty members, everyone is close.

"And he's been patient with a greenhorn like me."

"The great Jack Westwood, a greenhorn?"

"Nobody's good at everything." He shoots me a wry grin. "I know rodeos, but ranching is a completely different story. I left home for the circuit before I really learned the ranching business. Your dad's help has been immeasurable."

I look across the barn lot at my dad, noting for the first time that his once auburn hair is spattered with gray. "He knows a lot about cattle."

"He knows more than cattle," Jack says and walks slowly over to Jennifer and Dad.

I stand there for a minute and stare after him, thinking about his last words. Dad does know more than cattle, I'm sure. But unfortunately, he doesn't know me.

Or maybe he just doesn't want to.

~

I don't know how I ended up by myself with Mom. I guess subconsciously, when faced with the choice of watching Jack climb onto the back of a bull up close and personal or this, I considered leaving Jennifer with Dad at the Lazy W and driving the half mile to my parents' house the lesser of two evils. Now that I'm here on the doorstep, staring into Mom's startled face, I'm not so sure this was the best decision.

"I thought I'd go ahead and get that box out of your way," I say with a nervous shrug. "I'm sorry I didn't find it when I got everything else." When I moved back from Georgia eight years ago, Victoria came out and helped me get my things. She'd been unfailingly polite to my parents while I'd packed without really speaking. But I thought I'd gotten everything.

"They weren't in our way, Rachel." Mom stands back to let me in, but her voice is tight. "I just thought you might want them. Why not display them in your office?"

Right. Then people will say, "Oh, I remember you back then. Didn't you disappear from Shady Grove in the middle of your senior year? Where'd you go anyway?"

"Thanks."

Mom leads the way down the hall to my old bedroom and

motions to a big cardboard box on the bed.

"Oh wow. There are a lot of them. I didn't remember."

"Horses were your first love."

I nod and pick up one of the trophies. She's right. I was crazy about horses above all else. Until the first night I saw Brett Meeks. Then the horses and horse shows quickly became a means to an end. In my daydreams, Brett would be desperate to know my name but too shy to ask. Then I'd win, my name would be announced, and he'd know.

I pick up a few snapshots lying loose in the box, and my mouth twists into a bittersweet smile. Other than a few lines in my face and a lot more wisdom, I haven't changed much. At sixteen, almost seventeen, even though I was far from the anorexic shape that was so in fashion back then, I wasn't at all overweight, and it's hard to believe I thought I was fat. But I did. I fixed my hair a hundred different ways that summer and even wore blush, hoping for the illusion of cheekbones.

My gaze falls on a faded navy blue bandanna in the corner of the box. When I see it, I know why this box was in the attic and not with the rest of my stuff. My mind flashes back to the day I packed all my barrel-racing stuff away and took it up to the attic. Where it had stayed until now.

Chapter 8

ad memories?"

I stuff the bandanna deep under the mass of trophies and spin around. Mom is still standing in the door, her eyes suspiciously moist. I nod. "Mostly. It's never pleasant to remember how foolishly I acted." *And how much you and Dad hated me for it.*

"I wish..."

I want to hear what she wishes, but at the same time I'm afraid to. I turn back toward the box and slide the photos into it. "The past is the past. I'll keep the trophies and throw the rest away at home."

"Yes. Looking forward is always best, I guess," she says, and I hear her shoes clicking down the hallway.

I don't see her when I carry the stuff out to my car, but Jack's truck turns into the drive, and he, Dad, and Jenn climb out.

It hits me that Dad must have walked over to Jack's place. I feel bad he and Jenn had to ask Jack for a ride home. I open my mouth to apologize, although it wouldn't have hurt Dad to tell me that he was depending on me to bring them home. But before I can say anything, Jack rushes across the yard to take the box from my arms. Unless I want to wrestle him to the ground for it, I have no choice but to let him have it.

"Aunt Rach," Jenn yells. "You should have seen Jack ride the bull. He stayed on until the buzzer went off, and then he jumped off. Twister almost stepped on him."

"Cool," I call to her then glance at Jack. "Couldn't bear to 'jump' off without qualifying, huh?" I ask softly, referring to the eight seconds that makes a successful bull ride.

He shrugs as well as he can with the box in his hands. "No sense in bruising my body *and* my pride."

I lead the way out to my car and open the back door. "Thanks," I say as he sets it on my backseat.

"No problem." He nods toward the trophies. "Wow. I'd almost forgotten what a barrel-racing champion you were."

"I guess. Back in the day." I try to laugh.

He closes the car door and turns to face me. "Did you hear about Ron?"

Guilt clenches my gut as I shake my head. I meant to call and check on him, but when Jenn showed up, everything else took a backseat. "What's going on with him?"

"He's definitely looking at surgery."

"Oh no!" I feel awful for him. And not so great for me, either. I was counting on him being back for the committee meeting next week and me bowing out gracefully. "When do you think they'll do it?"

"Early next week. Then six to eight weeks of recovery."

I want to whine, but at least I'm not the one who's having surgery. I told Ron I'd take care of things, and I will. "Think your mom and I can handle it? With your help, of course?"

He grimaces. "Actually, Mom has gone to Batesville to stay with my sister."

"Let me guess. Your sister's pregnant."

He raises his eyebrows and draws them together at the same time. On him it's a cute look. Trust me. "Not that I know of. Why?"

"I just—" I wave my hand. "Never mind. Is it going to be a long visit?"

"I don't know. She's staying there to be close to Ron, since he has no other family nearby."

Of course she is. I hope Ron appreciates it, but somehow I doubt it. "So I guess I'll be the committee for a while," I say without thinking.

He frowns. "You sound like that's a death sentence."

I give a half smile. "Sorry, but you have to admit our first 'committee meeting'"—I put air quotes around the words with my fingers—"didn't go so well."

His brown eyes gaze at me intently, and for once he doesn't smile. "Rachel, don't write us off just because we had a rocky start."

I know he's talking about our working relationship as committee member and rodeo producer. Surely. But the way he says "us" sends a shiver down my spine.

"Okay, okay." I force a smile. "I guess it's too late to get new bids now. I'll give it a shot."

He swipes his hand across his forehead. "What a relief."

I swat toward the brim of his hat. "Yeah, I know you were worried."

He ducks and feints away, a slow grin spreading across his face. "Worried might be an overstatement, but it's nice to know my future is financially assured now that I'm going to *get* to produce the Shady Grove Centennial Rodeo."

"Oh yeah." I return his grin as I remember my hotheaded comment at Coffee Central. "Sorry about the whole nepotism crack. I know the town appreciates you giving us a deal."

We're joking. And it's fun. The realization makes me stiffen. As if in direct response, Jack stiffens, too, and his smile fades.

"I wanted to ask you. . ." He looks toward the house then back at me. I can't believe my eyes. Jack Westwood is nervous. I brace myself for a really personal question.

When he doesn't speak, I snap, "Ask me what?"

"If you'd like to go out with me this Saturday night."

"Out?"

He motions with his hand but doesn't really look in my eyes. "Out to eat. To a show. Bowling. Whatever people do on dates around here."

I stare at him. This cannot be happening. Jennifer's here full of questions, I'm thrust back into regular contact with my parents, and now, the drop-dead-gorgeous cowboy I have been trying desperately to avoid asks me out. And here's the worst thing. I'd like to say yes. And that's all the more reason to say no. "I'm sorry. But I can't."

"Oh." He looks down at the ground. "You are in a relationship?"

Because obviously that's the only reason he's ever been turned down.

"More relationships than I can handle."

He winces.

I relent. "But not a romantic one. I just don't have time"—*or trust*—"to spare right now. Thanks for asking though."

"I understand. Probably just as well."

I don't say anything because I'm afraid I'll scream, "Wait! I changed my mind."

"Tell your folks I had to get home." He turns and walks slowly toward his truck.

"I will." I stand and watch him pull out of the driveway. "It would have been fun," I say to the air.

~

"Maybe you should have said yes. I think it would have been fun." Allie tosses me the Frisbee and reaches over to get a bottled water out of the cooler.

I throw the neon green disc to Lark, who promptly pitches it over her shoulder toward the kids. Cocoa and Shadow both run for it, but Allie's youngest daughter, Katie, grabs it as she and Dylan, Victoria's son, take off to the open area next to the fountain, with the dogs at their side.

Katie motions for her older sister to come play, but Miranda is engrossed in conversation with Jennifer. Even though there's more than two years difference in their ages, they hit it off immediately, and they're walking along the paths talking. "I've tried 'fun.' It didn't work out."

"You were a kid. Besides, all cowboys aren't created equal, Rach," Lark adds. "He seems nice."

"He seems it. But we all know I've dated men who *are* really nice, and it never amounts to anything."

"Wonder why?" Allie asks, as she spreads out a tablecloth on the picnic table.

I give her an appraising look. Is she being sarcastic? Or serious?

"You tell me," I say, not caring if I'm a little flippant.

Allie concentrates on smoothing a wrinkle out of the red and white plastic.

"Because you never date anyone you're really attracted to," Lark says. Allie kind of gasps, and Lark shoots her a defensive look. "You know it's true."

"Well...," Allie starts, with a worried look at me.

Okay, I know Lark's nerves are on edge while she's waiting for the adoption agency to call, but I have to protest.

"That is *not* true."

Lark puts her hand on her hip and waves her Diet Coke bottle at me. "Name one man you've dated in the past fifteen years that you had the slightest desire to get to know better."

"There was—" I stop, running through the short list of names in my mind. All nice guys. But none of them rang my bell, as Lark's granny used to say. Still, I'm not about to admit it. "How did we get started on this?" I ignore Lark's smirk and turn to Allie. "Have you picked out our dresses yet?"

Allie gives me a dreamy bride smile. "I was hoping we might do that together a week from Saturday."

The opening notes of Martina McBride's "This One's for the Girls" blast out from the other side of the table. Lark almost knocks Allie over as she sprints to grab her purse. She fumbles frantically with the Velcro clasp and yanks her phone out. "Hello?"

I shoot Allie a worried look. "The waiting is getting to her, isn't it?" I whisper.

She nods.

Lark's shoulders fall. "Oh. Hi, Marsha."

"Craig's sister," Allie mouths.

Lark walks up to the top of the hill to get a better cell signal, and Allie and I start putting the food out. "We should do a spa day when we go to buy dresses," Allie says. "I think we're all pretty stressed."

I realize how much I've been consumed with Jennifer since she's been here. "Is Vic okay?" Victoria Worthington is one of the most "together" women I know. But sometimes I'm sure we take that for granted.

"Actually, yeah, she seems to be doing great. But she'd never turn down a spa day."

Lark yells, and we look up. She's running over toward Craig, motioning him to meet her. He hurries to her and she talks, waving her arms, talking with her hands in true Lark fashion.

"Looks like his sister had big news," Allie says.

"Good news, I hope."

Just as we finish setting the food out, Lark comes barreling down the hill, clutching her cell, a big grin across her face. "Okay, guys, I need you to pray like you've never prayed before. There's a chance we're going to be able to adopt a baby."

Allie looks up from where she's stirring the potato salad. "Really? Did the adoption agency beep in?"

Lark shakes her head. "That was Craig's sister in Batesville. A woman she works with has a friend in Shady Grove who is pregnant. She's not married and wants to give the baby up for adoption."

Allie hurries to hug her. "How old is she?"

"Thirty."

I hug her, too. "Why isn't she keeping the baby?" I say, caution tempering my joy.

Lark frowns. "She can't afford to. But the good news is Marsha told her about us and she wants to meet us."

"That's wonderful." I try to keep the concern from my voice.

"You sound like you're not so sure."

I'm saved from having to respond when Victoria jogs over to us, her blue polo shirt and khaki shorts spattered lightly with water. "Adam wanted to have a water fight." She nods over her shoulder to where the guys are barbecuing, and Allie's brother, Adam, is wringing water out of his T-shirt. "He lost."

Allie grins. "He never gives up, does he?"

"Never grows up is more like it," Victoria grumbles as she sinks onto the blanket and snags a sports drink from the cooler. "So what did I miss?"

Lark drops down beside her with her baby news, and

Victoria completes the round of Pinky hugs with her own enthusiastic contribution.

Allie sits across from her. "Rachel's cowboy asked her out."

Victoria's face lights up, and she salutes me with her sports drink. "When are you going?"

"I'm not."

She looks at me in disbelief. "You're saying no to him?"

"Already did."

"Wow. You've got willpower."

Allie laughs. "You make him sound fattening, Vic."

"He's worse than fattening," she says. "He should come with a surgeon general's warning: May be addictive."

Something unfamiliar wrenches at my gut.

I'm satisfied with how I look, and some people consider my red hair and green eyes "striking," but Victoria is supermodel material. If she set her sights on Jack, I wouldn't have a chance.

As soon as I think it, I realize how ridiculous the thought is. With or without Victoria, I don't have a chance. Because I'm not going out with him.

End of subject.

Chapter 9

Monday evening, I hurry up the steps to Allie's house to pick up Jennifer. We're supposed to be at the Lazy W in thirty minutes for her to watch a bull riding practice, but my last patient recently lost her husband, and she needed to talk. Some things can't be hurried. Then to top it all off, I had to get Norma to give my car a jumpstart. All I need is a new battery, probably, but trying to find the time to get one is another story.

Allie opens the kitchen door as soon as I knock. "Hey, girl. Come in. The kids are back there somewhere." She nods toward the bedrooms.

I give her a quick hug. "Thanks again for inviting Jenn to 'babysit' while she's here. You're a lifesaver." Besides being a major distraction to Jennifer's quest to find her birth mother, her having this job makes it easier for me to concentrate at work. I don't have to wonder if she's bored at the office or okay at home alone.

Allie waves her hand in a "no worries" motion and snags us both a bottle of water from her fridge. "My mom loves the girls, but I know she's glad to have a break." She hands me the water and gives my jeans a look. "You having casual day at the office now?"

"No, I haven't given in to Norma on that yet. I changed before I left work so I'd be ready to take Jenn out to this insane bull riding practice." I hold up my wrist to show two black elastics around it. "Still need to get my hair out of my face though." At the end of the day, I usually pull my curly mane back in a ponytail, but I guess the thought of going to Jack's arena brings out the cowgirl in me. Today I'm in the mood for braids. I split my hair into two sections and quickly braid one.

"So you're heading out to see Jack?" Her casual tone doesn't fool me.

"Only because of Jenn." I slip a ponytail holder off my wrist, fasten the first braid, and start the second.

She shrugs. "Of course. I was just asking."

Yeah, just asking. Why is it that when a seemingly happy single friend finds true love, she can no longer believe that her own seemingly happy single friend really is happily single?

I secure the second braid and toss it over my shoulder. "I'd better get Jennifer so we can get going."

Down the hall, I glance in the open doorway of Miranda's room. Katie is perched on the bed, and Miranda is standing behind Jennifer. Their backs are toward me and they're concentrating on a laptop computer open on the desk.

"Hey."

Jennifer jumps and slams the laptop shut.

An uneasy feeling worms its way through my chest. "Ready to go?"

She shrugs. "Sure. Cute hair."

"Thanks."

She hugs the girls and Allie good-bye, and a few minutes later, we're on our way to the ranch.

As we turn down the lane, I can't contain myself any longer. "It was a little obvious that you didn't want me to see the Web page you were looking at back there."

Her face reddens, but she doesn't speak.

"You know I'm not one to play the heavy, Jenn, but the Internet can be a dangerous place."

She crosses her arms and gives a little humorless laugh. "Don't worry. I wasn't chatting with strangers or giving out my personal information."

"Then what?" I glance over at her resolute expression.

"Every time I ask you to help me find my birth mother, you put me off. I thought maybe I could find some info online."

My heart aches for her, and for a split second, I wonder if I'm doing the right thing. "And did you?"

She looks down at her lap and shakes her head.

I knew the answer, but relief still seeps into my tense muscles.

"Do you know who she is?"

I keep my eyes on the road. "I know your mom explained to you that it was a closed adoption. I can't answer that question even if I did know the answer. So it's not fair to keep asking me." Not that I'd expect her to be fair. She's a fifteen-year-old, for Pete's sake.

She blows her breath out in obvious exasperation. "I'm a teenager. I don't have to be fair."

And way too smart for her own good.

I turn down the tiny barn road and slow to a crawl. "If your birth mother had wanted you to know who she was, she'd have gone with an open adoption. But she didn't."

"Maybe she's changed her mind. You don't know."

Unfortunately, I *do* know.

I pull into the wide-open dirt parking area in front of Jack's barn, kill the motor, and turn in my seat to face her. "Sometimes you just have to move on, hon. You have your whole life ahead of you."

She yanks the car door open and jumps out, her blondish-red hair swinging. I'm still clutching the steering wheel when she leans back down to get in one last parting shot. "It's kinda hard to move on when you don't know where you've been."

She slams the door and strides toward the barn. I open my own door slowly and put my feet on the ground. My legs are as trembly as a new colt's as I jog to catch up with her. I knew this wouldn't be easy. I have to keep reminding myself that she's better off with a little unfulfilled curiosity than she would be with the harsh reality. Isn't she? Tears prick my eyes. If only I could be sure it's Jenn I'm protecting.

When we enter the covered arena, Jack looks up from where he's standing next to the corral fence talking to a young cowboy. A grin lights up his whole face, and he raises his hand in greeting. The chill that invaded my heart on the way here recedes a little.

He turns back to the cowboy for a brief moment then walks toward us. "I'm glad you came," he says to Jennifer, but his brown eyes seek mine out as he finishes.

Jenn turns to me. "I'm going to say hi to the horses, okay?"

"Sure," Jack and I say together.

She flits over to the stalls and reaches through to pat one of the mares.

"She seems happy," Jack says.

I glance up at him then back to Jenn. "Yeah, she does." Which is amazing. But typical for teenage years, I guess.

"I really *am* glad you came. I thought you might chicken out."

"Why should I?" I shrug. "I'm not considering climbing up on one of those crazy bulls."

"Speaking of that, you asked me about the plan. Here's the idea. Your dad brought Sweetie over today."

"My Sweetie?"

Jack nods. "He thinks that if you do a little barrel-racing exhibition before the bull riding, Jennifer might decide she'd rather do that."

I cringe. The thought of riding in front of people again makes me feel nauseated. It's been so long. I glance around the arena. It's not too bad—there are only a half-dozen cowboys milling around. But there's Jack. Unfortunately, I can't forget him. "Okay, I guess it's worth a try."

"Good. I had Dirk saddle Sweetie. She's waiting for you."

I raise an eyebrow. "That doesn't sound like you thought I'd chicken out."

His dimples flash. "Not really." He reaches over and flips one of my braids. "You may look like a carefree teenager tonight, but you strike me as a woman who does the right thing at all costs."

I used to be that woman. I glance toward the horse stalls where Jennifer pats a bay mare's neck. Or at least I thought I was. "At all costs" is an innocuous-sounding phrase until the cost becomes too high to pay. Then what?

"You okay?"

I look up, and Jack is staring at me, concern written plainly on his handsome face.

I nod and toss my braids over my shoulders. "Let's get this show on the road."

He motions to the young cowhand he was talking to earlier, and the teen heads to the stalls. "Do you know Dirk?" Jack asks me.

I shake my head.

"He works part-time for me and part-time for your dad."

"I'm usually at the barn pretty early—"

"And gone before anyone shows up. Yeah, I know."

I raise an eyebrow. The dark-haired cowhand walks up, leading Sweetie. Jack introduces us, and Dirk hands me the reins. "Nice to meet you, Dr. Donovan."

"You, too, Dirk."

When he leaves to set up the barrels, Jack pats Sweetie's neck. "You barrel race on her?"

"Not competitively. Her mother was my barrel-racing horse." An old pain stabs my heart. "She died when I was away at college. But she left us a real nice colt."

He runs his hand down her smooth nose. "She sure did. It's tough to lose a horse, though."

"Yeah, it is." I guess I lost so much during those years that I considered it par for the course.

"So Sweetie doesn't know the barrel course?"

I feel my face burn. "Actually, I've taught her the basics on my early morning workouts over the last eight years." I grimace. "Silly, I know."

He shrugs. "Same workout. Only the audience is different. And I guess the prize money isn't too great either."

I take a deep breath and step up into the saddle. "You think this will work? Jennifer has her own reasons for wanting to ride a bull." I pray he won't press me for those reasons, and he doesn't.

"Don't we all? Let's just hope hers aren't solid enough to make her dig her heels in."

"Let's hope."

Sweetie and I make some warm-up laps around the arena. When I'm feeling ready to face the barrels, I glance over to Jennifer, standing next to Jack. At least I have her attention. And not just hers. All the cowboys have gathered around the white metal fence. Toby Keith's voice blares out over the loudspeaker singing "It's a Little Too Late."

I hold Sweetie for a few seconds at the front, gauging the distance to the front barrel and giving us both time to focus. When I'm confident that the barrels are set up in the usual way, I lean forward in the saddle. "Let's show 'em how it's done," I whisper.

She takes off like a shot. We round the first barrel and make a beeline for the second, cutting it clean and close. Again, at the third barrel, I'm careful not to swing too wide. Adrenaline pumps through my body as we ride wide open back to the gate.

I've been to big-city rodeos with less whooping and hollering. Amid the whistles and clapping, I see Jennifer beaming.

I ride over to her and slide off Sweetie. Dirk appears to take the reins. "Thanks," I murmur and pat my horse on the neck as I hand her over.

"That was incredible," Jennifer breathes.

"Thanks." I've always considered myself happy not to be the center of attention, but I can't deny the thrill of pleasing an audience.

"It looks so complicated."

I come back to earth with a jolt. Here it is. The whole purpose of this little exercise in showmanship. "It is. But it just takes practice."

"Cool." She hitches her thumb toward the stable. "I'm going to go check on Sweetie."

She hurries off to see the horse, apparently not even noticing that the bull riding is about to begin.

Jack's voice comes from behind me. "Looks like your dad knew what he was doing this time."

I swing around to face him. "We'll see."

"You're still amazing in the arena."

"Thanks, Jack. It was fun."

"So I guess we don't have to wonder who'll win the senior barrels event."

I frown. "Do you mean me? No, I just ride for fun."

"You're not going to compete? Why?"

Haven't I already answered this question this week for Jennifer? I shrug. "Not my thing."

He narrows his eyes and gives me a measured look, then nods. "Well, you did a good job out there."

"Thanks." Again.

"You going to hang around and watch the bull riding?" He motions toward the practice pens. "Or do you think your mission is accomplished?"

"You riding?"

His dimples flash. "That depends. Are you staying if I do? Or staying if I don't?"

I laugh. "Neither one. I was just curious."

He readjusts his hat. "In that case, I wasn't planning on riding. I just open up the practice pens on Monday nights for the guys."

I'm still trying to decide whether to stay or go when Jennifer joins us. "Are they about to start bull riding?"

Jack nods. "Better get you a good seat. I have it on good authority that these bulls don't aim to be ridden tonight."

"Who told you that?" Jennifer asks.

"My horse. He overheard it earlier." Jack winks at us and motions toward the gates. "I'd better go get things started."

Within seconds, the opening line of one of Chris LeDoux's many rodeo songs blares from the speakers next to us and the gate swings open. I watch Jennifer's expression as the bull bucks and twists, a cowboy clinging to the saddle horn, trying valiantly to keep his hand in the air. Fear and fascination war across her face. I pray that the fear wins out.

"That is a *big* bull," she whispers in my ear.

"I hope this fence is solid," I say, as the twisting pair nears us.

"That's what I was thinking."

We both jump when the cowboy lands right in front of us, hitting the hard dirt with a thud. The bull barely misses stomping on his head. The cowboys in the arena deftly herd the snorting animal into the pen on the far side.

After the third man hits the ground long before the eight-second buzzer sounds, Jennifer looks over at me. "Think Grand-daddy will ever let me live it down if I don't try bull riding tonight?"

I smile at her. "I think he'll be eternally grateful. I imagine your grandmother would have banished him to the guest room or worse if you had."

We stare in morbid fascination as a fourth guy doesn't even make it all the way out of the chute on the bull. The music has mellowed into "My Heroes Have Always Been Cowboys."

"I will ride a bull one day," she says. "Just not today." I look over at her lifted chin, and terror chills my heart.

Chapter 10

J enn, I think I know why you really wanted to ride a bull."

A wary look crosses her face. She raises her eyebrows.

"When I was a little younger than you, I tried to ride a wild horse."

She whips around to look at me. "Why?"

I shrug. "It seemed like if I could do something so impossible, I could handle anything."

She turns her gaze back to the arena. "Did you do it?"

"I got on it but ended up with a busted collarbone."

"So you took up barrel racing instead?"

"Yeah."

"It looks hard." She glances over to where the next cowboy is preparing to ride a bull. "Maybe not as hard as bull riding, but hard."

"It is. In a way." I look over at Jennifer. "But you can do it. You come from a long line of barrel racers."

She frowns. "By adoption, you mean."

Now what do I say?

The truth as much as I can. "I think this is something that's in your spirit more than your blood. And you have the

Donovan spirit." *And would, even if you weren't blood-related,* I finish silently.

She shrugs. "I guess it wouldn't hurt to learn to barrel race while I'm getting up the nerve to bull ride."

"No. Doing one doesn't rule out doing the other, but—"

"Can I learn on Sweetie?"

I nod. "Of course you can. She seemed to like being in the limelight."

"Thanks, Aunt Rach. You're the best."

I can't count the number of times she's said that over the last thirteen years since she learned to talk. I think she says it without even thinking. But I've never taken one time for granted. And even though I know it's not true, especially now, it still makes me feel better hearing it.

Cowboy number five falls at our feet, and I nudge Jennifer. "Since you've decided to leave bull riding to another day, what do you think about us getting out of here and leaving these men with their dignity?"

She giggles. "Sounds good."

I'd like to slip out unnoticed, but good manners demand thanking the host, so we make our way over to Jack. He sees us coming and walks to meet us. "Leaving so soon?"

"We wanted to thank you for all your trouble." My words sound stilted. I guess I talk with him that way sometimes to make up for how relaxed I feel around him. I need to keep a balance.

"No trouble at all. It was my pleasure." He looks over at Jennifer. "What did you think about your aunt's barrel-racing skills?"

"Cool," Jennifer says with a broad smile. "I've decided I want to try to learn."

"I think you'll be a natural," he says.

"Thanks. But I *am* still going to learn to ride bulls, too." She looks over his shoulder and her eyes light up. "I'm going to run tell Dirk bye." And before I can say a word, she hurries toward the young cowboy.

I spin around and watch the dark-haired boy doff his hat as she approaches, and the two of them laugh and talk. Panic rises in my chest. What have I done introducing her to this world? I brush past Jack and march over to her. "Jenn, we have to go."

She frowns at me. "Why?"

"We just do. I have some things to do at home."

She rolls her eyes, and her face reddens. "Whatever. See you later, Dirk."

Not if I have anything to say about it.

Jack is still standing where I left him, a strange look on his face as we hurry out of the arena, my arm hooked in Jennifer's. When we walk out into the dusky darkness, she stops. "What was that all about?"

I look at her, the moonlight glinting off her hair and sparkling in her eyes. How can I possibly explain? "Cowboys. . . You can't—" I sigh. "I'm sorry if I embarrassed you, but it's time to go home."

Her mouth tightens, but she follows me to the car and doesn't bring it up again.

~

"She's got a crush on a cowboy, Tammy." I lean against the deck railing and stare unseeing into the darkness as I press the phone against my ear.

"A crush? She was just talking to him. Besides, she's fifteen. She's old enough to like boys."

How can she sound so calm? I grip the phone. "Maybe you didn't hear me. He's a cowboy."

"Rach," her voice softens, "he's what? Sixteen? Seventeen at the most? He's just a kid. And if Dad hired him, he must be a good kid."

I sigh. "I guess you're right. Seeing her laughing and talking with him tonight. . .it was déjà vu all over again. I freaked out."

"That's understandable, given your history."

"I guess." Even though Tammy and I have been through a lot together, the past is a subject we normally avoid. Unfortunately, the present is making that more and more difficult.

"I'm a lot more worried about the fact that she's determined to ride a bull," Tammy says.

"Can't you just tell her she can't do it?"

Tammy laughs. "Do you remember what it was like when you were fifteen? Did you always listen when Mama and Daddy told you not to do something?"

"Pretty much."

"Yeah, well, most of us didn't. But I will tell her no. Then you'll have to do your best to keep her from disobeying me."

I'm not worried. If her parents tell her riding bulls is out of the question, I'm sure she'll let it go. In fact, I think she'd welcome her parents' ruling as a dignified exit from something she really doesn't want to do anymore. "I notice Jenn's been calling you every day. How's that going?"

"Good." Tammy sounds happy. "She's coming around. I apologized for not telling her she's adopted. And she apologized for running away. She has a lot of unanswered questions, obviously"—

Let's hope it stays that way.

—"but she's healing."

"Which is all the more reason not to hurt her again by telling her the truth about me."

Silence.

Finally she says, "Russ and I have been praying about that, and we've decided that decision is up to you. We did a closed adoption with the understanding that we wouldn't tell Jennifer you were her birth mother unless we all agreed to someday. Obviously, you haven't agreed, and we're sticking with our deal."

Tears sting my eyes. "Thanks."

"It's the least we can do considering"—she clears her throat—"what a gift you gave us."

"You and Russ have given me a gift, too. The gift of watching her grow up in a Christian home with parents who are able to take care of her and look out for her. I appreciate y'all. And I need to thank you, too, for letting her stay here for a while. I'm really enjoying this time with her."

"Good. We miss her."

"I know you do." I clear my throat. "Hey. . ."

"Yeah?"

"Did. . .is. . .do you think she's having a good time with me?"

"Rach, she loves you. She's thrilled to be there." She hesitates. "Except for one thing. . ."

"What?" My heart is in my throat.

"She can't understand how anyone can live in a house without sugar."

I blow out my breath. "Very funny. I have sugar."

"Yeah, but only a tiny bit of organic sugar in the sugar bowl. You don't have any snacks or desserts with sugar in the house."

"I never told her she couldn't have sugar."

"That's a relief. Then you won't kick her out if you find her contraband M&M's and Dove Promises?"

I smile in the dark. "She'd better watch it. If I have many more days like I've had lately, I'll be confiscating her stash."

"I'm sure she'll be glad to share."

"Let's hope it doesn't come to that." I glance back over my shoulder. "I'd better get back in the house before she comes out looking for me."

"Okay, but do me a favor."

"What?"

"Next time Jenn talks to a cowboy, relax a little."

I sigh. "I'll try. It's hard to realize she's even old enough to notice the opposite sex."

Tammy laughs. "Oh, believe me, she's old enough to notice. But she has a good head on her shoulders. And you have to realize all cowboys aren't the same."

"In theory, I know that."

"Take Jack Westwood." Tammy's voice is overly casual. "He sounds like he grew up nice."

"What do you know about Jack?"

"Mama and Daddy say he's a really good neighbor."

Since when do we talk about Mom and Dad's neighbors? There has to be more to it than that. "And?"

"And Jenn has mentioned him a few times."

"What did she say about him?"

"She said he's nice, and she thinks he likes you."

"He doesn't—"

"Oh, and that he's drop-dead gorgeous for an old man."

I laugh. "Yeah, well, she's got that right. Which is just another strike against him."

"I didn't realize he was up to bat," she says.

I gently slap my forehead. Why did I say that? She'll never let it drop now.

"You know, Tam, there's a reason people use the phrase 'devastatingly handsome.'"

"Isn't that a little judgmental?"

Only a sister knows how to hit where it hurts. I can't stand for people to judge without basis. "What do you mean?"

"Well, you don't like him because he's a cute cowboy. What would you call that?"

"Smart?" I pop off then sigh. "I know you're right, but there's more to it."

"Something to do with the past?"

I lean against the wooden railing of my deck and dial my voice down a notch. "He was there that summer. He was part of Brett's crowd. I'm afraid he knows."

I close my eyes, and for a brief second, I actually see him—a thinner, ganglier Jack, laughing with Brett's crowd. Reckless. Cocky. Maybe, hopefully, oblivious.

"Does he act like he knows?"

I close my eyes against the tears that are pricking. "No. But even if he doesn't, he might remember more than he realizes. He might eventually put two and two together."

"God's forgiven you, Rach. You've got to let it go and forgive yourself."

I let out a trembly laugh. "If I had a piece of chocolate for every time you've told me that. . .but it's hard to let go of the past."

"You know what, Rach? Don't let go of it. Your past made you the amazing woman you are today. But you still need to embrace the future, free of shame and guilt."

I hear her fumbling around, and I open my eyes and grin. "Did you just write that down?" Tammy's a speechwriter, and sometimes her speeches flow over into her conversations. Or rather, her conversations flow over into her speeches.

She gives an embarrassed chuckle. "You know me too well. But I meant it. Call me later. Love you."

We hang up, and I linger for a few minutes to watch the fireflies playing tag in the dark.

I tilt my face to the night sky and close my eyes. *Lord, You know I don't know what I'm doing. Please forgive me of the past. And help me.*

The back door creaks. I swing around. Jennifer stands in the doorway squinting to adjust her eyes to the darkness. She's almost as tall as I am. How did she grow up so soon?

"Aunt Rachel?"

"Yeah?"

"Will you walk with me out to the car? I left my iPod out there, and I'm scared to go by myself."

I grin, relieved in spite of myself. Maybe she's not so grown up after all. "Sure."

Chapter 11

I'm a few minutes early for the next committee meeting, but Jack is waiting. He jumps up to pull out my chair.

"Hey," I say and plop Ron's notebook onto the vinyl-topped table. "So, how do we get a real meeting started? We never made it that far last time."

Jack clears his throat. "Um, before we get started, I gotta tell ya that a reporter called me today and asked when the next meeting was. I figured we could use all the media exposure for the rodeo we could get, so..."

"A reporter?" Uh-oh. "What reporter?"

"There she is now." Jack pushes to his feet again.

I turn to look at the door and groan. I should have known.

Channel 6's *Wake Up, Shady Grove* has a reality show segment called "Get Real, Shady Grove." Blair Winchester, the station's star anchorwoman, has decided it will be great fun to stick her nose into—I mean, get impromptu footage of—the various workings of the centennial celebration. I'd gotten my fill of her on-air manipulations when she'd followed Allie's landscaping crew, including me, around with a camera, trying to make us look stupid. I'd really hoped the rodeo preparations would escape her notice, but apparently not.

I stand and brace myself as she approaches our table with a cameraman right behind her. "Blair," I murmur in way of greeting, but I needn't have bothered.

She ignores me and swoops in on Jack like a starving buzzard over roadkill. "I'm Blair Winchester. It's such an honor to meet you. I've watched you ride bulls so many times and never thought I'd get a chance to meet you in person."

Jack's face reddens, and he ducks his head. "Nice to meet you too, Mrs. Win—"

She throws back her head and laughs, a musical trill that she definitely practices at home. "You can call me Blair. But it's *Miss*. I'm single. And I'm planning to stay that way." She bats her heavy-with-mascara lashes at him then has the audacity to give him a sly wink. "Unless I meet someone who makes me an offer I can't refuse."

Oh, brother. Can we say obvious?

Blair slides into the chair opposite me. As Jack sits back down between us, she scoots over close to him and pats his hand, showing off her signature long red fingernails. "I'll just be a fly on the wall. You won't even notice I'm here."

Her perfume alone makes that an impossibility, but I sit down and open my notebook.

She motions the cameraman to start rolling. "Sooo," she purrs to Jack, "what time do you think the meeting will start?"

He looks at me and raises a brow. "You ready to get this done?"

I nod.

Blair frowns, but I notice her forehead doesn't wrinkle. Oh, the wonders of Botox. "Where is the rest of the committee?"

"For right now, I'm it." I tap my notebook and look at Jack. "First let's talk about the concession stand."

"Wait," Blair interjects, the buzziest fly on the wall I've ever seen. "Do you mean our fair city's centennial celebration committee consists of one person?"

"No, but the other members weren't able to make it tonight," I say through clenched teeth. No use in even telling her that I'm just filling in.

"Weren't able to make it?" she asks. "Why not?"

"Personal reasons." She's a reporter; let her figure it out. "Now if you'll excuse us, we need to get a few details taken care of."

She sits back in her chair and crosses her legs. Could that suit skirt be any shorter?

I start with the concession stand items, partly because I figure this is the least controversial, and I'm not about to fuel Blair's apparent love of tabloid-style reporting.

Jack pulls out two pieces of paper from his folder, keeps one, and gives me one.

I read the list of conventional concession stand items: hot dogs, popcorn, nachos, candy.

"Uh, Jack, I was thinking that maybe this year, we could, you know, maybe add some healthy alternatives. Sliced apples? Salad in a bag?" I put down the sheet. "I saw this company that makes vegetable wraps, and they looked so—"

"You're kidding, right?"

I expect the words from Jack, perhaps, but not Blair, who has apparently lost all attempts at objectivity. "Health food at a rodeo?" She leans back, shaking her blond curls, one eyebrow cocked. "Puh–lease."

I glance at Jack. I see what looks like a small battle waging on his face, between agreeing with her and not wanting to make a scene on local television.

Oh yeah, that's right. *Local television.* I shoot a glance at the camera and pick up the sheet of concession items.

"This is a good start, however."

Jack gives me the briefest of dubious looks before he says, "Our company orders the food and provides people to work the concession stand."

I remember what Ron said about saving money. "I thought we'd have volunteers do that." Oops, more controversy. I force a smile.

He shrugs. "If you want to, you can, but most people find it easier to let us do it."

"For a larger cut of the profits." I lower my voice as I say this, though. Maybe they won't catch it on camera.

"Well, yes." A wry grin edges his lips upward. "We don't do it for free."

"Normally I'd say let's do it the easiest way, but I crunched some numbers earlier, and unless we figure out a way to raise the attendance figures above average, we won't be making much of a profit anyway. So I vote volunteers."

"Whatever you think," Jack says.

See, that wasn't so hard. We'll get back to the food later. Meanwhile, I turn to Blair. Might as well make use of her presence. "If you could put out an on-air call for concession stand volunteers. . ."

She smirks. " 'Get Real, Shady Grove' is about the funny side of the celebration preparations. It's not a charity drive."

"I thought you might want to do something useful for a change," I mutter.

She seems to take that as some sort of subtexted line in the sand, because she leans forward, pushes her microphone in my face, and asks sweetly, "The last time we saw you involved in the centennial celebration, you were showing off your very amateur landscaping skills."

It takes all my willpower to return her smile, but I remember how skillful she is at editing these clips. "Yes, I worked with my friend Allie Richards of TLC Landscaping. She won the competition and is now in charge of the landscaping for the city of Shady Grove."

Blair's nostrils flare, but she quickly recovers. "So is this another case of helping someone you care about? What"—she gives a pointed look at Jack—"or should I say who, has fired your passion for the centennial celebration rodeo, Dr. Donovan?"

I give her my best professional smile. "Maybe we can do an interview later, but right now we're in the middle of a meeting."

Jack is grinning.

Blair shoots me a glare.

Jack's smile dims. He clears his throat and hands me a new paper. "Here's the proposed program order."

I look down at the straightforward list of rodeo events.

"I wrote these out in the usual order, but if we have a lot of contestants in the junior events, maybe we should consider doing ten-ten-ten."

I give him a benign smile, determined not to show my ignorance in front of Blair.

He apparently picks up on my confusion—hopefully the camera doesn't—because he jumps in to expound. "We'd start off with the little guys mutton busting, but then we'd have ten contestants in the sorting, ten in the goat tying—"

"Goat tying?" I shake my head. "Are we locked into these events?"

"Why?" Jack asks.

"Because I've always thought goat tying was barbaric." I must sound like a softhearted idiot, but I can't help it. "Have you seen one of those little goats? Poor little fella. After the contestant unties him, he lies there and pretends he's dead—"

I break off as I notice Blair motion the cameraman to zoom in on me. Oops, again.

"We can discuss it later."

Blair pastes on what I'm coming to think of as her buzzard smile. She has an unerring radar for weak spots. "Dr. Donovan, I would guess that your committee needs publicity for the rodeo. If you don't let us have a behind-the-scenes feel, then how can you expect to raise interest?" Apparently it's a rhetorical question, because she turns to Jack. "I've never seen goat tying, but it certainly *sounds* barbaric. What do you think?"

He gives me a level look that I roughly translate into "Why did you get me into this crazy mess?" then turns his gaze back to her. "I guess it just depends on how you look at it. Goats are known for being stubborn, and they're certainly not mistreated in our rodeos."

"Do you feel they're mistreated, Dr. Donovan?"

Oh good grief. Jack cocks his head as if he's truly interested and not holding himself back from strangling me. Committee meetings—more fun than a barrel of goats.

I keep my voice cool. "It's been a long time since I've been to a rodeo." I run my finger along the list of events and stare for a second at my short, unpainted nails. Prada versus practicality—that's Blair and me. But I will not rise to her bait. "You were explaining the ten-ten-ten schedule," I remind Jack. Code for "Let's keep going and get this over with."

Jack nods. "Yes, so after the mutton busting, we'd just have ten contestants in each event, the barrels, the poles, and so on, until the bull riding. Then, after we do all the bull riders, we'd start over with the remaining contestants in the other events and call out the winners."

I frown. "What's the logic in doing it that way?"

He leans forward. "Keeps the crowd from getting bored.

Most people are waiting for the bull riding."

"Says who?"

Okay, so that sounds a little junior-highish, but as a former barrel-racing champion, I'm insulted to the tips of my figurative cowgirl boots.

Blair's laugh trills through the room. Clearly, I'm also hilarious.

Jack shoots her a look.

"Well, she's right. It's not about the bull riding." She leans close to Jack and touches his arm. I see him freeze, even if she doesn't. "Everybody knows it's the big brave bull riders we want to see."

"I didn't mean—" I start, but Jack is already on his feet.

"I think our time's up for tonight. Thanks for coming, Ms. Winchester."

She bats her eyes at him. "Aren't you going to finish discussing the program? I'm sure you need to know—"

"We'll take it up next meeting." He looks at me and touches his hat. But his eyes are cold. "Good night."

I can't help but feel confusion as I watch him leave. I know Blair comes across a little—okay, a *lot*—strong, but isn't he used to gorgeous women throwing themselves at him?

Blair watches him leave then turns back to me. "Does he always call the shots? I thought he works for the committee."

I consider the best answer and my gaze falls on a menu. "Blair, have you tried Daniel's new Absolutely Amazing Allie Cappuccino?"

She purses her lips, probably remembering how hard she tried to get her talons into Allie's fiancé back when they first met. He was a cameraman then, and Blair had him practically jumping through hoops until he got tired of it.

"No, I don't believe I've tried that one. But I think I'll

pass. Some of Daniel's concoctions are sickeningly sweet." She stands and motions the cameraman to wrap it up. "Let me know when your next meeting is."

Fat chance.

She and her tagalong leave in a huff, and I'm gathering my papers when, to my surprise, Jack walks back up to my table. "Is she gone? For real?"

Uh-oh. My heart does this little jump in my chest that has nothing to do with being startled. "I thought you left."

"I hid over in the Christian romance section."

"Learn anything interesting?"

"Christian girls like cowboys."

Oh. Well, just to keep him honest, I snort. "Not all Christian girls."

"That's too bad." He watches me as I finish putting the papers in my bag, as if he might want to say something. I sling the bag over my shoulder then turn to him.

He looks past me, out to the parking lot. Night has fallen, and with the glare from the windows, I know he can't see a thing, so I guess he's gathering his thoughts. Finally he speaks. "Listen, I'm sorry about what I said earlier. Of course people come to see all the events. She was twisting everything we said, and I just wasn't thinking."

I have to forgive him. For one thing, at least he sees Blair for what she is. That's more than I can say for most men. "Well, I know a lot of people *do* come to see the bull riding, so I'll let it slide."

"While I'm 'hat in hand,' I guess I should be apologizing about inviting her. We need publicity, but that was clearly a bad move on my part. I'll figure something else out for that."

"Good idea."

He sighs, and for a second, he's got twelve-year-old sheepish boy all over his face. It's so endearing, all my anger vanishes in a flash.

"Now that she's gone, do you want to finish our meeting?"

"Sure."

We make it through the next half hour with no disagreements, but I'm keenly aware of the intimate feeling of working with him alone on this project.

"Do you think I should try to find some other committee fill-ins?" I ask as we put away our papers.

He raises an eyebrow. "You're doing fine. If we run into another problem, we'll hash it out."

"Okay." I pick up my notebook and start to stand. He reaches toward my arm but stops short of touching me. "Rachel, would you let me buy you a latte?"

It's the way he says it that stops me. With a sort of softness in his voice.

I will not be swayed by charm. "Thanks. But I really need to get home." Even I can hear the insincerity in my voice.

He finds my eyes. "Stay. Because I don't believe in accidents."

"Accidents?" I'm still not sure where he's going with this.

"I've been trying to catch your attention since we were fourteen or fifteen and never have been able to. I figure this committee thing may be God's way of giving me a chance to finally get to know you. What do you think?"

Chapter 12

I sit back down almost without realizing what I'm doing. I've never met anyone quite so straightforward. "I don't know what you mean. You know me. We've known each other since we were kids."

And it's true. I've known Jack practically since we were born. I don't remember our first "meeting," but I know we played together in our kitchens while our mothers canned for hours when we were tiny. And even though he was a grade ahead, we were in 4-H together. His smile is certainly familiar to me, at least the teasing element. Not so much the heart-stopping-dangerous part. That came after he left town apparently. And I remember how he could hang on to a bull, or get thrown and come up smiling. We were buds, certainly.

Then there was Brett. And from that night on I had no choice but to avoid Jack. But that doesn't mean I don't know him. "Really, Jack. I know you."

Is that desperation in my voice?

"That's what you think." He leans toward me. "What's my favorite color?"

I grin, drawn to him in spite of myself. "Green?"

He shrugs. "Lucky guess. But I don't know yours."

I cross my arms. I'll play, but not willingly. "Red."

Upon hearing this, most people say that I like red because my hair's red. But Jack looks at me and nods. "Because red is the color of being alive and healthy?"

I blink. I couldn't have said it better myself. "Yes," I say quietly.

"All time favorite song?" he asks.

"Oh, that's a tough one. There are so many."

"I'll narrow it down," he offers. "All time favorite country song."

I shrug, not willing to think too hard and give this man more of an insight into my soul. He already seems to have a clear view. " 'Mississippi Squirrel Revival' by Ray Stevens."

He leans back, and his eyes widen. "Your all-time favorite song is about a squirrel that gets loose in church?"

"Hey, I think it's hilarious. And my brain freezes when you put me on the spot. So, Mr. Know-It-All, what's yours?"

He pauses. "I'm not sure."

I shake my head with a laugh. "You're not getting off that easy. Name one."

His brown eyes twinkle. "Now it's my turn for brain freeze. Ask me something else, and I promise I'll answer."

He should really be more careful with his promises. Because one thing has been bothering me all evening. "Okay. What was that all about with Blair a while ago?"

The relaxed expression on his face disappears immediately, and his jaw muscle tightens. "She was messing up our meeting, so I decided it was best to get rid of her."

I'm not buying that. I've had too many patients pull that innocent act—"No, Doc, I have no idea why I'm hurting. All I did was weed the garden and vacuum." I narrow my eyes and reply, "You obviously have her wanting to start a fan club, but the minute she turns on the charm, you take off in a run."

"I wasn't running."

"I practically got whiplash. And I'm the only person in town who can fix that, so that wouldn't be pretty." I smile, trying to take the edge off my words, but he doesn't match it.

He shakes his head. "I've known women like Blair. All she sees when she looks at me is the thrill of danger."

Oh. I know that's probably true, but my stomach clenches. Oh please, I'm not jealous, am I? "And that's bad?"

"No, it's fine. Probably just what I should expect. So what's your favorite movie?"

I laugh. "Nice try. But they didn't call me 'bulldog' in chiropractic college for nothin', pal." I give him my best tough-guy glare, and he finally gives me a small grin. "Seriously, why does that bother you so badly? I guess I always thought bull riders wanted the girls to see them as a walk on the wild side. A good time."

"Maybe I don't want just a good time." His gaze is even. "Maybe I want to be seen for the guy I am, not the image."

Ah. "What was her name?" As soon as the words slip out, I regret speaking. If I'm going to maintain distance with this man, the last thing I need to do is pry into his past. And what if he decides to return the favor?

He looks up at me, his eyes dark. "I. . .really, what's your favorite movie?"

I could give in. But a dangerous, even wild, thread, the one that probably got me into trouble in my youth, makes me speak. "You can tell me, Jack. I know how to keep a secret."

Understatement of the year.

He regards me a long moment, during which I wonder if he'll make me give him a secret in exchange, which I most certainly won't do. So I'm surprised when he answers, "Maggie."

"Maggie," I repeat softly.

He takes a deep breath. "She was doing one of those coffee table books on rodeos. We dated for a year and a half. Me, her, and her camera." He tries to grin, but the pain in his face is evident.

"A photojournalist?"

"I thought we had a future, but when the book was done, so were we, as far as she was concerned."

Ouch. "I'm sorry."

He runs his hand along the tabletop. "I reacted pretty stupidly at first. But we won't go there."

Not going to stupid things we did in the past. I can so relate. "Okay. So where were we? Oh, *Steel Magnolias.*"

He meets my eyes and smiles. "Incredible strength encased in a soft Southern accent and a tight circle of girlfriends. That makes sense."

I never thought of it that way, but of course, he's right. I lift a shoulder, but I feel as if I've told him way more than I should have. "Actually, I haven't had time to see a movie in years. That was just a favorite when I was younger."

He smiles at me. A sweet, curious smile that has my heart thumping. This must be what speed dating feels like. I've never done anything so impulsive in my life. A shadow creeps over me and my sudden good mood. Yes, I have. Once.

As if he can follow my train of thought, he says, "You probably don't even remember, but I called you right before I left town for the rodeo circuit."

My muscles tighten all over my body, guarding against his words as if protecting myself from a physical attack. "I remember." When the phone had rung, I'd thought sure it was Brett, magically remembering me and my phone number.

But it had been Jack, calling to see if I'd go to the county fair with him.

He grins. "I spent the next several months hoping maybe you just didn't like county fairs. By the time I got home for a short visit the next summer, you had already gone off to Georgia to school."

I certainly can't tell him I was a little too preoccupied with a positive home pregnancy test at the time to think about cotton candy and tilt-a-whirls. I force my stiff lips into an answering smile. Apparently, my attempt is a failure, because he frowns.

"I'm sorry I've yammered on so long. You probably just didn't want to go out with me. Tell me what you want to drink, and I'll run get it."

If he has no suspicions about that summer and my speedy exit from Arkansas three months later, then I should definitely stay and visit longer. Just so none arise. But I can't. Can you be seasick on dry ground? That's how I've felt ever since he mentioned that summer. "Actually, I'm not feeling well." I put my hands on the table and push to my feet.

My words have the effect of rain on a sunny day. His face falls. "Did I say something wrong?"

"No. . .it's just been a long day." I push to my feet, gather my bags.

He stands immediately. "Are you gonna be okay?"

I nod. "I'd better just get home."

"Should I drive you?"

He looks so worried. "No, thanks, Jack. I had a nice time." I motion to the table so he'll know I meant during our getting-to-know-you-again session.

He smiles. "Me, too. I hope you're not coming down with something."

"I'm probably just overtired."

"Maybe you're not getting enough rest. Your niece is still visiting, isn't she?"

Was that a normal question? Idle curiosity? Or is he trying to figure out why Jennifer's with me? Just in case, I ignore the question and respond to his comment. "Yeah, I need to rest more."

He insists on walking me out to my car and seeing me safely inside, which is nice, actually. The night air seems to blow away all my "wooziness," and I thank him.

"My pleasure," he says.

Mine, too, I think. And that's the problem.

~

"So you're resolving not to be so paranoid about Jack?" Allie asks.

I nod. "It's not his fault he was around that summer."

"No, it's not. You grew up together, for goodness' sake," Lark says. "And it was one thing when you were just avoiding him, although I personally thought that was silly. But now that you have to see him on a regular basis, you might as well be friends."

Allie gives me a sideways grin and holds up a beautiful cream lace wedding dress in front of her. "Or whatever you want to be."

"Friends," I say firmly. "Just friends. Nice dress."

"Hey"—Allie slides the dress back onto the rack—"do you think Jenn would like to sit at the guest book?"

"Oh, I'm sure she'd love to, Allie, but you don't have to include her just because she's staying with me."

"I'd love to have her. I'll ask her next time I see her."

"Look at this one," Victoria says from a few feet away. She slides a simple off-white tea-length dress out from the rack and holds it up for us to see.

Allie gasps and lunges toward it. "That's the one."

"Don't be shy. Tell us how you really feel," Lark says dryly.

"Try it on." Vic passes it to Allie, and we all traipse back to the dressing room to wait.

In a few moments, Allie comes out, the elegantly simple dress the perfect complement to her long blond hair and blue eyes.

I stare at her. "You look like Sleeping Beauty."

"Only awake," Lark adds.

"It is the one, isn't it, Al?" Vic asks.

She nods. "Mission accomplished."

Lark pats her stomach. "In that case, let's get started on the next mission."

"Bridesmaids' dresses?" Allie asks, her voice muffled in the cubicle.

"First things first. Bridesmaids must eat."

"Luckily," Allie says, as she comes out of the dressing room wearing her regular clothes and smoothing down her hair, "we can kill two birds with one stone, as Lark's granny always said, and go see Mama Ruth." She looks at the time on her phone. "I told her we'd be there between ten thirty and eleven."

Victoria nods. "Brilliant."

The rest of us quickly agree, and ten minutes later, we reconvene at the huge kitchen table of Shady Grove's quintessential wedding planner. Mama Ruth has been planning weddings since long before it was vogue to have or be a wedding planner. She calls it "putting on." She "puts on" a wedding and handles everything but the wedding dress.

After we pick out the fabric and pattern for the bridesmaids' dresses, Mama Ruth brings out a huge platter of doughnuts and a hot pot of coffee. I ignore the doughnuts but go for the caffeine. Everything in moderation, after all.

Mama Ruth pats my shoulder as she passes out napkins. "Doc Rachel, it looks like we'll be planning your wedding next," she says.

"Is there something you're not telling us?" Victoria mutters beside me.

I glare at her then smile up at the older woman. "No wedding plans for me," I say, infusing my voice with cheer.

She shakes her head. "Soon. I saw you on TV the other morning. There were enough sparks between you and Jack Westwood to start a forest fire."

Victoria bursts out laughing, and Allie and Lark quickly put their hands to their mouths, no doubt to cover their own smiles.

I groan and cover my face with my hands. "Don't believe everything you see on TV, Mama Ruth."

She pours me another cup of coffee. "Denial is normal at first."

I peek at her through my fingers. "Jack and I are just friends."

She looks over at Allie. "Isn't that what you kept telling me about you and your Daniel? That you were 'just friends.'"

Allie nods mutely. Her hand is still in front of her mouth, but her eyes are dancing.

Mama Ruth nudges me. "See? Don't forget me when it's time to make the wedding plans."

I just nod and take a big gulp of coffee then push to my feet. "If we've got the details all ironed out, I'd better go."

I wave at everyone then drop a kiss on the older woman's wrinkled cheek. "Thanks for the coffee."

As I let myself out, I hear her say, "Denial. But that's normal."

My friends—the traitors—all laugh.

Chapter 13

I tap gently on the hospital room door then peek inside. Ron is lying in the bed, unmoving; no one else is in the room. The big man looks smaller somehow. Beneath his hospital gown, his leg is heavily bandaged. I motion Jennifer to follow me, and we tiptoe in. I set the flowers on the rolling tray beside his bed.

"We'll come back later," I whisper to Jennifer.

"No need for that; you're here now," Ron says dryly from the bed.

I spin around. "I thought you were asleep."

His brown eyes look tired, but they're twinkling. He pushes up to a sitting position. "That's what you were supposed to think. If you were Alma."

I grimace. "I thought she was helping you."

He grunts. "Depends on what you mean by helping."

I introduce Jennifer, who smiles politely and accepts Ron's invitation to the TV remote control and a place on the mini-couch in front of it.

I motion to Ron's heavily bandaged knee. "So, how are you?"

"Had to practically take my whole kneecap off and put it back on. But they say I should be able to go home Monday."

"That sounds really painful. But it's wonderful that you'll be back home soon."

He shrugs. "I guess. But at least here I have some protection. Alma's bound to want to take care of me at home."

"What's wrong with that?"

"Have you ever seen *Misery* with Kathy Bates? Alma could be that woman's evil twin."

I laugh then cut it off when he glares at me.

"Why else do you think she's here, if not to make me miserable? She's getting me back for every time I've ever disagreed with her since this whole centennial thing started."

"Maybe she just wants to help you."

He snorts.

"Good morning," comes a cheery voice as the door swings open. Alma, holding a cup of coffee out in front of her, stops when she sees me, her smile growing broader. "Dr.—Rachel, what a happy surprise."

"Hi, Alma." I introduce Jennifer, who looks up from the TV with a smile.

"What a beautiful girl."

"Thank you." Ever since Jennifer's been here, I've been afraid someone will remark on the resemblance between us, but thankfully, either the resemblance is a figment of my imagination or no one finds it worth mentioning, since she's my sister's daughter. Either way, I'm relieved.

"How are you doing?" I ask Alma.

"My arthritis is acting up a little in my left hip, but I'm doing well, considering." She hands Ron the coffee. "I finally found that coffee shop you like. Half caf, half decaf, just like you ordered." Alma's voice is lilting and sweet.

He takes a sip then sputters. "Did you put two sugars in this?"

"Yes, and one creamer, just like you said."

He sets it on the tray, and she immediately picks it up. "What's wrong with it?"

He shrugs. "It needs more sugar, but it's all right. I don't have to have coffee."

She smiles and sets the coffee back down. "I'll tell you what. Since you've got company anyway, I'll run down to the cafeteria and get a few packets of sugar, and you can fix it like you want."

"I can do that—," I start to say, but she holds up her hand.

"It'll do my hip good to get some exercise."

"You might as well bring more creamer, too, if you're going," Ron says.

When she's gone, I turn back to Ron. "Oh, I can see how she's making you miserable."

He nods. "It's awful. She can talk the spots off a leopard. Never quiet."

I shake my head. "I was being sarcastic."

He looks startled and then a sly gleam comes into his eyes. "You in cahoots with her? Drove all the way down here to make fun of a sick man?"

This time I snort. "Actually, I came to check on you. And to talk to you about the rodeo."

"What about it?"

"Did you see *Wake Up, Shady Grove* this week?"

He nods. "That was some good publicity. Did you two script that?"

"Hardly. My patients couldn't quit talking about it. Blair made me look like a lunatic."

"Now that's a little strong. It's her job to play up the conflict."

"Everything that wasn't conflict is apparently lying on the cutting room floor."

"Conflict sells. And we need to sell tickets to the rodeo."

"Blair aside, I need some input. I think I'm in over my head."

I ask about workers for the concession stand, and he shakes his head. "Too hard to get volunteers. Let Westwood handle it. Make the money back by using Blair's show to get us as much free publicity as you can. If she wants to see a soap opera between you and the cowboy, give it to her."

I ignore his last advice. "What about Jack's ten-ten-ten idea?"

"Sounds logical. He's right. Most people do come to see the bull riders. Discuss it further. But no matter what he says, if you don't want to do it, stand your ground." He glances at the door and lowers his voice. "Can't let this family push us around."

I clear my throat. "How do you feel about goat tying?"

He laughs. "It's always been a part of the rodeo in these parts. Next thing you know, you'll be wanting to do away with mutton bustin'."

I can feel my face grow hot. "I do want us to be careful about our weight limit on the mutton busting. Mama or Daddy setting the little tots on the back of a sheep is not a big deal, but I've seen some kids want to give it a try who weigh as much as any of the sheep do. Nothing fun about watching a sheep collapse as soon as Junior gets on his back."

"Get you some scales and weigh those little darlings."

I grin. "How soon can you come back to the committee meetings?"

He reaches over and pats my hand. "You're doing a fine job. If all goes well, I'll be there the opening night of the rodeo to cheer you on. Might be using a cane, but I'm planning on being there."

"I hope you can be."

"You getting along with Westwood okay?"

"About as well as you are with his mama."

He cringes. "Ouch. That bad?"

I raise my eyebrows. "Well, let's put it this way. He's not bringing me coffee then running his legs off to make sure it's fixed the way I like it."

I see a hint of chagrin in his expression, but before he can reply, Alma comes back in. "It's our lucky day. I found both sugar and creamer down at the nurses' station."

She hands them to Ron, and he nods.

"Alma?" I say. "Are you coming back to the committee meetings?"

She frowns. "I don't think so. I'll have my hands full taking care of our patient here."

"I'm sure Ron can get an in-home nurse and free you up—"

A loud groan comes from the bed, and we swing around to see Ron holding his knee. "Spasm," he chokes out, his eyes locked on Alma's face. "Pillow?" he asks pitifully.

She hurries over to tuck a pillow under his knee then turns back to me. "I can't leave him. I'm so sorry, dear. But you and Jack will do just fine."

I'm almost positive I see a grin flit across Ron's face, but when I take a second look, his grimace is firmly in place.

~

When the phone rings, I instinctively sit up in bed and grab it from the nightstand. "Hello."

"Dr. Donovan, it's Judy Costin."

Relief courses through me just as it does every time a patient calls in the middle of the night and it's not Tammy or my parents. That puts being awakened at—I glance at my alarm clock—2:00 a.m. into perspective. "Hi, Judy. What's wrong?"

I push my hair back off my face and swing my feet around to the floor. Cocoa and Shadow jump instantly to their feet.

"I'm okay, but Bobby rolled over a while ago and he musta pulled something. He didn't want me to call you, especially in the middle of a thunderstorm."

Lightning makes my bedroom look like daylight for a split second. I hadn't even realized it was storming.

"But that stabbing pain between his shoulders..." She stops, and when she speaks again, it's almost a whisper. "He's been crying, Doc, or I wouldn't have called."

"How soon can you be at the office?"

"Fifteen minutes."

"I'll meet you there."

"Are you sure? I've been watching the weather, and they say the worst of the storm is over. But there's still going to be a hard summer rain. If you want to wait until it quits completely, that's fine."

"I won't melt." I flip on my light switch and search through my closet. "I'll be right there."

"I'm sorry."

I stop in midmotion. "Don't be sorry, Judy. I'm glad I'm here to help. I'll be praying for Bobby on the way over, and you be praying that God will guide my hands."

"We sure will, Dr. Donovan. See you there."

When she hangs up, I fly into hyper mode, and within four minutes, I'm dressed and brushing my teeth. I snag my lip gloss from the drawer and freeze. I forgot about Jennifer. Do I leave her here? Get her up and make her go? Fifteen is surely old enough to stay home by herself. But what if she wakes up and is scared? I glance out the window at the sheets of rain coming down. Especially in this weather.

I tiptoe to the door of her room. She's sprawled out on

the bed, and it hits me again as it did the other night out on the deck. She's full grown. Physically, at least. She stirs, and I whisper, "Jenn."

Both dogs, apparently taking my whisper as a cue, leap up on the foot of her bed. Jenn jumps and sits up. "What?" Her voice comes out loud and forceful in the dark room.

"I have an emergency patient, so I have to run to the office. It's still pouring, so it doesn't look like Allie will need you to babysit tomorrow. If you want to go with me, you can sleep in when we get back."

She flips on her bedside lamp and pushes her hair back from her face. "You want me to go?"

Part of me does. So I'll have the company. So I won't have to worry about her being home alone. But she's a kid. And it's not her responsibility to go out in the middle of the night. "It's totally up to you. I thought you might not want to stay alone."

She shrugs and yawns. "I've got the dogs. I'll be fine. I stayed at home alone last month when Mom and Dad went to a conference."

I have a sudden vision of my mom leaving me at home at sixteen while she went to Georgia. My dad was there, and I still managed to find trouble. Tammy and I need to talk.

I guess she reads my face, because she says, "Lissa spent the nights with me, but I was by myself a lot of the time." She looks at the rain beating against the window and snuggles back down amid the covers with a dog on each side of her feet. "If it's okay with you, I'll just stay here and sleep. Unless you need me," she says, sleep already slurring her tone.

"I always need you," I whisper and drop a kiss on her forehead. "I'll be back in just a little while. You go back to sleep." I reach over and flip off the lamp switch and tiptoe out the door.

When I'm almost to the street that the clinic is on, I see blue lights ahead. I slow to a crawl and lean up to peer through the windshield. A man with a flashlight and a slicker motions me to go around a car that's crashed into the bridge guardrail. I recognize him and wave. He gives me a two-fingered salute, and I smile. Jack may be a reckless, bull-riding cowboy who leaves broken hearts in his wake, but he's also a dedicated public servant—I'll give him that.

Five minutes later, I pull into the office parking lot, my headlights reflecting off the wet asphalt. Soon after I kill the motor, a car swoops into the lot behind me. How's that for timing?

I grab my umbrella and prepare to walk up to the door with Judy and Bobby. A spotlight shines in my face through the window, and I instinctively shield my eyes. A second later, Jack Westwood taps on my window.

Chapter 14

I open the door, thankful that his huge black umbrella shields me from the torrent. "Emergency call?" he hollers.

"Yep." I step out and pop my own umbrella and use it as a shield in front of me.

We splash up to the front door and set our open umbrellas down on the covered porch. I turn the key in the lock and flip on the light, then turn back to look at my knight in shining rain suit. "Thanks."

"Glad I was around."

"Me, too, although I'm sorry about the poor guy who hit the guard rail. He okay?"

"Yeah, he's probably back home by now. I was just waiting for the tow truck. They came up right behind you."

"Do you always work the night shift?"

"I'm a light sleeper, so I don't mind." Headlights flash across us, glaring off his clear vinyl rain suit. "Want me to wait out here until you finish? I don't like the idea of you going back out to your car alone."

"You don't have to do that." I nod toward the car pulling into a parking place next to mine. "I can walk out with them."

"I'd rather wait, if you don't mind."

"Suit yourself. But I have to hurry home. I left Jenn there, and even though she's old enough, it still worries me to leave her." And the fact that I'd bring her up to him is a sign of how much it worries me to leave her.

He frowns. "I'm sure she's fine, but if you want me to, I can drive by the house a few times then come back in time to escort you to your car."

"Jack, you don't have to do that."

"No problem," he says firmly and picks up his umbrella. "I'll be waiting in my car when you finish. In the meantime, don't worry about Jenn. I'll make sure she's safe and sound."

"Thanks," I call as he darts through the rain and slips into the patrol car.

The reflection of his taillights as he pulls out onto the road casts an eerie red glow across Judy and Bobby walking slowly through the rain.

"You in trouble with the police, Doc?" Bobby jokes as they come in the front door with him leaning heavily on Judy.

"Yeah, I got in trouble for working over a patient who waited longer than he should have to get into the office," I fire back.

"You know how to kick a man when he's down. It's not my fault I've been pulling long loads and haven't had time to get in. When I do get home, it's late, and I leave early." He shakes the water off his hair with his free hand then gasps as a shooting pain apparently takes his breath away.

"And heaven knows, he wouldn't want to call you out after hours," Judy mutters, but I can see the loving concern in her eyes.

I snatch his file from the vertical cabinet. "Come on back."

Thirty minutes later, adjusted and iced down, Bobby grins. "You're a miracle worker, Doc."

"I'm afraid not," I say. "But I am here to help you." I sit down at Norma's appointment book. "You need to get back in tomorrow before you go back out on the road, okay?"

"That would be great."

I schedule him for late morning, and he pays then tries to pay me extra for coming in after hours.

I shake my head and smile. "I don't charge extra for after-hours visits unless someone takes advantage and starts coming in at two in the morning for the fun of it."

Bobby clutches his wallet and frowns. "I'd feel better if you'd take some extra."

"I don't guess you're a Beatles fan, are you?" Judy asks.

I nod. "I definitely am. They were before my time, but I love most of their music. Why?"

She fumbles in her purse. "We had these tickets for the Liverpool Legends concert tomorrow night. It's at the Omaha Center in Cherokee Village."

She pulls out two tickets and shoves them into my hand.

I look down at the cardboard rectangles. Who says this is a thankless job? "Judy, are you sure? I heard they were sold out. Everyone says they're the next best thing to the real deal, so I meant to buy a ticket, but. . ." But Jennifer showed up, and this whole centennial committee thing happened, and I completely forgot until it was too late. "Thank you."

"Thank *you*," she says, as they follow me to the front door. "You have no idea how much it means that you came out tonight to help Bobby. Since he hurt his back, we weren't going anyway. It would be a shame for them to go to waste."

I shut down the lights, and we walk out the door.

"At least the rain has let up for a little while," Judy says.

Bobby motions toward the parking lot as Judy and I are folding up our umbrellas. "Looks like the law decided you were still on shaky ground, Doc. Either that, or he just wanted to see you again. He's back."

"What'd I tell you?" I banter to hide my embarrassment. "Better not miss your appointment."

"Don't worry," Judy says, looking up at her husband. "He'll be here." She grins at me. "Maybe Jack Westwood would enjoy going to the concert."

I feel my face grow hotter. But that is a sort of pay-it-forward idea, considering Jack's literally gone the extra mile to make sure Jennifer and I are safe tonight. And this week's committee meeting went unbelievably smooth. Not to mention the fact that when it was over, I mentally lamented that it might be another week before I saw him. "We'll see."

They head toward their car. I watch them for a minute. Bobby isn't leaning as hard on Judy now. I'm so thankful that God put the ability inside our bodies to heal. And I'm extremely grateful that He lets me play a little part in helping patients get better.

I turn to go to my own car. When I approach, Jack opens his door and gets out. "Everything appears to be calm out at your house."

A wry smile lifts my lips as I think of Jennifer's determined search for her birth mother and me with all my secrets. Looks can be deceiving.

But she's safe for now, and I'm thankful Jack drove by. For a second, I close my eyes and lift my face to the light breeze. The air has a rain-cleansed smell. I open my eyes to see him staring intently at me. "Thanks for driving out there. Knowing you were checking on Jenn made it easier for me to keep my mind on what I was doing."

"I'm glad. You really put yourself out for your patients, don't you?"

I shrug and start to make a tongue-in-cheek remark about getting free concert tickets out of the deal, but he speaks again.

"Couldn't you have told him to go to the ER?"

"What?"

"Your patient. Wouldn't it have been easier on you if he just went to the emergency room?"

I laugh. "The ER is a wonderful and worthy place, but not if you've got a vertebra that needs to be put back into place. My patients know when to go to the ER and when they need me. If it's something I can take care of, they call me."

He frowns. "No matter the weather or time of day?"

"No matter. Neither rain, nor sleet, nor— Why should their health be less important than delivery of the U.S. mail?"

"But if you had a family...," he says.

"What about you?" I counter. "You're out in the middle of the night. What if you had a family?"

He looks startled then shrugs. "My wife would accept that as part of my job."

"I'm guessing my husband would have gotten my rain slicker out of the closet for me and would have a cup of chamomile tea waiting when I get home."

He chuckles. "Or been really irritated that the phone blasted him out of a deep sleep."

There went his invitation to the concert. I open my car door. "You know, that's probably why I'm not married." I slide in. "Thanks again, Jack."

He looks like he wants to say more but just touches the brim of his hat. "Glad I could be here."

As I drive home, I think about our conversation. I *am* awfully settled into my life. All these years, I've had warm, fuzzy daydreams of a wonderful partnership, but maybe a husband *would* just be irritated by my job. Of all the men I've ever known well, I'd have expected Jack to be the most understanding. I'm sure he's had to call doctors out in the middle of the night plenty of times.

I snort. I must be delirious from lack of sleep. What difference does it make to me what Jack thinks about my schedule?

~

The dogs meet me at the front door when I get home then follow me down the hall to Jenn's open door. She's sound asleep, and the guard light outside the window casts a golden glow across her face. Her eyelashes are so long they almost touch her cheeks, and her bow mouth is slightly open. Has it really been eight years since I made the second hardest decision of my life?

As soon as the baby was born, I'd gotten my own apartment five miles down the road from Tammy and Russ, closer to the chiropractic college. In spite of Tammy's protests, we both knew it was for the best. Every day I stopped in, just to watch Jenn grow.

Jenn shifts and I freeze. What teenager wants her loony aunt watching her sleep? I can hear her now—"That's just creepy." Her left foot peeks out from under the blanket. I smile. I was blessed to witness that little foot—well, that foot that used to be little—take its first step, to hear her first word. And my sweet sister asked my opinion on everything from preschools to Jenn's sleep habits.

She'll be going into tenth grade when school starts. Her first day of high school. I shake my head. Seems like yesterday was her first day of kindergarten. Tammy and Russ invited me to go, but that momentous event was one for parents, not an aunt, no matter how doting. I'd tried to stay busy all day, but

I cried that night for the first time in years. I knew right away what I needed to do. In one of those things that must surely be God, my childhood chiropractor called to tell me he was selling his clinic. I made him an offer and moved back to Shady Grove.

A longing tightens inside me. What would it be like to truly be her mother?

I push the longing away. Not my path. My path is to keep the promises I've made. Promises to my sister, to myself, and most of all to my baby Jenn, whose life will turn upside down when she finds out the truth.

Lord, what do I do?

I don't linger for an answer, because, really, I'm not ready for it.

"You made it back, huh?"

I jump and look into Jenn's green eyes, open wide. "Um, yeah. I was just checking to see if you were okay."

"I made it fine. Barely knew you were gone." She smiles sleepily. "But it's good to have you back."

"Thanks, kid. Night." I drop a kiss on her forehead and walk quickly from the room.

Chapter 15

The next morning, as I slip into my clothes, my gaze falls on the concert tickets sitting next to my jewelry box. I freeze as I remember a wild thought I had as I was drifting off to sleep. Surely in the light of day, there has to be a different person to invite.

Not Jenn. She's barely heard of the Beatles. And Allie is too busy making last-minute preparations for her wedding. Victoria has a standing Friday night thing with her parents. I could ask Lark. That might get her mind off babies for a few minutes. And get me off the mental hook my crazy idea has put me on. I reach for the phone then draw my hand back. Lark isn't a Beatles fan, and I know it. She was country when country wasn't cool.

I pace on the Oriental rug in front of my dresser. Cocoa and Shadow pace beside me, both looking puzzled. Only a few minutes before I have to go to work. If I'm going to call and ask, now's the time. I close my eyes and pray. This could be a first step. A bridge. Not a huge steel interstate one, admittedly. Maybe just a shaky rope job hanging over a deep precipice, but a bridge nonetheless. And God expects me to build bridges when I can. I snatch the phone up before I lose my nerve, then punch in the number and wait.

"Hello?" Mom answers, in her energetic morning voice. When we lived at home, Tammy and I used to laugh at the way Mom could wake from a deep sleep with a perky hello if the phone rang.

"Hey, how's it going today?" I scratch Shadow behind the ears and try to relax.

"Rachel?" The incredulous note in her voice makes me want to slam the phone down. It's not like I *never* call. Rarely, I'll admit, but not never.

"Yes, it's me."

"Is Jennifer okay?"

"She's fine."

"Oh. Well. That's good."

Silence. A part of me—probably the very childish part—wants to just let her wonder why I called, but I can't stand the silence.

"Have you ever heard of the Liverpool Legends?"

"The Beatles?"

"Not exactly. They're impersonators, I guess you'd say. A tribute band. George Harrison's sister put the group together."

"I've never heard of them."

"The reason I asked—a patient gave me two tickets to their concert tonight in the Village." I love saying that. It sounds so New York. Of course I'm talking about Cherokee Village, a community right down the road from Shady Grove, but still, it *could* be Greenwich.

"Oh? And you can't go?" Mom sounds genuinely puzzled.

This is harder than asking a man out, I think. Not that I know for sure.

"I can, but I wanted to know if you wanted to go, too."

"With you?"

Is this how Jack felt that day he asked me out and I acted like such a goose?

"Yes, with me. I'm sorry it's so last minute. They just gave me the tickets."

"I'd love to," Mom said, her voice quivering slightly. "But wouldn't you rather take a date? Or Jennifer?"

"Jenn might enjoy it," I say, ignoring the "date" comment, "but not as much as you would. She's happy staying with Allie's girls. And it's only fair you should have to go with me. After all, you're the one who played me all those albums when I was sick with the chicken pox."

"I was desperate to get your mind off the itching."

"And to get that 'inane boy band' off my boom box, if I remember correctly." I say, relaxing a little. "You wanted to show me what a real boy band sounded like. And from that moment on, it was Paul, John, George, and Ringo for me."

"You had good taste for an eleven-year-old."

"No doubt I inherited it from you." How's that for bridge building? At least a four-lane with concrete posts.

"Oh"—she clears her throat—"that's very sweet."

"Great. I'll pick you up at seven."

She laughs. "It's a date."

~

As I'm tearing off the face paper after the last patient leaves, Norma comes in, grinning. "You sure are humming a lot today."

"I'm going to a concert tonight." I wad the paper into a ball and toss it through the little basketball hoop over my trash can.

She puts her hands on her hips. "You sound excited. Big date?"

"I wouldn't say so. At least not where she or my dad can hear you."

Her brows draw together, and she shakes her head. "You feeling okay?"

I just nod. "Fine and dandy."

As soon as she's gone, I go back to humming "She Loves You." I hurry home and change into jeans and a green top. But when I pick up the brush to give my hair one last going over, I clutch it like a microphone and blast out, "Yeah, yeah, yeah." Good thing Jennifer's already at Allie's. She'd fall on the floor laughing.

When I get to the ranch, Mom meets me on the porch, and I smile. As we settle ourselves in my car, I look over at her. It must have killed her to leave her blouse untucked so that it hangs out beneath her vest. But the stylish effect is worth it. "Nobody would believe you're old enough to be my mother," I say after she's buckled in.

She blushes.

I pop in my Beatles CD, and the opening notes of "I Saw Her Standing There" fill the interior of the car. When they sing about her just being seventeen, Mom clears her throat. And I fumble with the forward button. Unfortunate choice. "The Long and Winding Road" starts. Much better.

Mom smiles. "Great mood setter."

We ride without talking. By the time we reach the Omaha Center, the knot in my stomach is gone.

We enter the auditorium early and find seats in the fourth row. Most of our fellow audience members are roughly twice my age, with a few teenagers and tweens scattered throughout the arena. I probably should have offered the other ticket to Dad. He's not a fan, but at least he's from the right era.

When the curtains open, I quickly forget second-guessing myself. The fast-paced show keeps me on the edge of my seat.

The performers may not look exactly as I remember John, Paul, George, and Ringo looking on my parents' album covers, but they sound much as I remember the voices on the albums sounding. And they encourage audience participation. At first I don't look at Mom as I sing softly, but soon we're leaning together, belting the familiar tunes out like we did that rainy chicken pox summer.

At intermission, Mom heads to the bathroom while I wait out in the foyer examining some archaeological finds in a display.

"You a fan of the Fab Four?" a deep voice behind me asks.

I spin around to find Jack, his brown eyes twinkling.

I nod. "Yes. You too?"

"Guilty as charged."

"I had no idea." As soon as I say the words, I realize how silly they sound. Even though we lived next door to each other through grade school, junior high, and high school, I found out more about him during our little crash course in "getting to know you" at Coffee Central than all the years before. I'm sure there's much I still don't know. Intriguing thought.

He flashes his dimple. "That's understandable. We didn't cover our favorite '60s' bands the other night."

"Oh, Jack. . ."

I jerk my head around to see Blair waving. Jack seems ready to ignore her, but I know from past experience that doesn't work. "Better wave at her so she'll go away."

Jack ducks his head, and his face reddens. He raises one hand. "Be right there."

"Be right there?" I blurt out before I think.

"I ran into her this morning, and she had these tickets. She said if I wanted to go, we'd discuss rodeo publicity on the way over here."

"Your noble sacrifice on behalf of the rodeo amazes me."

Okay, I will not stoop to sarcasm again. He might think I'm jealous.

He frowns. "It was better than allowing her at another committee meeting. Who are you here with?"

I raise my eyebrow. "Someone who is probably wondering where I am. I'd better get back in."

"Rachel, this. . ." He waves his hand toward Blair. "She knows. . .it isn't a date."

I just shrug. "Like Lark's granny always said, 'There's no accountin' for taste.' It's a free country. Enjoy the show."

If only I could take my own advice. The second half is another incredible performance, complete with Sgt. Pepper's Lonely Heart's Club Band costumes, but no matter how much I know I shouldn't care, I find myself scanning the crowd for Jack and Blair.

"I had so much fun," Mom says as we walk out to my car.

"Me, too."

"Really?" She leans forward and peers at my expression under the glare of the parking lot lights. "You seem distracted."

"No. I had fun." I hit the clicker and unlock the car, then slide into the driver's seat. When I turn the key in the ignition, the motor turns over but refuses to start. "Uh-oh."

"Uh-oh what?" Mom says, her brow furrowing.

"It's been acting funny lately, but I haven't had time to get it down to Buddy's for a new battery."

"Your dad would've been glad to put a new battery in for you. All you had to do was ask."

I pound out a rhythm on the steering wheel and try to relax my shoulders. "Buddy doesn't mind doing it." For a much lower price than the cost of depending on my parents for everything.

"Well, at least you should have said something. We could have brought my car."

"I know. But I didn't think it would actually give up the ghost." I try again, and we listen in tense silence to the *rrr, rrr, rrr* of the uncooperative motor.

"If only you'd said something." She sighs and gets her cell phone out of her purse. "I'll call your dad."

"No!"

She shoots me a startled look, but I shake my head and reach down to pop the hood.

"It's a twenty minute drive for him. All we have to do is find somebody with jumper cables." I peer out my window at the end of the line of cars streaming out of the parking lot. There are only a few vehicles still parked, but their owners have to show up eventually. With that in mind, I get out and open the hood all the way. While I'm examining the situation and trying to remember if my mechanic's number is in my cell phone, I hear a throat clear behind me.

"You need some help?"

I spin around. Heat rushes up my face when I see Jack. "I was just about to call a mechanic then try to find a cab."

"What's the problem?"

"Battery, I think."

He waves at my mom and looks back at me. "It'd be a shame to ruin a girls' night out by having to get a ride home."

Is it my imagination, or does he smirk a little when he says "girls' night out"? I didn't actually say I had a date when he asked me in the lobby earlier.

"I've got jumper cables in the back of my truck. Why don't we see if that works before you have someone come out?"

I look behind him. "Where's your date?"

He narrows his eyes. "Don't have one."

"Right. Where's Blair?"

He motions across the lot to where she's talking with two

men stashing equipment into a white van. "They just finished up an interview. Let me get my cables."

I relax a little. "Thanks, Jack."

"No problem." He takes off at a jog across the parking lot.

When he gets out of his truck in front of my car, he hands me one black and one red cable end. I hook them onto my battery while he connects the other ends to his.

I send up a silent prayer as I climb in and give the key a turn. The motor roars to life.

Jack puts the cables away and comes over to my window. "You need to get a new battery."

I nod. "Believe me, that's on the top of my to-do list for tomorrow." I point over his shoulder. "Don't look now, but your non-date doesn't seem to be too happy."

He turns his head, and for a second, we watch in silence as Blair strides across the parking lot, her high heels clicking in the quiet summer night.

He looks back at me and Mom and doffs his hat. "See y'all later."

I roll the window up right before Blair reaches Jack.

"Better to dwell in a car with a dead battery than in a truck with a contentious woman," Mom says softly beside me.

I jerk my head around to look at her.

Her grin twinkles in her eyes, and she shrugs. "Just paraphrasing."

I return her grin and turn on the Beatles CD. "This was fun."

"This time you sound like you really mean it."

"I meant it before."

"But seeing Jack with Blair soured things for you a bit."

I shrug. This is my mother. What I say can and probably will be used against me later. "Thanks for going with me."

"I was surprised you asked me. But I'm glad you did."

Just as I'm settling into our first comfortable silence in fifteen years, she clears her throat. "About your car. . ."

"Yeah?"

"Come over for lunch on Sunday, and your dad will put a new battery in it while we're cleaning up the dishes."

I keep my eyes on the road. "I'll get Buddy to do it, I promise."

"Jennifer is our granddaughter any way you look at it."

"I know that." I grind my teeth. Why do conversations with her have to be so hard? "What's that got to do with my battery?"

"Don't you think we'd like to spend a little time with her while she's here?"

"We've been over."

"Should I have to go out to the barn to visit with her?"

I glance up at the little Drive Friendly angel clipped onto my sun visor. Forget road rage. What about passenger rage? "No, Mom, you shouldn't. She can eat lunch with y'all on Sunday."

"But our own daughter would rather drive through the burger joint than sit down at the same table with her parents. Or eat dinner at someone else's mother's house."

I often eat with Allie's mom on Sunday, but I didn't realize my parents knew that.

I should have known the master of guilt wouldn't miss a chance to add an arrow to her arsenal. She probably has spies all over the country. As soon as I have the thought, guilt shoots through me. See what good aim she has? Why should I feel guilty? They basically disowned me when they found out I was pregnant. Are they truly trying to reclaim me at this late date? My jaw clenches. Some situations are lose-lose from the beginning. "We'll be there Sunday as soon as we get out of church."

Mom smiles. "We'll look forward to it."

Chapter 16

ost people are surprised to find I'm not a morning person. Something else I guess I inherited from my mom—a certain perkiness that gives the illusion that I'm Miss Morning Sunshine. I keep up the facade during the week. But Lark knows me. And she knows my aversion to anything that happens before the dew dries on Saturdays.

So when I pull into her driveway at 9:00 on Saturday morning, I give myself a minute to ponder Lark's wake-up call two hours earlier that got me sitting here instead of out on my deck drinking a cup of hot green tea. I look over at Jennifer, whom I dragged along with me, because, after all, why should I get to have all the fun?

"I still can't understand Lark's urgent need to clean out her junk room today." I also can't understand just why I felt like I needed to be a part of the chaos. Maybe I just needed a good dose of someone else's reality to get my mind off What's His Name and the Channel 6 blond.

See, cleaning will be good for me.

"You didn't have to say yes," Jenn grumbles beside me and stuffs her hair up under her Braves cap.

I frown at the sight of Victoria's luxury car and Adam's old truck in the driveway. Lark called out the cavalry. "She wouldn't have asked if it weren't important."

"Fine. We're here." She motions toward the simple one-level brick house. "Let's get this over with."

"Check the attitude at the door, please. Lark's my friend, and I don't intend for you to give her any grief."

"Dirk's my friend, too. But I'm sure it 'gave him grief'" —she puts air quotes around the words—"when you wouldn't let me spend the day with him."

I look through my purse, searching for who knows what. Mostly a place to look that isn't a scorching glare. "You're fifteen. Spending the day alone with a cowboy is out of the question."

"Alone? He wanted to take me to look at a horse." She huffs and crosses her arms. "Why do you say 'cowboy' like it was 'scuzzbucket'?"

"I didn't say it like 'scuzzbucket.'"

"Did too."

I bite back a "Did not" and sigh. "The horse he wanted to show you is two hours from here. Your mom left it up to me, and this is my decision." Actually, Tammy had suggested that I invite Dirk to spend some time with us today instead, but she hadn't pushed it when I balked. I soften my voice. "It's just one day, Jenn. Why not try to make the best of it?"

She grunts in what I hope is reluctant agreement. I won't hold my breath, though, especially when she gives the car door an extra *umph* when she closes it.

Lark opens the door with a sunny smile. "I'm so glad you came." She hugs me and pulls Jenn into a stiff embrace as well.

"Why the sudden urge to clean out the junk room?"

She giggles, and I grab her arm. Lark is not a giggler. "Lark?"

She bounces up and down. "We're having a baby!"

I hug her again and jump with her. "Whoo-hoo! Congratulations."

She nods. "Sheila—she's the woman that Marsha called us about who's pregnant—contacted us last night, and she definitely wants us to take the baby."

A baby. I can't believe Lark is going to be a mom. My happiness for her pushes tears into my eyes. "That's wonderful."

"I know. I can't believe it! We have so much to do!"

Her words make me glance down the hall where a pile of empty boxes waits. "So we're going to get started on the nursery today?" Even though the due date isn't for another four months, I can totally understand Lark being so eager.

Lark's brow wrinkles, and for a second her eyes dim. "Actually, there's a small catch."

"The baby's coming early?"

She shakes her head. "Sheila has no place to stay, so I told her she could move in with us until the baby is born."

That happy feeling inside me deflates. "Whoa. That's a big step. Did Craig agree?" The plumber is the silent type normally, but if he had strong misgivings, he'd express them.

"It all happened so fast. She just poured her heart out to me, and I asked her. Craig's okay with it." She hesitates. "Well, he *will* be, anyway."

Uh-oh. "Lark—"

"Really. He'll come around." And by the look on her face, I believe her. How could anyone put a pin into that bubble of joy?

"When do you think she'll move in?"

She doesn't say anything. Why does every question I ask produce a feeling of dread?

I frown at Lark. "Do you know when she's moving in?"

She gives an unsteady laugh. "Yes. . .I know. She'll be here at five."

"Five? Today five?"

"Yeah." Her eyes plead with me not to make a big deal out of this.

"We'd better get busy then." I start down the hallway with Jenn trudging along beside me.

"Rach?"

I turn around to look at her. "What?"

"Thanks for not telling me how stupid I am."

"Hey, you're smart enough to get us all here to clean out your junk room on a Saturday morning. Who am I to judge?"

The front door opens, and Allie comes in juggling bags and a tray of coffee cups, her long blond hair pulled up on top of her head in a ponytail.

"What took you so long?" she says and grins.

"I beat you."

"I got here earlier, but I ran out for our doughnuts and coffee fix."

I smirk at the sight of the Coffee Central bag. "Your Daniel fix is more like it. He working this morning?"

She gives me a sheepish grin. "Busted." She waves a bag at Jenn. "Would you mind taking these to Katie and Dylan? They're out in the yard."

"Where's Miranda?"

"She slept over at a friend's house, but they should be dropping her off here pretty soon. You can take these out to the kids and come back in and help us until she gets here if you want."

"Sure." Jenn takes the bag then glances at me with a subtle pursing of her lips. "If it's okay with Aunt Rachel for me to go outside."

I meet her level gaze and nod. "Sure, honey, run along and play."

"Ouch," Lark says as soon as the door closes behind Jenn. "Was that sarcasm I heard?"

"Definitely."

"Trouble in paradise?" Allie asks as we walk down the hall.

I lead the way into the junk room and wave at Vic, who's sitting cross-legged in the corner sorting through some papers. "Trouble with a capital *T*. Dirk called to ask Jennifer to spend the day with him."

Lark tosses me a box of black garbage bags and motions for me to share them with Allie. "Dirk, the cowboy? And you wouldn't let her?"

I shake my head and pop the box open. "Do I look crazy? She called her mom, but Tammy left it up to me."

"So you got to be the bad guy," Victoria says. "Fun."

"For once, I didn't mind."

Vic holds up a stack of postcards. "Lark? Store these? Or keep them out?"

Lark frowns. "Granny sent them to me when she took that cross-country train trip." She squared her shoulders. "But I have to make room for Sheila. So I guess pitch 'em."

Vic shakes her head and drops them in a small box. "If a few postcards bother her, then she needs to get a hotel room. We aren't throwing away your granny's postcards."

"These we can throw away." Allie holds up a huge stack of magazines. "Or at least recycle."

Lark groans. "Every kid in the neighborhood has sold me at least one subscription. I promise you there are duplicates in there even."

Allie laughs and holds up three identical magazines. "She's right. Look at this."

Victoria grins. "What could be better than three Matthew McConaugheys?"

Allie tosses her a mag, then one to me just as Jenn walks in the door.

"Hard at work?" Her smile is a little cooler than normal, but at least she's not being belligerent.

"You know it," I answer. "Did you take the doughnuts to the kids?"

She nods and picks up a magazine.

"Black garbage bags for trash, white for recycle, and these for keep and store," Lark says and hands Jenn a box of clear bags.

"Why don't you do the trash, Lark?" I suggest. "That way you can look at everything one last time before it goes."

"Are you going to tell the baby it's adopted?" Jenn says suddenly, keeping her eyes fixed on the glossy magazine in her hands.

Uh oh. The room goes still, and I think, for a second, I can hear the air being sucked out. My friends freeze.

Lark gives me a slow, one-eyebrow-up look, silently asking for the right answer.

Don't look at me. I don't have a clue what she should say. I shrug, hopefully imperceptibly.

Lark takes a breath, and I appreciate the calm in her voice. "Rather than have a big sit-down talk where we tell him, we hope to make it a fact he always knows. Like the existence of God."

"Will you tell him about his birth mother?"

Lark's face turns red, but Jenn is too busy nonchalantly flipping through the pages to notice, I think.

"Craig and I are going to leave that up to Sheila. If she wants us to tell him, we'll definitely leave that option open for the right time."

"Oh." Jenn closes her magazine and drops it in the recycle bag Allie is holding. She looks at Lark, unaware that she just took out my heart and gave it a squeeze. "What do you want me to do?"

"Why don't you clean out this bookshelf? We're moving it to the garage."

Jenn nods and walks over to the shelf.

Some days I think Jenn has forgotten her great quest for truth. Then something like this happens to remind me that I'm living with a time bomb. My knees tremble as I sink down beside Victoria on the floor.

She gives me a sympathetic look and pushes a bin of shoes toward me.

I look down at the mishmash of sneakers, heels, and sandals. "How do I know what to keep?" I mentally congratulate myself on my steady voice.

Lark glances at me. "If it looks tired or out of style, get rid of it."

Allie snorts. "I need to be careful not to wander into that bin. I'd be thrown out for sure."

I toss a sandal with a broken strap. "Prewedding exhaustion?"

She nods. "But I guess that's better than prewedding jitters."

"No second thoughts?" Lark speaks up from where she's sorting through a stack of clothes.

"Not unless you count wondering why we didn't make the date sooner."

"In a week, you'll be Mrs. Daniel Montgomery," Victoria says. "Are the kids upset that they're going to have a different last name than you?"

"Actually. . ." Allie lowers her voice. "Daniel's going to adopt them."

I look up in surprise. "Really? Did you tell Jon's parents?"

Allie's in-laws, always difficult, haven't gotten any easier since their son's death several years ago.

She nods. "They took it hard at first, but the girls explained that it's what they want and assured them that they will never forget Jon."

"Miranda *wants* to be adopted?" Jenn is incredulous.

No one speaks for a few seconds. I can see that Allie is afraid she'll say the wrong thing.

"Being adopted is a good thing," I finally say. "It means you're chosen."

Jenn lets my words sit for a moment, and I can't read her face. Then, "I'm gonna go see if Miranda's here yet." Jenn drops the book she's holding and walks out.

"That went well," I say. Even I can hear the sarcasm tingeing my voice.

"Sorry," Allie says. "I shouldn't have brought it up around her."

I throw a worn-out pair of sneakers into the trash bag. "We can't watch everything we say. She's obviously thinking about it today, regardless of what we say. . .or don't say."

"When are you going to tell her?" Lark asks, but a loud noise in the hallway saves me from answering.

Craig and Adam come in carrying a bed frame. "Where do you want this?" His voice screams that maybe he's not as thrilled as Lark about their upcoming houseguest. I stare at the easygoing plumber. Even when he first broached the topic of adoption and Lark came to stay with me for a while, he didn't act like this.

"Just lean it against the wall in the hall. Hopefully by the time you get everything carried in, we'll be ready for you to set it up." Lark's voice is breezy and light, in full ignore-my-husband's-bad-mood mode.

This is going to be a fun day.

They set it down, and Craig disappears. Lark gives a loud sigh and follows him.

Allie's brother, Adam, is younger than everyone, even me, but for the most part, he fits into our group. He loves to tease Victoria. Especially about her family's wealth. And she gives it back as good as she gets.

He walks over to where she's still packaging up old greeting cards and letters. "Getting some experience in case your stock goes belly up and you have to take a mail room job?"

Vic tosses her hair over her shoulder. "No. If that ever happens, I'll sit on the couch and play video games with you."

Considering Adam's company did go belly up, and he did end up playing a lot of video games afterward, Victoria isn't pulling any punches. I look over at Allie and mouth, "Ouch."

She shrugs and whispers, "Like Lark's granny always said, 'Don't dish it out if you can't take it.'"

Suddenly I remember my conversation with Jack at Coffee Central after the committee meeting. That little tidbit of wisdom is exactly why I have no business encouraging him to share secrets from his past with me. From now on, I need to keep things strictly on a professional level.

If the concert didn't teach me that, then common sense should have.

I'm paying attention. . .now.

~

By noon we have the room almost completely organized, and the guys put up the bed while we make some sandwiches. We've only been back to work a little while when Katie and Dylan come running in with Miranda and Jenn following slowly behind them.

"Some lady's here." Katie's voice sounds worried.

"I think her car is about to fall apart," Dylan adds quietly.

"It's going *bump, bump, bump* all the way up the driveway," Miranda says, and Jenn nods.

Lark's face freezes in panic. "Sheila's early. I've got to get the bed made, at least." She throws the clean sheets onto the bed, and we each grab a corner. Within seconds the bed is made.

I step back and take in the cozy little bedroom. Hard to believe it's the same place we threw junk out of this morning.

The doorbell rings, and Lark puts her hand to her stomach.

"Buck up, girl," Allie says. "You know she's more nervous than you are."

"Want us to slip out the back door?" I ask, partly out of fear that Jenn will have more pointed questions, and this time in front of Sheila. Neither Lark nor I am ready for that.

Lark glances at Craig's stony face. "I'd really rather y'all stay. Please."

"You two let her in, and we'll rustle up some snacks," Adam says. As we file through the doorway, he locks his arm in Victoria's. "Come on, Vicky, let's see what you can do in a kitchen that doesn't come complete with a cook."

She jerks her arm away. "Like I have a cook."

He raises an eyebrow and grins. "Surely you borrow Mommy and Daddy's chef from time to time."

"Unlike *some* people I know, I live my own life. . .with a whole separate address from my parents," she says.

Adam clutches his heart and staggers backward.

Allie laughs and reaches out to catch her brother. "Cease-fire, please. We're supposed to be helping smooth things out."

Adam rolls his eyes. "Brides. They're such Pollyannas."

Vic snickers, and the rest of us, including Allie, join in the laughter. It dies to a trickle when Craig and Lark usher a heavyset woman into the kitchen.

She nervously twists the bottom of her black Chez Pierre waitress uniform top then stops herself. But within seconds, her finger is twirling her lank, shoulder-length blond hair. I cast a surreptitious glance at her stomach. She's heavy all over, so it's hard to tell how pregnant she looks. She offers a tentative smile, and my heart goes out to her. I remember what it felt like to be pregnant and unable to keep the baby. And I was in my sister's home and knew I was loved.

"Everybody, this is Sheila Mason. Sheila, these are our friends. They've been helping us get your room ready."

"Thank you," she says softly. "I'm sorry to be so much trouble."

"Don't be silly," Lark says. "I invited you. You're no trouble!"

Craig's knuckles are white on Sheila's suitcase handle. I'm hoping she doesn't notice.

Victoria offers Sheila a tray of crackers and cheese, but the woman shakes her head and touches her stomach. "I'm really not feeling well. That's why I'm early. They gave me the rest of the day off."

"Let me show you your room." Lark takes her arm and guides her down the hall. Craig follows stiffly.

"It was nice meeting you," Allie calls after her.

The rest of us chorus our agreement.

"Y'all, too." Sheila's voice drifts back to us.

The room is thick with an uncomfortable silence, and finally I clear my throat. "Y'all, Jenn and I are going to go. Tell Lark and Craig we said bye."

Victoria, Allie, and Adam all speak at once, as if we'd been playing the quiet game and I'd lost. Now everyone could make their own excuses and leave.

When we're in the car on the way home, Jenn glances over

at me. "Wonder if that's what my mom is like."

What—? Before I can stop it, exasperation shoots through me. "Your mom is a wonderful Christian and a successful speechwriter who lives with your incredible dad in a beautiful house in Georgia where they spend a large portion of their time making sure your needs and wants are met."

She looks surprised, and I don't blame her. I'm pretty surprised myself. And not a little ashamed. What am I thinking, striking out at her with my adjective-laden tirade? This whole mess is my fault in a dozen different ways. My fault for falling into Brett's arms. Not that I can wish that never happened when we wouldn't have Jenn if I hadn't. My fault for being too big a coward to let Tammy tell her the truth.

"I guess you're right." Jenn's soft voice startles me from my self-recriminations.

"I didn't mean to be so blunt."

She continues as if I didn't say a word. "I've been upset with the wrong person. My biological mom is the one who didn't want me. She's the reason I don't know who I really am. She's the one I should be mad at, the one I should blame."

We ride in silence the rest of the way, because what can I say to that? Just dig a hole and toss me in.

Chapter 17

So you made up with the Grands?"

I juggle my broccoli casserole and gallon of tea and ring the doorbell. The sun is high in the sky and a mockingbird calls from the high grasses around the house. "Yes, we made up, in a manner of speaking."

"What did y'all fight about anyway?"

And I thought her questions were tough when she first got here.

"We didn't really fight." I nudge my hair back from my face with my forearm.

"Here, I can take that." She smiles at me as she takes the glass dish from my hand and slides her plate of brownies on top of it. Yesterday on the way home from Lark's, I told Jenn we were eating lunch here today. She spent the evening in the kitchen singing and making brownies. Whatever mood bit her on the way over to Lark's, Jenn shook it by the time we returned home.

Thankfully, it hasn't returned. Yet.

The door swings open. "Jennifer, Rachel! Come in. Come in." My dad has his reading glasses in one hand and his Sunday paper in the other. I'm always amazed at how little he changes, with the exception of a few more lines and graying hair.

"Hi, Dad."

He pats my arm.

"Hi, Granddaddy."

I take the casserole back, and Jennifer gives him a hug with her free arm.

He drops a kiss on her forehead. "How's my favorite granddaughter?"

A grin spreads across her face. "Fantabulous."

"Em," he yells toward the kitchen, "she's making up words. He'd better get here soon."

"Who'd better get here soon?" I ask, suspicion making my voice edgy.

Jenn shrugs, her eyes wide.

"You girls come on in the kitchen," Mom calls.

"What is he talking about?" I hiss at Jenn as we walk to the kitchen.

Jenn ignores me and steps back to let me go in first.

Mom looks up from the stove, and a frown creases her brow. "Rachel, I told you there was no need to bring anything." Her gaze lights on the plastic gallon jug of tea with the store label. "You bought ready-made tea? I've never tried that."

Ouch. But I'm not going to let her put a chip in our bridge. I find a tough smile, slide the casserole dish onto the counter, and plop the jug down beside it. "You always taught me not to go anywhere empty-handed."

She looks over my shoulder. "What is this?" she says playfully, pointing to the plate Jenn is carrying.

"I made some brownies for dessert."

"How sweet!"

"They definitely are," Jenn says with a saucy grin. "Aunt Rach almost had a heart attack when she saw the sugar content."

"Good thing we had those nitroglycerine tabs handy," I pan.

Mom jerks her head to look at me.

"Just kidding," I mumble.

Why is it a crime for me to bring something, but Jenn can offer death on a plate and suddenly I'm the bad guy? "She might be exaggerating a little, but they *are* loaded with sugar." Really, they should be warned, right? But back to the subject at hand. "So who was the *he* Dad was talking about?"

Mom and Jenn meet each other's gaze then instantly look away, but not before I see.

"When did your father say, 'Who'?" Mom asks.

Apparently I'm in the old Abbott and Costello routine. "Let me spell it out for you. Who is the 'he' that had better show up soon?"

Mom purses her lips as if I am a difficult child. Which, come to think of it, I guess I am. "Jenn, why don't you set the table, honey? The plates and silverware are already in there."

Jenn casts me a worried look, and suddenly I know *exactly* who's coming to dinner. No guessing needed.

"Mom!"

Jenn skitters out of the kitchen without a backward glance.

"Now look here. She just suggested that I might enjoy inviting Dirk for lunch. And I agreed. Your dad and I have visited with him many times and always find him to be good company. He loves my lemonade."

"Well then, by all means, let's bring him into the family if he loves your lemonade."

"You don't need to shout, Rachel."

"I'm not shouting."

The kitchen door swings open, and Dad walks in, still clutching his paper. "What's going on?"

"Nothing," we snap at the same time.

He holds up his hand. "Doesn't sound like nothing."

"Are you in on this. . .matchmaking?" I sputter. "Good grief, she's only fifteen!"

His brows draw together and, inanely, I notice again the touch of gray in his hair. Where has the time gone? "A dinner invitation doesn't constitute matchmaking."

"Again, did you hear the *fifteen* part?"

He looks puzzled. A pang of worry interrupts my outrage. Why is he acting so confused? Is his memory so dim that he's forgotten what happens when you turn an impressionable girl loose with a cowboy?

Or, apparently, they think that Jenn is not me, that she won't make my mistakes.

Yeah, well me, too. But I'm not going to tempt fate.

"Alton"—Mom puts a hand on Dad's arm and one on mine—"you should go on out and be ready to answer the door. I'll handle this."

I jerk away from her as Dad leaves the room. "You'll handle this? This? I'm a person, Mom." I lower my voice to a terse whisper. "And living proof that teenage girls don't have good judgment when it comes to boys."

"Dirk's a nice Christian boy," Mom says. "We should have had him over before now, actually."

"He's a *cowboy*. They know how to be whatever they need to be to get the girl."

Mom frowns. "You're making much too much of this, Rachel. You'll see."

Tears prick my eyes. "You know what? I've lost my appetite. I'll be out in the barn when Jenn's ready to go."

Mom looks at me, shock on her face as if she can't believe how I'm overreacting.

I'm not overreacting. I slip out the back door and let it slam behind me. A shuddering sob racks my chest. In every other area of my life, I'm successful. Why am I such a failure at being a daughter?

She doesn't come after me. Not that I expect her to. I escaped to the barn many times after that night with Brett, and she didn't come after me then, either. Of course she didn't know what was wrong, but she didn't ask.

Sweetie nickers with surprise when I walk up. Horses are creatures of schedule, and she knows as well as I do that I'm not supposed to be here right now.

I run my hand across her mane. "Your mama dried a lot of my tears that autumn," I whisper.

Her ear flicks as if she understands.

Odd how my rebellious teen times started with that night at the rodeo and ended when I decided to give up the baby to Tammy and go to chiropractic college. From that day forward, I've been the picture of steady and easygoing. But when I'm with my parents, it's like the defiant girl never left. I'm a stupid, irresponsible teenager all over again.

I've read all the scriptures about forgiveness. I've prayed for God to forgive me, for my parents to forgive me, and for me to forgive them. But so far, nothing. I know that God can forgive me, but will He as long as I hold a grudge against Mom and Dad? I drop down against the wall of Sweetie's stall and close my eyes.

Lord, You know how many times I've been here, in this painful place in my heart, over the years. How many times I've asked You to take this whole thing away. What am I doing wrong? I don't want to cause my parents any more pain than I already have. And I don't want to see Jennifer get hurt like I did.

Suddenly, my eyes pop open. If Jennifer did the same thing

I did, would I be able to forgive her? In a heartbeat. Without hesitation. I love her that much. For the first time in years, cleansing tears spill down my cheeks as I continue praying.

Oh, Father, how could I be so blind? I've heard the sermons, I've read the scriptures, but all I could see was my own unworthiness and pain. How much more do You love me than I love Jennifer?

My heart thuds against my ribs. I pull my knees up to my chest and drop my head onto them.

Am I wrong about my parents, too? Please help me find the truth, once and for all.

A truck door slams out front. Dirk, no doubt. I take a shaky breath and push to my feet. If I hurry, I can get in the kitchen door before anyone has to make excuses for my absence.

Be good, Rachel.

I will, for Jennifer's sake. For all our sakes.

Maybe this bridge *is* salvageable.

I slip inside the kitchen just as the doorbell rings at the front of the house. Mom looks up from the stove, her eyes wide and red-rimmed. "Forget something?"

"Yes." I cross over to her and put my arm around her shoulders. "I. . .uh. . .I forgot to tell you I'm sorry for overreacting."

Her blue eyes soften, and she reaches up and covers my hand with her own. "Believe it or not, I understand. I'm sorry, too. We should have told you—"

"Since I'm a bit of a control nut, it usually helps me to have advance notice of things." I flash her an apologetic grin. "Gives me time to wrap my mind around something." I walk over and grab the casserole dish. "Are we ready to put the food on the table?"

"Yes, but—"

"Well then, let's go see if this cowboy is as nice as you two—make that you *three*—think he is."

"You need to—"

"Don't worry, Mom. I really am going to give him a chance." I rush out the door into the living room–dining room area before Dad has a chance to tell Dirk I'm not here.

And bump right into my own cowboy.

Whoa. I need to get a serious grip on my thoughts. Jack is definitely not "my own" cowboy, nor is he supposed to be here. But for a second, no, a long moment, all I can do is gape up at him, caught in the vortex of my mixed emotions.

I shouldn't be this happy to see him. Should. Not. Has my good sense completely disengaged?

Jack has a grip on both my elbows. I guess to stop me from smearing broccoli casserole down the front of his nice red shirt. "Where's the fire?"

He smiles at me, and my heart pounds as my gaze meets Dad's over Jack's shoulder.

Dad's face reddens. "Rachel, how are things coming in there?"

"Fine." I force a smile and extricate myself from Jack's grip. "We're getting ready to put the food on the table." I look over to where Dirk and Jennifer are sitting on the sofa talking. "Hope y'all are hungry," I say, with about as much warmth as an Ozark mountain winter.

So much for my newfound determination to make peace with my parents. Apparently our lives are rigged with land mines. I should have seen this one coming, though. It all makes sense now—even Dad's puzzlement about what I was mad about earlier. He assumed I'd found out that Jack was invited. That they were matchmaking on *my* behalf. And in the kitchen just now Mom was trying to break the news to me.

I'm going to be gracious if it kills me.

Chapter 18

A few minutes later, as we all sit down at the table, I'm thinking I might choke on graciousness.

"So, Rachel," Mom says as she passes me the rolls, "Allie's wedding is next Saturday? I guess everyone is excited."

I stare at her and nod. Mom barely knows my friends. My choice, but still. . . "Yes, they are. *We* are."

"Are you taking anyone?"

Taking. . .anyone?

Dirk and Jennifer stop their murmured conversation, and everyone at the table is suddenly watching me. "I'm taking Jennifer," I say quickly and pass the rolls to Jack.

"I mean a date."

Of course I knew exactly what she meant the first time, thanks to the thinly veiled matchmaking efforts of this dinner. Still, my face reddens. I concentrate on buttering my bread. "Dates aren't required. I'm a bridesmaid."

"Why, I know they aren't required." Mom waves her napkin in the air as if to wipe away such a silly notion. "But you don't have a date, even for the rehearsal dinner?"

"No, ma'am," I say through gritted teeth.

"Jack, you know Daniel, don't you?"

I set my butter knife down. Okay, that's *e-nough*. "Mom—"

"Yes, ma'am," Jack answers.

I give him a "Don't encourage her" look, but he ignores me. "We rode the same bus in elementary school."

She smiles at me as if everything is oh, so simple now that Jack has a childhood connection to the groom.

"And of course I know him from Coffee Central, too," Jack continues. Stop, please, Jack.

Mom nods. "Such a nice place."

"You've been to Coffee Central?" I can't hide my surprise.

"Our scrapbook club meets there once a month. I noticed he named a drink after you. Rachel's Special Soy Latte. I even ordered it." She twists her mouth with distaste. "Once."

Everyone—except me—laughs.

"Aunt Rachel's taste buds are psycho," Jenn explains to Dirk. "She doesn't do sugar, and she's always eating tree bark and stuff like that."

"I like sugar," I say a little defensively. "For special occasions. And I don't eat tree bark."

I hear a little hiccup or something from across the table and catch Jack in midchoke. He's coughing and my mother is slapping him on the back.

I love Sunday dinners.

Somehow we manage not to discuss my dating—or lack thereof—or the wedding for the rest of dinner. I quietly listen to my father's inquiries about Jack's unofficial rodeo school and Dirk's enthusiasm about his improved bull-riding skills. But the question of the wedding date lingers, like a bean casserole no one wants to touch.

Considering that the last time I saw Jack he was out with Blair, I'm not inclined to invite him anywhere. Not that I have a right to be mad. I'm just annoyed. Which I don't really have a right to be either.

Mentally I stamp my foot. There has to be some emotion that's on the approved list when you see a man who has been trying to sweep you off your feet out with a blond bombshell.

"Jennifer, would you and Dirk mind helping with the dishes?" My mother's voice yanks me out of one dilemma right into a new one. "It's such a beautiful day out. A lovely day for a walk."

Mom is looking at Jack, but she's talking to me.

"I could use a walk after that delicious meal," Jack says obediently. I feel like I'm in a soap opera. "I'd like to show you something, Rach. Will you come with me?"

Do I have a choice?

It is a beautiful day, however, and the sweet scent of Mom's crepe myrtles finds me and unlatches the hold my parents' matchmaking has on my mood. I shove my hands into my jean pockets and find my own gait, aware that Jack has shortened his stride to match mine.

He says nothing until we've hiked up the back pasture toward the thicket that once upon a time served as my favorite hiding place.

"Apparently, only one of us knew what plans your mother had on her mind today," Jack says finally as we slip into the cool alcove of the trees.

I lean against a big hickory. Our horses graze in the pasture behind our house, and a few cattle lounge in the summer pasture. From here I can see clear over to the Lazy W, Jack's beautiful red barn, the horses in his corral.

Jack notices the direction of my gaze. "I can see your parents' house from up there," he says, pointing opposite his barn to a hill that climbs up to a jagged cliff. "Ever since I was old enough to want to be by myself, I'd hike up there and spend some time.

Time with God and with my own thoughts. Sometimes I'd see you out riding and wonder if you'd ever notice me as more than just that pesky guy next door."

"I didn't think you were—"

"Since I moved back, I've seen you ride in the early mornings some. I've wondered if you've been avoiding me on purpose."

I pray he will attribute my red face to the hike.

"I guess that's why I felt like maybe you ending up on the centennial committee was God's doing."

Ron and Alma's doing, more likely. But Jack's speech touches me. And that scares me. "You've watched me?"

Jack's brown eyes shine as he answers me. "I wouldn't say 'watched.' I'd say. . .'noticed.' And that's nothing new. I've noticed you—from far away and up close—since I was old enough to notice any girl."

Oh. My throat is thick. This is the second time he's alluded to my past—and the fact that he was there when. . .well, when everything went south. But I don't feel the same fear as a couple of weeks ago. Now I just feel warm, down to my toes.

I push away from the tree and deliberately shove away the warmth. I climb up past the woods, to the path that leads along the ridgeline. "You said you wanted to show me something?"

I know this land like the back of my hand, but I'm still surprised when Jack veers off the path and cuts through the rock, taking a route toward his place.

"I'm sorry you got the wrong idea at the concert, by the way," he says over his shoulder.

I ignore him.

"But it wasn't a date. She had tickets. And if I had known you were a fan—"

"You wouldn't have gone?" Oops, that's too hopeful. "I don't want you to—"

"I would have gotten tickets and asked you to go with me."
Oh.

We have descended a small gully, in a wash that borders the back side of his land and butts up to a small offshoot of Spring River. I've been here a few times years ago, but back then this was just a brook. Now it seems to have cut away the bank and become more of a shallow creek meandering over mossy rocks, tucked inside a wooded glen of hickory and oak.

I stop and breathe in the smell of summer skimming through the forest. The birds chirp, the water burbles, and I want to stay here forever. "I'd forgotten this place was here."

Jack holds out his hand. "C'mon. We need to cross." He doesn't wait for me to consider, just grabs my hand and pulls me across stepping-stones to the other side before I can resist.

It seems, with Jack, that happens a lot.

"Where are we going?"

Jack looks at me, still wearing that dangerous smile. "You've been around this land all your life, Rachel. But I think you haven't a clue what you might be missing."

I don't have time to give him a skeptical look as he turns and continues along the other side of the creek. He doesn't let go of my hand, however.

And, stupid me, I don't let go either.

The walls of the forest rise up on either side like great fortresses protecting us in our special place. Or giant monsters looming. Depending on the day and the company. "When I was about eight years old, I hiked over the ridge. This was about as far as I got before I turned back, afraid the trees were going to kidnap me. I've never been any farther."

Jack squeezes my hand, as if he knew that already.

I'm not going to speculate. He veers away from the water and toward an opening in the rock that runs parallel to the creek. "You'll have to turn sideways, but it gets roomier once you get inside."

Turn sideways? But I don't have time to ask before he disappears into the crevice in the rock. He still has my hand and gives it a tug.

O-kay.

The little cave is shadowy, with only the light from the slit in the rock to illuminate the room. Jack's hand is tight around mine as he moves us through. The cool air is damp and smells of moss and lichen. I touch the sides then pull my hand back. "Where are we?"

"Right at the edge of where my land meets your folks'. Billy Blake and I found this place when we were kids. We spent more than one summer playing *Gunsmoke* in here. I was Matt Dillon, and he'd be a different bad guy every time."

I grin at this. Makes sense. I can't imagine Jack playing the bad guy. "Figures."

"This place is one of the main reasons I bought the land when Mom got ready to put it up for sale." He tugs on my hand. "We have to go through a little tunnel. Just hold on to me. I know where I'm going."

I'm not sure why, but those words rush over me, and I pull them in, close to my heart. Here in the dark where I can't see my footing, I need to know that I can trust him. And I do.

I see a spray of light and hear a rushing. The air feels cooler, wetter.

"It's just around this bend." Jack's hand guides me toward the source. And then, suddenly, we're in an amazing wonderland.

A waterfall tumbles over bumps of white rock, crystals that reflect the light from a high-up source. A spray of water from the splash catches in the sunlight and refracts a rainbow prism. It's as if the cave has collected jewels, right here on the back side of our land.

"It's gorgeous, Jack."

He turns to me, and I feel him edge closer. "Yep. See, you never know what's hiding right in your backyard."

"Okay, fine. I give up."

Jack turns to me. The light, shiny around his head, picks up all the highlights in his hair. And perhaps there's a lack of oxygen down here, because I'm getting a little woozy.

"Will you be my date to Allie's rehearsal dinner and wedding?" Yep, definitely woozy.

Jack smiles, and it's a slow, sweet smile. "Well, Blair already asked me to the wedding. But since you asked me to both, I'll ditch her for you."

"Ha ha. You are soo busted. Allie would never invite Blair to the wedding."

Jack makes a "You got me" noise and grins. "I just wanted you to know that I'd choose you."

He'd choose me.

See, I knew cowboys were trouble.

Chapter 19

If I ever get married, I want a night just like this to celebrate with my friends. Breathtaking, as if God reserved this day just for Allie as His special gift to her. The sun lingers on the horizon, spilling out lavenders and rose-golds across the park, soothing the heat with a soft breeze.

On the picnic tables, Allie has arranged purple passion flowers and accented them with white orchids that add elegance to the casual barbeque rehearsal dinner. Daniel's collection of cool jazz plays on the boom box out of sight. A perfect mix for an eclectic evening. Allie is sending off a glow of joy that feels catching. I'm not sure if I want to get near her or not, thanks to my own current confusion about Jack.

Allie's girls are hanging on Daniel. Soon he'll truly be their dad, and their feelings are evident by their beaming faces tonight.

God certainly surprised them all with Daniel.

Yeah, if I ever get married...

Okay, enough of that kind of thinking. Because I'm not getting married...ever...maybe.

The word *married* makes my gaze fall on Jack as if I'm a

smart bomb zeroing in on my target. I'm still in shock that I asked him to be my date for tonight. I've decided to blame it on the way he kidnapped me, brought me into his lair, and hypnotized me with the ethereal beauty of the waterfall.

It's a good thing he hadn't tried to kiss me.

Or is it?

Yes, it definitely is, because my powers of resistance are crumbling. And it doesn't help that he cleans up well, in a surprising attire of black jeans, pressed designer shirt, and sports coat. It's getting hard to think of him as just the boy next door.

Apparently, he's spent his rodeo winnings well.

"So, what made you decide to bring Jack?" Lark glides over to me, staring at Jack. She also has a glow, and I know it has to do with the baby coming. Everyone's glowing these days.

Am I glowing?

Oh boy. "My mother made me ask him."

Lark eyes me. "Okay, are we in middle school? Did she threaten to ground you? Take a wooden spoon to you?"

"She practically asked him herself at Sunday lunch." Jack looks over, meets my eyes, smiles at me.

Am I still standing? Because I feel as if the earth has moved under my feet.

"Yeah, I can see you were forced," Lark says with a shake of her head. "Too bad he's such an ugly cowboy."

I ignore her massive sarcasm and focus on the last part. A cowboy! I'm out with a cowboy. See, I should carry note cards to remind myself.

"I don't know what I'm doing, Lark."

I'm not sure where that confession came from, but Lark seems to, because she weaves a hand around my waist and leans her head against mine. "I do. I think you're finally starting to forgive yourself."

I step away from her, shocked at her words. But she smiles at me and nods. "It's time, Rachel. Time to let go of your guilt and forgive yourself for your childhood mistakes. God obviously has—look at that incredible, uh, niece you have. And Jack, well, by the way he's looking at you, I think he thinks you're his own gift from God."

He does seem to smile at me whenever he looks my direction. And I have absolutely no control over my reaction, because every time he does, my heart performs a little two-step.

"How are things going with Sheila?" I've been dying to know but haven't seen Lark alone until now.

She frowns. "Not as great as I'd hoped but probably better than Craig expected."

"Are you and Craig okay?"

Her gaze flickers to where her husband is chatting with Adam and Daniel. "We are. He's having a hard time understanding. . . . Sheila is apparently having a difficult pregnancy. She's missing work most days and doesn't feel like doing the most basic things— like picking up her dirty towels off the bathroom floor."

"So you're waiting on her hand and foot? She's only five months pregnant. She seems nice enough, but can you keep this up for four more months?"

"Do I have a choice?" Lark takes a sip of her punch. "Where's Jenn? She looks so pretty tonight, her hair down, wearing that sundress. She said it was one of yours. Are you two the same size?"

I recognize the subject change for what it is, but I play along anyway. "I used to be her size. It's an old dress." Who knew that someday my daughter might be wearing the green summer dress that hung in the back of my closet all those years?

My *niece*, I mean, not my daughter. My niece is here visiting for the summer and happened to try on a dress I had when I was younger. If I try hard enough, can I forget the rest? Not as long as her unwitting comments continue to make me feel as if I've betrayed her instead of having made the hardest choice of my life in giving her up. I just want to put a pillow over my head and scream. Do I really have to tell her?

I know the answer to that question. I just don't know how. Or when.

And deep inside I keep thinking that maybe it will all go away.

"I don't see her," I say, slowly scanning the crowd. And it is a crowd. I think Allie invited everyone she knew.

There's Vic, and of course Adam, probably verbally sparring over some trite issue. And Allie on Daniel's arm. The smell of barbeque has my stomach wishing it was time to eat.

"She was with that cute cowboy earlier."

I glance at Lark. "What cowboy?" But already I know the answer. *The* cowboy. The one who definitely *wasn't* invited. But the one Jenn can't seem to stop talking about. The one who flirted with her Sunday as they did the dishes. I know, because I walked in on them having a towel-snapping contest, Jenn all breathless and laughing.

I know exactly where that kind of laughing leads. "I need to find her. Now." I leave Lark standing there and march over to Jack.

He glances at me with a smile. "What?"

"I think Jenn is off with him."

He quirks an eyebrow. "You're going to have to be more specific with your pronouns, Rachel."

"Him," I say, and my teeth are clenched to keep my voice down. "Him...Dirk."

Jack grits his own teeth in a comical imitation of me and repeats, "Dirk?"

"Yes," I say, glancing around. "She likes him, and I think they left together."

"Calm down," Jack says and puts his arm around me, veering me away from clumps of eavesdroppers. "So what. They're good kids. She's fine."

"She's not fine," I hiss and instantly put a clamp on my tone. Force a smile. "She's not fine. She's with *Dirk*."

"I got that part. And?"

"He's a. . .a. . ." Just how much do I have to spell it out? Jack is looking at me, waiting, eyebrows raised. I lower my voice. "A cowboy."

"No," he says, an incredulous tone in his voice.

I blow out my breath, exasperated that he isn't taking me seriously. "You know what kind of—"

"Guys cowboys are?" Jack finishes for me.

And yes, while I was thinking that, I can't bear to admit it.

"What kind of trouble girls can get into with cowboys." Oh no. Like that was better? Why did I say that to Jack of all people? After wondering forever, suddenly I'm not the least bit ready to find out if he knows what happened that summer or not.

His brown eyes are full of compassion. "Dirk's a great guy. A Christian. And he has lots of integrity."

I can almost hear between his words. Dirk's not Brett. But as I look up at Jack and see the concern on his face—concern, and perhaps a little anger—I notice it's void of judgment.

Maybe. . .maybe he doesn't know.

"He's not that kind of cowboy," Jack says softly.

Oh. My throat tightens, and it's almost on my lips to ask him straight out what he knows about that summer. But he's shaking his head, and something like disappointment crosses his face. "When are you going to stop judging every cowboy you meet? I think it's time you learned to trust someone, Rachel."

I know he's right. Why was trusting him easier in a dark cave where I couldn't see my feet? Was it because I had no choice then? Because out here in the sunlight, it's hard not to overanalyze and scrutinize every motive.

He stares at me, as if he's waiting for a response. No, not just waiting, begging for one.

I shake my head. "I'm going to look for her." And without a backward glance, I head over to the nearest group of people.

Ten minutes later, my heart is pounding. I'm about to raise a real alert when I hear my name.

"Aunt Rachel!"

I turn and see Jenn weaving her way toward the picnic area through the crowd. Miranda is beside her.

"Jenn!"

She comes up, her face flushed, holding a sweater at the neck around her shoulders. "Do you have a safety pin? The strap on your old dress broke, and Miranda and I tried to fix it, but it won't stay tied."

Oh. So then she wasn't. . .off. . .with—oh boy.

"Sorry, I don't have a pin. Mama Ruth will though." She turns to go, and I touch her arm. "Lark said she saw you with Dirk."

Jenn frowns. "I wasn't—" She laughs and slaps her palm with her forehead. "Actually, yeah. He stopped by for a second right after we got here to give me a CD he wanted me to listen to. Some new country singer. I keep telling him I'm not a country girl, but he's convinced I can be. I told him some things never change."

Clearly, she's right. Like prejudices and fears and all around stupidity. While she and Miranda head off to find Mama Ruth and a safety pin, I turn to try and make amends with my date, aka my own noble cowboy.

But Jack's gone. I glance around for him then cringe as I see his truck pulling out of the park.

Matt Dillon would never leave Miss Kitty high and dry, no matter how badly she acted. So much for my hero.

"Hey, Rach," Lark calls and waves frantically.

She looks like she's about to drop in her tracks, so I go toward her. "Yeah?" I'm still trying to wrap my mind around the fact that I've been ditched without a word.

"I've been all over the park looking for you. Then when I finally spotted you, you were all the way over here. Do you know how hard it is to walk in these heels?"

"I'm sorry, Lark. I didn't know you needed me." My words are automatic since my brain is still fixated on the truck I just saw leave.

"Jack asked me to tell you—" She chooses this minute to stop and bend over to catch her breath. "Whew."

"Jack told you to tell me what?" I try not to snap, but it's hard.

"He got a call. One of his horses is foaling, and apparently it's not going well. He had to leave immediately and couldn't find you. I think he tried your cell."

"It's in my car."

She nods. "Oh. He said to tell you that Dirk is the one who called him. I'm not sure why that was important, but he repeated that twice."

Heat creeps up my neck. "I understand."

"He also said that since you drove over, he didn't think you'd mind seeing yourself home."

Chapter 20

A couple of hours later, when Jenn and I get in the car, I'm not ready to go home. I cock an eyebrow at her. "Feel like riding out to the Lazy W?"

She looks over at me. "Is this a trick question?"

I chuckle. "No, it's for real. Jack had to leave to check on a mare. I'd like to make sure everything's okay, but I hate to call in case he and Dirk are in the middle of a birth."

She settles back in her seat. "Makes sense to me. We could stop by Coffee Central and get them a couple of iced cappuccinos just in case it's going to be a long night."

A peace offering. "Sounds perfect."

"You really like him, don't you?"

"Dirk?" I admit I'm stalling, but I don't know how to answer this question. "He seems nice."

"I mean Jack."

"Oh. He's nice, too."

She rolls her eyes. "He's obviously crazy about you."

"Oh yeah, the way he ditched me tonight is proof of that."

She looks over at me. "He ditched you?"

"He couldn't find me when he needed to leave. I was

off looking for you."

"Ah. When you thought I'd run off with Dirk."

"Pretty much."

"Why don't you trust me?"

I frown at the road. "I do trust you."

She crosses her arms. "It doesn't feel like it."

I swing into the Coffee Central parking lot. "I'm giving you a chance to see him again tonight." I park and kill the motor.

"Sure. With you right there." She waggles her eyebrows and grins as we enter the coffee shop. "Not that I'm complaining."

"Better not be looking a gift horse in the mouth, missy."

"I'm not about to."

We giggle with our heads together while we guess what flavors to get for Jack and Dirk.

"Too bad they don't have one called Macho Cowboy Cappuccino," Jenn says.

"We'll have to take that up with Daniel after the honeymoon."

In the end, we settle on iced white chocolate mochas, and soon we're turning down the lane to the ranch.

The barn lights are on when I pull in. "Looks like they're definitely still at work."

I push open the door, and Jenn follows behind me. "Jack?"

"Rachel? Down here," he calls, surprise evident in his voice.

When we reach the stall, Jack is kneeling beside a colt. The baby, still slick and new, its knobby legs wobbly, toddles toward its mama. The palomino mare lying on her side regards Jenn and me warily. Or wearily. I'm not sure. "Is she okay?" I whisper.

Jack nods. "Couldn't be better." He stands. "You want to get them settled in for the night?" he asks Dirk.

"Sure."

Jack steps out of the stall and washes his hands at the wall sink. Then he looks at me. "Feel like getting a little air?"

I look at Jenn, who whispers, "I promise not to run off."

I grimace. "I trust you," I whisper back. Plus, I won't go far.

As Jack and I walk outside, I hold up the cappuccino. "I came bearing gifts."

He gives me a sideways glance and raises an eyebrow. "Peace offering?"

"Exactly."

He takes the cup from my hand. "I accept."

"Seriously, I'm sorry for my major overreaction earlier. Dirk seems like a nice enough guy."

"He is. His dad works full-time for me, but he hurt his back a few weeks ago. Dirk already worked here part-time and is filling in for his dad this summer so the family doesn't lose any income. Not many sixteen-year-old boys think like that."

"No, you've got that right."

"I appreciate you coming out here. I wasn't expecting it."

I duck my head. "To tell you the truth, neither was I."

He grins. "I'm an impulse? I'm impressed."

"Don't be too flattered. Desserts are an impulse with me, too, but I rarely indulge."

"Ouch."

He puts his arm loosely around my shoulders, and I glance at his hand. "You have nice hands."

"Wow, you are impulsive tonight."

I nod. "A little. But I notice hands. That's why I held on to yours so long in the office that day when you came with your mom. I've always wanted to clear that up."

"Oh, so really you're just complimenting my hands to make

sure I know that you're not remotely interested in the rest of me."

My turn to raise an eyebrow. "Did you moonlight as a personal injury attorney while you were on the rodeo trail? You're twistin' my words a little there, cowboy."

He leans against the fence and pulls me around to face him. "Look up."

I obey and draw in a breath. "How did I not notice that?" The stars, so many the June sky seems like it might not be able to hold them all, twinkle brighter than I've ever seen them. And the full moon appears to be smiling benevolently down on the earth.

"Sometimes the most amazing things are right in front of us, but we never see them."

He tugs me toward him in a loose embrace. I know I should turn and run, but I lean toward him. He drops a light kiss on my forehead and releases me.

In a hopefully inconspicuous move to support my trembling legs, I clutch the fence rail. After we look up at the sky in silence for a minute, and I'm able to stand without support, I push away from the fence. "I'd better get Jenn and get home. We've got a big day tomorrow."

"Can I still be your date even though I deserted you tonight?"

I motion toward the barn. "Since you had a good excuse, I guess I won't rescind your invitation."

"Whew." He makes an exaggerated motion of wiping sweat from his brow. "I was afraid I was going to have to call Blair and beg her to reinvite me."

"You're a very funny man."

"I'm glad you know I'm kidding. She's called me several times to ask when the next committee meeting is."

I bet that's not all she wants, but I won't go there. "You

didn't tell her it was next week, did you?"

He shakes his head. "I told her I just show up when you tell me to."

I laugh then raise an eyebrow. "You really told her that, didn't you?"

"Yep."

I move toward the open barn door. "I've really got to go."

Jenn and Dirk are on their knees next to the colt when we reach the stall. Good thing that dress is old.

I clear my throat. "You ready?"

She nods and stands up. Dirk jumps to his feet and stammers a little. "Bye, Jenn. Thanks for the coffee."

Jenn smiles. "Cappuccino."

He nods. "I thought it tasted a little funny." His face reddens. "I mean it was good. Kind of cold, but good."

"It was iced cappuccino, goofy," she says.

"That explains it then. It was great."

"Think he'll be able to get his foot out of his mouth long enough to walk out to his truck?" Jack whispers in my ear.

I grin. "He reminds me a little of you."

He pokes me gently in the side, and I jump away.

"Good night, Jack."

"Good night, Rachel."

When Jenn and I are in the car, I glance over at her. "From that smile, I'd say you had a good time."

"Dirk is. . .awesome. He's different than any boy I've ever known."

"Yeah, that's part of the cowboy charm."

"I'm guessing you dated a cowboy when you were young, and it didn't turn out well."

Uh-oh. Is it just me or is there a big THIN ICE sign pointing toward this conversation? "Something like that."

"Is that why you never married?"

Crack.

I keep my eyes on the road, grateful for the darkness of the car interior. "Who knows why anything happens?"

"Yeah, but did you ever come close to getting married?"

I shake my head. "Not really."

"Why not?"

Okay, obviously I'm going to have to work a little harder to get back to safe ground. "I never married because I never met anyone I could imagine growing old with." A sudden vision of Jack, his brown hair peppered with gray, pops in my mind. I blink away the warm fuzzies and concentrate on what Jenn's saying.

"Oh. Well, there's still a chance you might."

Is she trying to comfort me?

I hunch over the steering wheel and give her my best old woman voice. "Yes, you young whippersnapper, I suppose anything is a possibility. Even at this late date." I roll to a stop at the light and wink at her. "Or I might decide that I like being single."

"I guess."

She doesn't sound convinced, but thankfully she drops it. Maybe the ice isn't going to open up and swallow me whole. . . tonight.

Chapter 21

"Whose bright idea was it to have an outdoor wedding anyway?" Allie groans.

Mama Ruth continues to deftly weave tiny glass beads and baby's breath through the gorgeous updo she just created. She gives us a subtle "Handle this now" look.

Lark, Victoria, and I just look at each other then back at this exquisite creature. We're more used to seeing Allie with a garden trowel in her hand and dirt smudged on her nose.

Finally Lark says, "Honey, it's just a tiny cloud. It's going to blow right over."

I smile. "She's right. Jenn and I heard the weather report on the way over here, and this afternoon is going to be sunny."

"Yeah, I've heard that before." Allie has her back to the dresser mirror per Mama Ruth's instructions. In her lap is a hand mirror turned facedown. Every time she tries to look in it, Mama Ruth gently slaps her hand. She casts a wary sideways glance at Mama Ruth and holds the mirror in her lap to keep it from falling as she motions out her bedroom window with the other hand. "Does that look sunny?"

I walk over and look out at the blue skies. "Honestly, it does.

There's just one little cloud here by the window."

"One little cloud?" Allie wails. "And it's outside my window?" Her blue eyes widen. "That's not a good sign, is it?"

We all laugh then simultaneously cut off in midchuckle as we realize she's at least semi-serious. "You know those pre-wedding jitters you were saying earlier you couldn't believe you hadn't had?" Victoria says.

Allie nods.

Vic grins. "I'm pretty sure you have them now."

"Really?"

"You know what you need?" Mama Ruth says and steps back to look at her handiwork.

"What?" Allie starts to pick up the large mirror on her lap.

Exasperated, the older woman snatches it away from her. "No lookin' yet. What you need is just. . .that." Like a painter putting the finishing touch on a masterpiece, Mama Ruth gives a tiny twist to a strand of Allie's hair then steps back with a sigh of satisfaction. "There. No jitters now."

She puts the mirror in Allie's hand.

Allie looks in it and gasps, then stands and faces the larger mirror. Mama Ruth holds the hand mirror so she can see the back of her hair and dress. "I look like a. . ."

"Princess?" Victoria guesses.

"Supermodel?" Lark adds.

Before I can guess, Allie shakes her head. "Like a bride."

"A beautiful bride," I say quietly, tears stinging my eyes.

She gives us a tremulous smile. "The most blessed bride in the world."

"And don't you forget it," Mama Ruth says, wiping her own eyes.

"Mom!" A knock pulls us all back to the present. "The carriage is here."

Katie pushes in the door, looking perfect in pink. "Can we go get in the carriage? Wow! Mom, you look awesome."

Miranda, beautiful in her purple dress, comes in. "When you knock, squirt, you're supposed to wait for someone to say come in." She sees her mom and stops. "Wow."

Behind Miranda, Allie's mother puts her hand to her mouth, tears spilling onto her cheeks. "You look beautiful, honey."

"Now that we have a consensus," Mama Ruth says, "let's get this show on the road."

~

When we get within sight of the beautiful white horse-drawn carriage in front of Allie's mom's house, Mama Ruth insists she'd rather take her car than ride in something that might turn back into a pumpkin at any minute.

Allie's mom laughs. "I think I'll go with you, if that's okay."

As they drive away, we walk over to the glistening covered carriage. The snowy white horses toss their heads as if in greeting.

"Mama Ruth is right," Katie says. "This is just like Cinderella's carriage."

"Only supersized," Jenn adds, as she climbs into the spacious cab.

When the seven of us are settled in, the driver shuts the door, and in a few seconds, we're listening to the *clip-clop* of horses' hooves through the open windows. "I feel like we're in a fairy tale," Miranda says. "I can't believe Daniel did this."

"He's pretty amazing, isn't he?" Allie beams, all traces of her earlier nerves gone.

"Surely after the wedding she'll be back to normal, don't you think?" Victoria asks Lark and me in a faux whisper.

I nod. "If she's not, we'll have to institute a new Pinky rule.

Number 4—No being nauseatingly mushy about the man in your life."

"Better be careful," Allie shoots back. "You looked a little mushy yourself last night with Jack."

"I—I d–did not!" I stammer.

"You should have seen her after the rehearsal when we went out to his place," Jenn pipes up.

"Traitor," I say under my breath, but I can't hold back a grin.

"To his place?" Victoria leans back against the padded seat. "Do tell, shugah. We've got all the time in the world."

For the next few minutes, they tease me mercilessly about Jack. My own feelings are such a jumble I don't know what to say or how to react. I let out a sigh of relief when Allie gives me a wise look and changes the subject.

"The carriage did come with a price," she says.

"I imagine it cost a pretty penny." Vic runs her hand over the plush upholstery.

Allie laughs. "I mean Daniel and I made a bargain. He got me this carriage, and I agreed to leave the reception on the back of his motorcycle."

Jenn looks up suddenly. "You're going on your honeymoon on a motorcycle?"

"Not our Allie," Lark says. "How far down the road do you have to ride?"

Allie grins. "We're going to stop by his place and get his truck. But for him, me riding the motorcycle is symbolic."

"I'm proud of you," I whisper to her. Her fear of motorcycles and anything risky almost kept her and Daniel from getting together. She's come a long way.

She squeezes my hand. "If I can find a happy ending, you can, too."

But happy endings aren't for everyone. Thankfully, the carriage pulls into the park entrance and I don't say my thought aloud.

"Look at the crowd," Katie breathes.

We all lean to look out the windows, and sure enough, the wedding guests are lining the path, watching our arrival.

"Might as well wave," Lark says.

"Feels like we're on a parade float," Vic grumbles, but she waves regally.

When all of us but Allie alight from the carriage—really, it is the only way to get down from a carriage, right?—I instinctively look around for Jack. And I'm not disappointed. There he is, standing with his mother and Ron near the folding chairs. He gives me a discreet thumbs-up, and I feel myself blushing.

Jenn hurries to take her place at the guest book table, set up to the side where the green carpet aisle begins.

Mama Ruth claps her hands. "Ladies and gentlemen, family and friends, if you'd like to take your seats, the ceremony is about to begin."

Everyone obeys immediately. That woman has an amazing knack.

When all the guests are seated, Adam, in a tux and for once totally serious, takes his mother to her seat. Daniel's sister, Candice, is escorted to her place by her husband, just home from Iraq and handsome in his dress uniform. Allie said Candice didn't want to be in the wedding party because she wanted to be sure everyone knew that Daniel had family in the audience.

We get in line, the music starts, and Dylan takes Katie's arm. They lead the way down the aisle to where Daniel, resplendent in his tux, stands beside the preacher. Daniel's nephew, Elijah, escorts Miranda, and we Pinkies look at each other. Our turn.

Allie not only refused to choose a maid or matron of honor

but also decided to have Lark, Victoria, and me walk down the aisle together instead of having Daniel find three friends to escort us. "It's our wedding," she'd said. "And we want our closest friends and family in it without having to worry about tradition."

In keeping with her wishes, the three of us make our way down the aisle arm in arm.

When we're all in a row next to the flower-lined arch, "The Wedding March" begins. Everyone stands and turns toward the carriage as Adam opens the door and offers his sister his arm. When she alights, the crowd draws a collective breath.

I glance at Daniel. A broad grin splits his face, but his eyes are moist.

Join the crowd, buddy. Everyone seems to be sniffling and passing tissues. I'm sure most of the men would claim allergies, but the truth is Allie's Cinderella story finally has a happy ending, and the whole town loves watching it unfold.

~

After the ceremony and pictures, we line up for the receiving line. Then while Allie and Daniel go to cut the cake, we walk over to where the tables are set up for the buffet reception.

"You girls look just like a flower garden," Alma says. "Whose idea was it for you to each wear a different color?"

Mama Ruth smothers a laugh. "They couldn't decide on one color. You should have heard them. They were arguing like junior high girls, so Allie suggested each wear her favorite color."

Jack's voice near my ear makes me jump. "I thought red was your favorite color."

I spin around. "Well, red was a little too bright to go with the others, so I settled for green."

"Ah." Jack gives me a knowing smile. "Good choice."

Is he insinuating that just because I know green is his favorite color. . . ? "I've always worn green a lot," I say in a low voice.

"I know. Why do you think it's my favorite color?" he whispers.

In spite of the fact that it's ninety degrees in the shade, I shiver. What if I'm losing my heart to this Casanova cowboy?

~

Jack and I balance our plates on the edge of the fountain. "So when are you going to go out on a real date with me?" he asks.

I almost choke on a mint. "I haven't heard an invitation lately."

"What time do you get off work Monday night?"

"Five."

"So by six thirty you'd be ready? Monday night then? Chez Pierre?"

"Chez Pierre?" I say.

A male voice behind me echoes my words.

I spin around.

Ron is standing there, a puzzled look on his face. "I'm glad to see y'all firming up plans for the next committee meeting, but don't you think Chez Pierre is a little outside the city's budget?"

I start to stammer an explanation, my cheeks burning, but Jack speaks before I can. "This one's on me, Ron."

Ron smiles. "In that case. . .bon appetit."

I motion toward his cane, desperate to change the subject. "How are you doing?"

"Better, but I'm not up to sitting through any committee meetings yet. Besides, French food gives me heartburn."

Jack winks at me. "Sorry to hear that."

"Speaking of food, I see your mama's got me a plate fixed. I'd better get over there before she gives it away."

"Sorry to hear that?" I say when Ron's gone. "What if he'd reconsidered and decided to go with us?"

"I'd have been more careful in scheduling our dates from now on."

"From now on? You sound awfully sure of yourself."

"Maybe I'm just sure of us. Speaking of that, was I right in thinking you didn't want Ron to know about us yet?"

Us? I barely know about us yet. I nod. "It's not that I'm embarrassed."

He reaches over and takes my hand. "You set the pace, Rachel. I'm just thankful that we're finally on the same path."

I wish I could be so sure.

Chapter 22

By the time I'm dressed in my one and only little black dress Monday night, I'm wondering if I should have insisted on Pizza Den. At least then I'd have on comfortable clothes and wouldn't be trying to tame this wild curly mess I call hair. As I fight the temptation to call Jack and break our date, my phone rings and an irrational fear stabs me. Maybe Jack has the same doubts and is acting on them.

"I know you're getting ready to go, but I had to call and tell you. Sweetie and I just broke my personal best time on the barrels." The breathless exhilaration in Jenn's voice makes me laugh as she rattles off her time. "You can do better blindfolded, I know, but I'm getting faster every day!"

I sink down on the bed and slip the strappy little black heel onto my foot. "Jenn, that's a fantastic time. . .for anybody! I bet the Grands are excited." Although I know it doesn't compare with how excited they were that she wanted to stay out at their house tonight.

"Granddaddy went up to the house to get Grandmom. Here they come now, running across the yard." She laughs, and she sounds so happy and carefree that I wish there were no secrets in her life. No ticking bombs waiting to explode in her face. I slip on my other shoe and blink away the sudden tears threatening my makeup. Like Lark's granny always said, "If wishes were horses, beggars would ride."

"That's great, honey."

"Bye, Aunt Rach. Have fun on your date."

"I will. Y'all have fun, too."

Just as I say good-bye, the doorbell chimes, and the dogs go wild.

I make them both sit so I can answer the door with at least a tiny bit of decorum. By the time I get the door open and Jack enters, we've about reached the limits of Labrador self-restraint. I decide to let Cocoa and Shadow beg for their good-dog pats from Jack to distract him as I scope him out. He looked really nice in his suit at the wedding, but tonight—in black dress pants and a red shirt with a black and red tie—he could easily top *People* magazine's "Most Beautiful People" list. For any year. Even his polished black cowboy boots with their silver tips are dressy. A smile flits across my face as I note that fact.

"What? You don't like boots with dress pants?" Oops—obviously not enough distraction. I should have let the dogs jump on him. He smiles and scratches Cocoa behind the ear. "This is about as gussied up as I get."

"You look super." Do I sound like a groupie? I tack on, "For a cowboy, I mean."

"You just don't know when to stop, do you?" He shakes his head. "You look okay yourself."

"Aw, c'mon, you're gonna give me the big head."

His dimples flash again. "For an incredibly beautiful woman, I mean."

I'm speechless. Finally I stammer out a "Thank you."

After one more pat for the dogs, I grab my little black bag, just big enough for a lipstick and my cell phone, and let him escort me out the door.

Jack offers his hand to help me into the truck, and I take it, trying to scramble in as elegantly as possible. Little black dresses were made for vehicles lower to the ground. But I love trucks. So I'm not complaining.

He turns on soft country music, and I stare out the window. I can't believe we're officially on a date. How did I let this happen? I didn't think it would be like this, but I have first-date jitters and everything that goes with it. And more. My heart is pounding out of my chest, of course, but I also feel like I can't breathe, like I might die at any second. At the same time, I feel more alive than I've ever felt before. How can love feel so much like a bad case of the flu?

Love. I stare at the streetlights reflecting on the fogged-up passenger glass. Uh-oh. I just thought the word *love*. What I really mean is. . .infatuation, right? Yes, that's it—a crush. I've got a crush on Jack. There. That's much more manageable. Like something I'll get over and then I'll be able to move on.

Relax, Rachel, and enjoy tonight. It's just a crush.

"I guess my red shirt was a bust, huh?"

I jerk my head around to look at him. "What?"

"I wanted to wear your favorite color to impress you, but since you didn't mention it, I figure you didn't notice."

"Actually, I was impressed. It's perfect. And I love the tie."

Stilted conversation, I admit, but it beats staring out the window.

He pulls into the Chez Pierre parking lot.

"Have you ever eaten here?" I ask then wish I hadn't. What if he always brings his dates here to impress them? What if he and Blair came here last week "to discuss rodeo publicity"? Wouldn't I rather not know?

"No. You?"

I shake my head. "No, but I've heard it's really nice."

When we enter the restaurant, Jack gives the hostess his name, and she scurries off to check on our table.

Reservations. I'm impressed.

And I'm even more impressed when the hostess guides us to the best table in the house—right in front of a wide window overlooking the river. She hands us oversized menus, murmurs, "Your waitress will be with you in a moment," and flits away.

Jack grins at me. "Hopefully she'll be able to interpret the menu. Unless you're fluent in French and you're not telling."

"Nope. I know a little Pig Latin, but that's it for me."

"When I take you to the Rib Crib, I'll have to remember that. Might come in handy."

He has a habit of talking in terms of our future. Part of me loves that. The other part of me remembers that I have a secret the size of Texas, and I really shouldn't make a lot of future plans.

When the waitress comes and takes our drink orders, I order water with lemon and so does Jack. As she leaves, he raises an eyebrow. "Water? You're a cheap date."

"Ha. Wait until I start on the food. You'll be begging me to stop."

As we look at the menus, he leans toward me. "Apparently we're not the only ones in Shady Grove who don't read French." He points to the English explanations of the dishes. "Subtitles."

I read over the main courses then lower my menu. Jack is watching me. I smile. "So, what looks good to you?"

His brows draw together, and he shakes his head. "Talk about fishing for compliments! I already told you how beautiful you look."

I immediately feel my face grow hot. "I'm pretty sure you

know I was talking about dinner."

He laughs. "Yeah, I know what you meant. I usually understand you pretty well. But I never was able to resist teasing you." His words turn back the clock, and I feel on firmer footing. This is my old friend Jack, not the handsome cowboy Jack.

The waitress smiles pleasantly as she sets our drinks and a basket of crusty French bread on the table. "Are you folks ready to order? The soup du jour is French onion. As for hors d'oeuvres, the chef recommends our sautéed foie gras."

"I'd love the soup, but I think I'll pass on the hors d'oeuvres," I say quietly to Jack.

"Duck liver doesn't sound too appealing to me either," he confesses. He smiles at the waitress. "We'll both just have the soup."

We finally settle on our main courses—Chicken Wellington for me and Filet Mignon for him.

When I hand my menu back to the waitress, my gaze falls on her uniform top. Suddenly I realize where I've seen that elegant gold monogram on black before. "Isn't this where Sheila Mason works?"

"You know Sheila?" She tucks the menus under her arm. "She sure is lucky, isn't she?"

"Lucky?" I must sound a little confused, because she frowns.

"You didn't hear about it?" She's eager to impart glad tidings. "She quit without notice a week or so ago." She grins. "You should have heard Pierre." She lowers her voice and leans toward me. "I don't speak French, but I'm pretty sure he wasn't wishing her good luck." She chuckles then muses for a minute. "Wish I could be so lucky."

"What do you mean by 'lucky'? Did she win the lottery or something?" I ask, an uneasy feeling working its way through my stomach.

She shakes her head. "Tanya said she saw her at Wal-Mart, and she said she'd found a cushy setup for a while. Something about a new family to take care of her." She shrugs. "Who knows what she meant? Maybe a long-lost rich uncle."

Yeah. Uncle Craig and Aunt Lark.

Our informative friend leaves to place our order. Jack scrutinizes my face. "You look a little like I felt when I got kicked in the stomach by a bull one time."

"Sheila quit her job to move in with Lark and Craig." I know I sound dazed. "She's pregnant, and they're going to adopt her baby."

"Do you need to go call Lark?"

"No. Let's just don't think about it tonight. I'll sleep on it and decide what to do about it tomorrow."

Jack leans closer to me and covers my hand with his. "Good. I was hoping maybe we could forget everything tonight and just get to know each other again."

I open my mouth to reply but stop short when a bright light illuminates our table.

"Is this how the centennial committee does business?" Blair drawls, motioning her cameraman in closer. "Candlelit dinners at Chez Pierre?"

Chapter 23

Jack scrambles to his feet, but Blair ignores him, speaking into the microphone. "Shady Grove citizens might be appalled to know that their centennial dollars are paying for extras like..." She turns and touches my goblet, and the cameraman zooms in on it.

"Water with lemon," I say through gritted teeth.

"Well, I'm sure there are more expensive items to come."

"May I speak to you off camera, Ms. Winchester?" Jack asks. Even in the dim light, I can see the jumping muscle in his jaw.

"Whatever you have to say to me, you can say to our viewers, Mr. Westwood."

"I have no idea where you got the idea this was a committee meeting."

"But"—she looks at me, taking in my little black dress, no doubt, then at him—"this isn't a committee meeting?"

He shakes his head.

For a second I see real chagrin flash across her face. I'm almost positive. Then it's gone.

"Oh my." She gives a fake giggle. "Shady Grove, aren't we embarrassed? I'm afraid we've crashed a date between our local rodeo star and our most beloved chiropractor. Dr. Donovan, tell us when the next committee meeting is, and we'll let you get back to your"—she looks at Jack, still standing, still stone-faced—"romantic evening." She sticks the microphone in my face.

I'm appalled by her nerve, but I can't think of a single quippy comeback. "Tomorrow night."

"Coffee Central Bookstore?"

I nod.

She waves. "See you then."

Her cameraman stops filming, takes one look at Jack, and hightails it out of the restaurant. Blair looks as if she wants to say something, but maybe even she has a modicum of sense, because she shuts her mouth and follows him.

The waitress scoots over to our table, accompanied by the maître d'. "I'm so sorry," she says. "She got here before I knew what was happening."

The maître d' puts up his hands in a conciliatory gesture. "Tonight's meal is complimentary, Mr. Westwood. It's never our intention for our guests to have their privacy invaded. Please accept our apologies."

Jack nods. "Thank you. I appreciate that."

As the two leave, Jack wearily scrubs a hand over his face, sighs heavily, and lowers himself into his chair.

"That was exciting." I try for a light tone, hoping to ease Jack's obvious embarrassment. My voice shakes a little, though, and gives me away.

"About as exciting as being in a pit full of rattlesnakes."

A laugh pushes out of me unexpectedly. "That's an apt comparison, actually."

"I'm going to go down to the station tomorrow and talk to Brad Mansfield. That was inexcusable and incredibly intrusive, even for Blair. You shouldn't have to put up with that."

I put my hand on his arm. "You know what? I think this is one of those 'the less said the better' situations. She may mention us in the morning on her show, but if she does, it's only going to make her look silly and unprofessional. It'd probably be best to just let it go and not make things worse by calling attention to it. So if you're going there for me, don't."

The waitress approaches with our food, and thankfully, Jack lets the matter drop.

"Do you mind if we pray?" Jack asks when she leaves.

"Not at all."

Reaching over and taking my hand in his, Jack bows his head, blesses the food, and then thanks God for this opportunity to renew an old friendship. Is that all this dinner is for him? Good thing I only have a crush, right?

When he finishes the blessing, he stares at me in the candlelight for a few seconds, still holding my hand.

I meet his gaze, my pulse jumping, my mouth suddenly dry. What is he thinking?

He gives my hand a squeeze and releases it, then picks up his fork and begins to eat. After a bite or two, he says, "Even when it's not some psycho reporter making groundless accusations, you just naturally avoid the limelight, don't you?"

Startled, I nod. "I guess."

"But you always loved barrel racing. That put you in the limelight. Competing, I mean."

I grin. "Barrel racing was one of those rare events that was worth putting up with the limelight."

"When you competed, you always looked like you were on top of the world. I never could understand why you quit."

I pick up my water goblet and take a sip, my mind racing. "I'm not a kid anymore."

"I didn't ask why you quit *junior* barrel racing. But there's no age limit on the senior division. People older than you enter all the time."

Okay. Time out. I take a bite then motion toward my mouth.

"The old can't-talk-with-my-mouth-full trick." Jack points at me with his fork. "I invented that."

I finish chewing, swallow, and then smile. "Caught me." I nod toward him. "What about you? How's retirement going? Are you missing the limelight?"

"Not a bit. There is the thrill of hearing the crowd cheer, but for me it was more about the challenge of staying on the bull."

"I always thought someone had to be half crazy to get on the back of a bucking bull." I grimace. "I probably shouldn't have said that aloud."

He laughs. "That's okay. The thing I always liked most about you, even when we were kids, was your honesty—you always said it like it was."

I stare down at my plate. That's me. Honest Abe. Yeah, right. Slick Larry, the used car dealer, is more like it. If only he knew. I poke around with my fork but can't bring myself to put another bite in my mouth.

"You okay?" Jack's brows draw together with concern. "Something wrong with the food?"

"No, it's good. I was just thinking." That's honest, at least. "Sometimes, just when you think you know someone, you find out you don't, really."

"You're thinking about your friend Lark's situation with the pregnant girl?"

I shrug. "That's one example. But how much do any of us really know each other?"

He caresses the back of my hand with his thumb, and I shiver.

"I know you, Rachel Donovan, but I'm hoping and praying that we'll have a long time to get to know each other better."

Talk about a catch-22. In the past, it was my honesty he always liked the most. Yet if I was honest about that past, he would most likely run as hard as he could in the other direction.

~

Running the other direction is exactly what *I* should be doing, instead of walking up onto my softly lit porch with Jack. Hand in hand with Jack.

I can't let him kiss me. I've already decided that. I know there's no guarantee he wants to, but just in case he does, I've thought it through, and he can't.

"Thank you for a wonderful night," I say when we reach the welcome mat. Inside, the dogs go bananas barking.

He smiles at me and examines my face as if searching for clues. Then he leans down and drops another kiss on my forehead. "I'm so glad you went with me. I hope we can do it again soon."

I nod, relieved and disappointed at the same time. Just a crush. A *crush*. "Only without Blair."

"Definitely without Blair."

I slide my key in the lock, and he stands motionless while I unlock the door; then he turns to go. "Good night."

"Good night, Jack. Drive carefully."

Once safely inside, I peek out the window before I turn on the light, and he's sitting in his truck, just looking up at the house. I'd love to know what he's thinking. Then again, I'm too chicken even to guess.

By the time I'm ready for bed, Jack's truck is gone. With Jenn at Mom and Dad's for the night, the house feels so empty. I've gotten used to her presence in the few short weeks she's been here. My daughter. In my house. The two of us—a family. Thankfully, my Bible catches my eye. I pick it up and flip to Proverbs. I'm feeling desperately in need of some wisdom. Regret and hindsight are two useless paths that won't lead me to a decision about whether to tell Jenn the truth.

As I finish my reading and climb into bed, my anxious thoughts about Jenn subside, but my mind turns to another question I'd like the answer to. I lie in the darkness, thinking about what Jack said on the porch. *I hope we can do it again soon.*

I know that could be taken for just politeness, but I don't think it was. Because I feel the same way. And I'm not being polite. But how can I go ahead with this relationship when I know I'm not going to tell him about the past?

Finally I say my prayers and settle in to sleep, but the moon shines in the window. I turn first one way then the other. Around midnight, Cocoa pads into the room and gets up on the bed, and Shadow jumps up on the other side.

"You guys love me, no matter what, don't you?" I pat first one then the other and drift off to sleep with my hand on Shadow's head.

When the alarm goes off at five, I sit up and stretch then smile at the dogs still flanking me. Some nights they sleep on the floor, but last night they knew I needed them close. If only all relationships were so easy.

As I drive out to the ranch to meet Jenn for our morning ride, I rehash last night again. What if he *was* just being polite? What if he never calls me again? I slam my hand on the steering wheel. *Rachel, get a grip.* If he never calls again, that's just a complication avoided.

My heart isn't fooled by that reasoning for a minute, though, and I find myself slowing down as I pass his driveway. In the dim light of the early morning dawn, I'm almost positive I can see a figure up on the hill sitting on a craggy rock. Is that Jack up there? Did he need time alone to think this morning? To think about this crazy thing we're doing?

Or is he taking inventory of his cattle?

I shake my head at my ridiculous thoughts and pull into the barn lot just as my cell phone rings. I glance at the caller ID and don't recognize the number. "Hello?"

"I had a great time last night." Jack's deep voice sends shivers up my spine even over the phone. I'm hopeless.

"Me, too."

"So the Fourth of July is Friday. Do you have plans?"

"We'll go to the lake, I guess, for the town celebration."

"Would you like to go together?"

"Sure." I glance toward the barn. "Jenn will be with me."

"Is it okay with you if I bring Dirk along then? Or would you rather I didn't?"

I sigh. There's just no getting around some things. If I say no, Dirk will probably show up on his own. It's a public event. This way I can keep an eye on him. "I'm sure she'd be thrilled. But they'll have to stay with us."

I climb out of the car and head on foot toward the barn. When I'm almost to the door, I hear voices. My pulse speeds up as I recognize Jenn's giggle.

"I've got to go for now, Jack. I'll call you back." I walk faster.

"Great. Don't forget the committee meeting tonight."

"How could I forget?" Blair and her cameraman. Joy.

We say good-bye, and I flip the phone shut as I walk into the barn.

Jenn is leaning against the rough board wall, and Dirk is

standing in front of her, smiling broadly. She looks up at him and laughs at something he says then catches sight of me.

Her grin fades. She murmurs something to Dirk. He picks up a bucket and goes toward the stalls without looking my way.

She walks toward me. "We were just—"

"Talking. I know. I saw." I force my mouth to relax into a smile. "Last time I checked, talking was allowed."

She shrugs. "Sometimes it's hard to know."

I feel a pang. Tammy's right, and so is Jack. I've got to loosen up a little about Cowboy Junior. Then a sudden thought hits me. "Did Dirk come over last night?" I strive for casual, even though my nerves are jangling as bad as a cowboy's spurs.

She nods. "We played Scrabble with the Grands."

"Sounds like fun."

"It was." She blushes. "Granddaddy walked Dirk to his truck when we were done."

Maybe my parents did learn something about teenagers. "I'm glad you had fun."

"It was just a spur of the moment thing." I look up, and her green eyes are serious. "Granddaddy asked Dirk for supper. As a surprise I guess. And he ended up staying awhile." She picks at an imaginary piece of dust on her shirt. "I just didn't want you to think I was going behind your back."

"Jenn, I'm sorry I've been so hard on you. I'm struggling a little with letting you grow up."

"Now you sound like my mother."

Chapter 24

I can feel all the color rush from my face. I bend over and grab Lady's saddle blanket and offer a trembly chuckle. "Aunts, mamas. . .either way, it's hard for us to see our little girls get to the old-enough-to-like-boys stage."

She laughs, and I relax a little. "Believe me, Aunt Rach, I've been at that stage for a long time."

"Well, since a certain someone has already saddled your horse, why don't you get on Sweetie and let's see your stuff on the barrels this morning, kiddo?" I toss the saddle blanket on Lady and reach for the saddle. "I've got to be at work before too long."

Jenn mounts Sweetie and grins down at me from the saddle. "Get ready to be impressed!" She gently nudges the mare and they head toward the barrels.

The sun is still a low orange ball barely peeking over the horizon when we take the horses out to rinse them off and brush them down.

"You're getting faster every day."

"And we didn't knock the barrels over once this morning, did we, Sweetie?" Jenn pats the mare on the neck.

Dirk comes around the side of the barn. "Want me to finish grooming for you?"

I glance at my watch and nod. "That would be great, thanks!"

"Thanks," Jenn echoes. I notice their hands touch when she hands him the reins.

Oh boy. "Why don't you run on up to the house and get your stuff? I'll drive around and wait for you in the car."

She frowns. "I thought you'd come in with me. Grandmom was making scrambled eggs and bacon, and I told her to make enough for you."

"I'm all dirty. . . ."

She rolls her eyes. "Like they care. This is a ranch, remember? They're used to it."

I know she's right, and I can't think of another excuse. "Okay, but we'll have to hurry. I still have to get in the shower before work."

As I drive around to the front of the house, I keep the windows down. An early morning breeze flutters through the pines, and high in their branches, birds cry out greetings to the new day. I would so love to have a clinic out here. It wouldn't be a far drive for my patients, and the peaceful countryside would be a balm for them and for me.

"Come on," Jenn says, waking me from my daydream. I barely have the car in park before she's jumping out. "Breakfast will be cold."

She bounds up to the front door and yanks it open. "Grandmom? We're here."

I smile as I follow more slowly. It doesn't take that kid long to feel at home somewhere. I feel a twinge of guilt. She should have come to stay a summer here long ago.

"Come on in. We're in here," I hear my mom call.

When we walk into the kitchen, my dad points at the small television on the counter. "I think you're going to be on TV."

"Me?" Jenn says.

My heart sinks. "No, me. Right?"

Dad nods. "Blair Winchester just said she'd be right back with some"—he frowns—" 'very enlightening' footage of Shady Grove's favorite chiropractor. I think she means you."

I cringe at the thought of her "very enlightening" footage. "I'm sure she does." Never mind that since Dr. Burt retired, I'm Shady Grove's only chiropractor. Blair has a way with words. And a way of always landing on her feet. Even when she makes a major faux pas, that woman is going to turn it into profit.

Mom looks toward the screen where a man is bragging about saving a bundle on his car insurance. "What does she mean? Is this another one of your committee meetings?"

"Not exactly. She crashed my date last night."

The theme song for the "Get Real, Shady Grove" segment of *Wake Up, Shady Grove* begins, and Mom shushes us.

We stand in a semicircle around the little screen as the camera pans to Blair's elaborately made-up face split by a picture-perfect smile. "Good morning, Shady Grove. Last night we got a hot tip from a very reliable source that those camera-shy centennial committee members were meeting at Chez Pierre without telling us." She frowns. "How can 'Get Real' bring you the coverage of the centennial celebration that we promised if our own committee members won't cooperate? So this reporter took matters into her own hands and went to the meeting."

The camera cuts away to a video of Jack holding my hand at our table at Chez Pierre. My mother gasps, and I see a grin flit across Dad's face. I'm afraid to look at Jenn.

Onscreen, Blair walks up to the table, and I brace myself for her ridiculous accusations about us spending town money on a

French restaurant. While the video shows Jack arguing with her and even me reluctantly telling her when the meeting is, we can't hear a word of it. Instead, we hear a voice-over of Blair. "Even though our reliable source was mistaken about the nature of the meeting at Chez Pierre, we did find something newsworthy. Apparently what started as collaboration on our centennial committee has flamed into a sizzling romance between our good doctor and the handsome cowboy who signed a contract with the city to put on the rodeo for our celebration. Can we say 'conflict of interest'?"

"Can we say 'yellow journalism'?" I mutter.

My mother reaches over and snaps off the TV. "The nerve of that woman."

Dad's face is dark and stern. "I've a good mind to go down there and tell them—"

I glance at the clock on the wall. "Jenn, we're going to have to go."

"Oh, I almost forgot. Breakfast is ready." Mom grabs the bowl of scrambled eggs and the plate of bacon from the stove and hurries to set them on the tiny kitchen table. "I thought we'd eat in here this morning since it's just the four of us."

"My bag is already packed," Jenn says, her eyes pleading. "Don't we have time to eat?"

I want to go lick my wounds in private, but short of making a scene, I don't see how I can get out of this cozy breakfast. "Sure. Let's go wash our hands and dig in."

When we're all seated around the tiny table, Dad reaches for Mom's hand on one side and Jenn's on the other. Jenn quickly slides her hand in mine. Mom and I look at each other for a millisecond then clasp hands. Holding hands at the little kitchen table during prayer has always been a Donovan family tradition. But I haven't eaten at the kitchen table since I left home almost sixteen years ago.

We bow our heads, and Dad says a beautiful blessing over the food. I love hearing him pray. He always says what I wish I could think to say.

Mom releases my hand when he's done and passes me the eggs. "They may not be salty enough."

"Thanks," I murmur and dip out a small helping.

Mom picks up the salt shaker and looks at Dad. "I think maybe you should go down to Channel 6, Alton. She should have been embarrassed for ruining Rachel's date like that, instead of—"

"She didn't ruin it." As I say it, I realize how amazing it is that she didn't.

My dad stops in the middle of buttering his biscuit and gives me a level gaze. "That's good to hear."

Heat rushes up my face. "I mean. . ." I don't know what I mean.

"Can she get away with that? What about that thing about 'conflict of interest'?" Jenn asks, worry shining in her eyes.

I give her what I hope is a reassuring smile. "The media has a lot of leeway. But I've seen Blair operate before, so this really isn't a surprise. Let's think positively. Hopefully no one will pay any attention to her inane reasoning."

~

By midmorning I've managed to make myself believe my own reassurances. No one has mentioned "Get Real, Shady Grove." Well, no one besides Norma, of course. I got an earful from her as soon as I cleared the front door of the clinic. But thankfully, my patients obviously have better things to do than watch a reality segment on the local morning news.

I smile brightly at the elderly woman waiting for her

adjustment. "Mrs. Swanson, come on in. How's your shoulder doing?"

"Pretty good. But my lower back is killing me."

I nod. "Been working in the garden again?"

A sheepish smile spreads across her wrinkled face. "You caught me." She shakes a playful finger under my nose. "Speaking of caught, are you sure you've got your mind on my aches and pains instead of that handsome cowboy you're so crazy about?" She trills a laugh at her little joke.

I force an anemic chuckle. "Mrs. S., all I have on my mind right now is you."

By the time my final patient for the day, elderly Mr. Duncan, arrives for his appointment, my good humor has gone from anemic to nonexistent. How could so many people watch "Get Real, Shady Grove"? Don't my patients have lives?

Still trying to think positively, I remind myself that Mr. Duncan is usually so busy listing his aches and pains, we don't discuss anything else. Why should today be any different?

Sure enough, as I write his complaints in his chart, my hand almost cramps. Just about home free.

"Let's get you fixed up," I murmur and lower the hi-lo table.

"So, young lady," he wheezes as he lies facedown on the adjusting table, "went out and got yerself a feller, huh? About time, I'd say." His raspy chuckle echoes through the room.

So much for home free. "It was just a date," I mutter.

"Huh?" he yells.

"Nothing." I refuse to let Blair ruin my professional life as well. I work on him in silence. Then when he's standing again, I smile. "You get to feeling better, Mr. Duncan."

He takes his hat from the hook on the wall and puts it on

his head. "I always do feel better after I see you. You're a fine doctor."

For the first time in hours, calm rushes over me. "Thank you."

He clasps my hand in his bony fingers. "I had a wonderful marriage for fifty years before my Sally went to be with the Lord," he wheezes. "Don't let some busybody reporter stop you from grabbing happiness if you get a chance."

My throat clogs with tears and I nod then reach out to pat our clasped hands with my other hand. "I won't. Thank you."

When he's gone, I sink down at my desk and rest my head on my arms. I don't have to let Blair keep me from happiness. I'm doing a fine job of that myself.

~

After I wallow a little, I pick up the phone and punch in Jack's number. He answers on the first ring. "Don't even think of backing out tonight."

"My throat," I croak, mostly joking.

"You'll have to try something else. I can do all the talking, but you still have to be there."

"Jack, I can't do it. Did you *see* that show this morning?"

"No, but I heard about it. I know how you feel."

"You do? So you've had patients teasing you about your 'romance' all day, too?" My face grows hot just saying the word to him.

"Well, no," he admits. "But so what? Romance is nice." His voice is husky. "And at least no one took Blair's accusations seriously. She ended up looking foolish just like you said she would, don't you think?"

I fumble with the calendar on my desk and think about his words. "I guess so."

"I know so. So I'll see you at Coffee Central in an hour."

"Jack."

"Yeah?"

"We have to get along on everything. We can't give her any ammunition for tomorrow morning's show."

He chuckles. "Are you sure we shouldn't argue to refute what she said this morning?"

I groan. "Does this have to be so complicated?"

"Not if we ignore Blair and concentrate on the job at hand. Listen, I'll figure out a way to distract attention from us. Trust me."

He makes it sound so simple that I feel silly arguing. "Okay, but be warned. I may contract some dread disease between now and then and not show up."

"Then I'll just have to come get you. You can run, but you can't hide. I'll *always* find you, Rachel."

Promises, promises. Thankfully I use a little discretion and don't say that aloud. I'm in enough trouble as it is.

Chapter 25

I slip in the door of Coffee Central ten minutes early. I thought about being fashionably late, but I decided I'd rather be manning my battle station when the enemy arrives. Jack waves to me from across the room, and I head that direction and then stop. Someone's already at the table. He turns, and I recognize Ron, who shoots me a rueful smile.

"Mayor Kingsley, nice of you to join us," I say coolly. It doesn't take a professional detective to figure out who filled Blair in on last night's rendezvous at Chez Pierre. Blair says "reliable source." I say "snitch," "fink," "stool pigeon." Take your choice.

He chuckles. "I figured I owed you one."

Jack clears his throat.

"And Jack figured I owed you one, too."

Before I can speak, Alma comes up holding two coffees. She sets one in front of Ron and leans over expectantly. He gives her a kiss on the cheek. "Thanks, sweetie."

"Thanks, sweetie?" I mouth to Jack over their heads.

He grins and shrugs.

"You two want to catch us up on the rodeo details before

the Wicked Witch of the West gets here?" Alma asks as she sits down next to Ron.

"Don't look now, but I think she just flew in," Ron says.

I'm laughing. I can't help it. "You two are so bad."

Alma looks indignantly at Blair and her cameraman making their way toward us. "If she thinks she's going to accuse my son of dishonesty and get away with it, she's got another think coming."

Jack pats the chair next to him, and I sit down. "Tonight we get to just sit back and enjoy the show," he murmurs. "And possibly feel sorry for Blair."

I shoot him a puzzled look, and he mouths, "Trust me."

When Blair approaches the table, she raises an elegant eyebrow. "What have we here?"

"A committee meeting," Jack volunteers. "Some of our members were able to make it back tonight."

"Well, in that case"—Blair smiles for the camera—"Shady Grove, let's talk rodeo."

"Actually, let's talk manners," Alma says. "And liability."

Blair whips around so fast I think maybe a hair came out of place. She makes a cut motion across her throat, and the cameraman drops his camera and steps back.

"First of all, we're volunteers, and you *will* treat us with respect, or we'll rescind our permission for you to attend our meetings. Second, if you ever accuse my son or Dr. Donovan of impropriety again, you'll be standing in the unemployment line. Do you understand?"

"Well, I—"

Alma draws herself up, her shoulders back, her chin high, and her eyes leveled on Blair. I feel a little nervous, and she's not even looking my direction. "Do you understand?"

"Yes, ma'am." Blair licks her lips and brushes her hair back from her face. "May we start filming again?"

Alma shrugs. "You could have filmed that if you'd wanted to. You're the one who told him to cut."

Blair nods then motions for the cameraman to begin filming again.

Thirty minutes later, we have all the current business taken care of, and I think Blair's cameraman is nodding off. Blair stands. "We're going to go."

"Come back anytime," Alma says sweetly.

"Yes, well, we'll see when we can fit it into our schedule."

When she's gone, I look at Alma and drop my mouth open. "Wow. Where did that come from?"

She laughs. "Years of teaching sixth grade. You learn how to tame bullies." She looks pointedly at Ron. "Especially the ones you care about."

Ron blushes. Wait, hold the phone—Ron *blushes*? He reaches over, takes her hand, and looks deep into her eyes. I hold my breath, sure I'm going to hear our crusty mayor declare his undying love for Alma Westwood. What comes out is no less proof of the taming of Ron Kingsley. "Alma, honey, can I get you some more coffee?"

~

When I get home from Coffee Central, I call Lark. As much as I'd like to, I can't put it off any longer.

"Saw you on 'Get Real, Shady Grove,' " she says first thing.

"Yep. We were at Chez Pierre."

"I wish I'd had you give them a piece of my mind while you were there."

"Really?"

"They fired Sheila because she was having some morning sickness."

"Really?" I know I sound like a broken record, but I don't know what to say.

"She'll find something else soon." A worried tone creeps into her voice. "I think."

"One of the waitresses mentioned her."

"That's odd."

"Well, I brought her name up actually. I just asked if she worked there."

"I bet they were embarrassed. Imagine—firing someone for being pregnant and sick."

Why is it so hard to tell her this? "The waitress I talked to said Sheila quit."

"Ha."

"She was serious. She said Sheila told one of the other girls that she'd found a cushy situation with a family."

Silence. "I'm sure she misunderstood."

Oh, what to say?

"Or maybe Sheila did say that to one of the girls to keep from having to admit she was fired."

"Yeah, maybe. But, Lark?"

"Yes?"

"Be careful."

"I am."

"I love you."

"Love you, too, Rach. I know what I'm doing."

"I'm praying for you."

"Thanks. And thanks for calling. I know it wasn't easy to tell me that."

"No problem. Good night."

When the connection is broken, I send up a prayer that God would make the truth known in this situation. So easy to pray for Lark.

But what if Jenn is praying the same prayer in her quest?

~

Fourth of July morning, the sweet aroma of cinnamon prods me to consciousness. In that little space between sleep and awake, I'm back at my parents' house, about to get up and eat some of Tammy's specialty—cinnamon toast.

I stretch and smile as Jenn pops her head into my room.

"Breakfast is served, Aunt Rachel!" Jenn has one of my aprons tied around her small waist.

I throw on my favorite hot pink robe and slide my feet into some slippers.

"It smells delicious. Cinnamon toast, right?"

She nods, her eyes sparkling.

"Just like your mom used to make."

A few minutes later, I pour myself some orange juice and plop down at the kitchen table.

"I used real sugar on the cinnamon toast." Jenn grins. "Hope it still tastes okay to you. I hated to ruin perfectly good cinnamon toast with your fake sugar."

I grab a slice from the plate. "I think once in a while, and in moderation, real sugar is fine." I take a bite and savor the taste. "And I don't use 'fake' sugar. What I use is an herbal supplement that happens to sweeten things."

"That's a matter of opinion." Jenn sits down beside me and heaps her plate with toast. "So what time should we leave for the lake? What kind of stuff does Shady Grove do for the Fourth of July?"

"Well, let's see. The community picnic starts at five, and then there will be games, music, and, a little while before sundown, the annual canoe race. I think the guys are coming to get us around four so we can get to the park in time to get a good table." I wipe my mouth. I won't admit it to Jennifer, but the real sugar tastes delicious. The Pinkies would have a fit if they saw me right now. "Then they'll set off a fireworks display over the lake as soon as it's dark."

"Are you gonna make me and Dirk stay with you and Jack the whole day?" Jenn finishes one of her slices and looks at me expectantly.

I laugh. According to everyone and his brother, it's time I cut her a little slack where Dirk is concerned. Today might be a good day to try giving her some room. Alone in a crowd, so to speak. "Maybe not the *whole* day. But it would be nice if you guys would at least eat with us, and I think if the four of us team up, we might just win the canoe race."

The expression on Jenn's face tells me I've just won a million cool points. Now if only I can put my money where my mouth is and let her spend some time with Dirk today without freaking out.

"Besides, you probably want some time alone with Jack anyway, right?"

Oh, now *that* was subtle. Not.

I narrow my eyes. "I don't really consider a community-wide picnic and fireworks display 'time alone,' but, yes, I am looking forward to our afternoon at the lake."

Surely the news of my date with Jack at Chez Pierre has blown over by now and people won't think much of seeing us together. Of course, the way things have gone lately, Blair will probably pop up from the bed of the pickup on our way to the lake, microphone in hand, wanting to question us about our rodeo budget. Maybe I should invite Alma to go with us as insurance.

"I guess you're right." Jenn smirks a little. "Although I'm sure if you wanted to, you could find a way for some time alone."

Now she looks at me curiously. "Aunt Rachel, how old were you when you had your first kiss?"

Uh-oh. Where did that come from? This conversation is heading in a direction I don't want to go, but I'm not sure there's a good way out of it. At least not one that I can see right now.

"I was a little older than you. Why?" Maybe I'm right to panic at the thought of Jenn and Dirk spending time together.

"No reason, really. I just wondered." She looks embarrassed. "I'm the only girl in my class who hasn't kissed a boy. I just wondered if I'm normal."

I reach over and touch her hand. "There's no need to rush into grown-up stuff. You'll have plenty of time for that later." Like when you're thirty.

"I guess."

"I think the barrel racing is really coming along well." There—how's that for a natural segue? Kissing. . .barrel racing. Well, okay, maybe not natural, but we're not talking about kissing anymore, are we? Mission accomplished. I take one last sip of juice and carry my dishes to the sink. "The rodeo's just a month away. Anything in particular you want to work on today?"

She shakes her head. "It's all so much fun! And I think I'm getting pretty good at it. Dirk even thinks I have a chance of winning my category."

Guess my change of subject wasn't so brilliant after all. At the mention of Dirk so soon after Jenn's curiosity about kissing, I feel myself stiffen. The thought of her falling for a cowboy still makes me sick to my stomach, even if everyone who knows him thinks he's a nice guy.

"We *all* think you have a great chance." I look at her over my shoulder as I rinse my plate and glass. "Your form is good, and you certainly have the skills. You just need to keep your mind on it. Don't get distracted," I say pointedly.

"I know, I know." Jenn rolls her eyes and starts clearing the table. "You've said it a million times."

I put my juice glass in the dishwasher. "Let's get ready. I know Sweetie will be happy to see you."

Chapter 26

Later that afternoon, I lay out a pair of khaki walking shorts and a green polo shirt on my bed. At the last second, I grab a navy shirt and swap it for the green. I don't want Jack to think I'm wearing his favorite color, do I? Wait a minute. Strike that thought. I don't care what Jack thinks.

But I know deep down that I do. I change the shirts back. I feel like wearing green today.

Our date at Chez Pierre has been on my mind all day. While riding Lady, I played our conversation inside my head over and over, obsessing not only over Jack's words, but the tone of his voice. Jenn thought it was hilarious that I kept getting distracted during our lesson, especially after all of my "keep your mind on barrel racing" speeches. Thankfully, she has no idea what was on my mind.

I finish dressing and look at my reflection in the mirror. Considering the sweltering heat that is July in Arkansas, I decide to put my red hair in a high ponytail. Feeling a little defiant, I tie a green scarf around the holder. See, I don't care what he thinks.

After a touch of makeup, I'm ready. And nervous. Am I

ready to be seen with Jack in front of the whole town? I'm afraid that maybe Jack is ready to confirm to Shady Grove that we're a couple, and he thinks this picnic will do that. At the same time, I'm afraid he's just clueless and thinks that this "double" date will stop any residual gossip resulting from Blair's report.

When the doorbell rings, I nearly collide with Jenn in the hallway. She looks very cute in denim shorts and a white top, with her ponytail sticking out of her Braves baseball cap.

She steps back and lets me go first. I opt not to say anything about the touch of mascara and lip gloss I'm pretty sure I detect.

"Sit, girls," I order Shadow and Cocoa as I open the door. And there he is. Mr. Cowboy. And behind him, Mr. Cowboy Junior.

"Well, don't you ladies look festive." Jack's suntanned face is in stark contrast with his even, white teeth. "Can we carry anything out to the truck?"

Out of the corner of my eye, I catch Jenn grinning at Dirk, who peers around Jack's shoulder. "We're ready to go. We just need to get the food. Could you help with the picnic basket and cooler? They're in the kitchen."

Jack follows me to the kitchen where our food waits. A glance backward tells me that Jenn is using this opportunity to introduce Dirk to Cocoa and Shadow. I have to admit, right now in his khakis and T-shirt, he looks pretty harmless.

When I turn back around, Jack is watching me, amusement dancing in his brown eyes. "Would we be able to relax more today if I hired a PI to follow Jenn and Dirk around and keep an eye on them? I'm afraid you're going to get a crick in your neck."

I slug him on the shoulder. "Very funny."

He lifts the lid on the picnic basket and takes a deep breath.

"Mmm. Smells like fried chicken."

"You got it." I pick the basket up off the table. "Not the healthiest of meals, but a picnic must. If you can get the cooler, we'll be on our way." Jack takes the handle of the rolling cooler and follows me back to the living room.

Jenn and Dirk grab the blankets, and the four of us make our way out the door, loaded down with our picnic supplies. We put our things in the bed of the pickup next to an assortment of sporting equipment. I see a football, soccer ball, baseball, and a couple of gloves.

"I wasn't sure what to bring." Jack opens the passenger door for me. "I thought we might want to play some games or something."

As I climb inside the truck, I see Dirk has opened the back passenger door for Jenn. Thank goodness for crew cabs. There's no way I would've let her ride in a car alone with Dirk. The two of them climb in the back, and we're on our way.

Jack turns on the radio and pulls out onto the main highway into bumper-to-bumper traffic. "Not something you see every day around here," he says as he leans forward to check out the long line of cars.

"Yep. Only traffic jam we have all year." I twist around to glance at Dirk and Jenn, who are carrying on a conversation in low voices. Jack looks at me and grins. "There's a mirror in that visor," he whispers.

"Don't be silly." But my neck is a little sore by the time we finally make it to the Lake Oriole sign and turn down the lake road. Jack pays the volunteer Lion's Club parking attendant, and just as we pull into a space, "The Star Spangled Banner" begins blaring from my purse.

Jack raises a brow. "Wow. Just because you wore green today doesn't mean you're not patriotic."

"I'm one of those people who likes to coordinate ringtones with holidays. Got a problem with that?" I snap, suddenly irritated with myself for not dressing in classic red, white, and blue. I flip the phone open without waiting for his answer.

"Rachel?" Lark's voice on the other end is a little staticky. All the trees around must interfere with the cell tower.

"Hey." I jump out of the truck and walk around a little to try to get a better signal.

"We've got a spot saved near the Shady Grove Idol stage. If you want to sit with us, look for the lime green blanket."

"Okay, we'll find you. Thanks for letting us know."

I flip the phone shut and stuff it back in my bag.

Dirk is in the back of the truck handing things down to Jenn. Jack walks over to me. "Everything okay?"

I nod. "Do you mind if we sit with Lark and Craig?"

Jack holds up the picnic basket. "It depends. Do we have to share your fried chicken with them?"

"No, honey, they'll have their own food," I say. My face flushes as I realize what I just said.

"So I'm your honey?" Jack asks next to my ear as we make our way through the crowd.

I walk faster. "I don't know where that came from."

He lengthens his stride to catch up with me. "You know what the Bible says, 'Out of the overflow of the heart the mouth speaks.'"

I keep walking, but I'm afraid he's right. My mind is taking things slow and easy, but my heart is rushing ahead.

I spot Lark waving to us from a little rise in the grassy area ahead. "Here we are, Lark," I yell, relieved to have a reason to end this conversation.

She walks to meet us. "Hey. Glad you found us in this crowd."

"In all this red, white, and blue, green stands out," Jack says, keeping his gaze fixed on me.

"Yup, it sure does." Clueless, Lark nods toward the bright blanket on the hill. "That's why we brought it."

"Speaking of blankets, is there room for ours?" I ask, still pointedly ignoring Jack.

"Yes. Plenty. We spread out so we could condense when y'all got here and still have enough room."

I turn to motion to Jenn and Dirk, who are lagging a little behind, on purpose I'm sure. And bump right into Jack.

The gold specks in his brown eyes sparkle in the sunshine. "Am I making you nervous?"

"No more than usual," I shoot back.

He frowns. "For real? Because I'm trying really hard."

I laugh and slug him. "You're hopeless, you know that?"

His dimples flash. "That would make me your hopeless honey, right?"

Before I can respond, he takes the picnic basket on up the hill.

Lark smiles. "I didn't catch all of that, but it looks like things are going great."

I shrug. "We'll see. I still have the same issues. So that hasn't changed."

She glances up the hill. "Yeah, we all have issues, I guess."

For the first time, I notice a grumpy-looking Sheila sitting beside Craig. "So Sheila came with you." I try to keep my voice even. I'm still a little suspicious of the unemployed waitress, no matter how pure Lark thinks her intentions are.

"Yep. We thought it would do her good to get out of the house for a little while."

It flits through my mind that Lark doesn't completely trust Sheila. That would make it difficult to leave her at home alone.

So I'm guessing Sheila came whether she wanted to or not.

Nevertheless, I smile and wave to her when we approach. She lifts a hand then picks up a paperback lying facedown on the blanket, pointedly and effectively cutting off any further conversation.

An hour later, Jack wipes his mouth and puts down a chicken bone. "That was delicious." He holds up the chicken pan. "Does anyone want more?"

"Now that he's full, he's feeling generous," Craig quips.

"You're one to talk. I saw the size of that piece of apple pie you had, man." Jack pushes to his feet. "Dirk, you want to give me a hand, and we'll take this picnic stuff back to the truck?"

Dirk looks reluctant to leave Jenn, but he stands. "Sure."

"I might as well help, too, since y'all have eaten all the good food," Craig grumbles.

"We'll leave our blankets here for Sheila to watch Shady Grove Idol and head on over to the field," Lark says. "Meet us there." She touches my shirt. "Look for Rachel. Her green should be easy to see."

Jack leans toward me as he walks by. "That's what I like about you. You stand out in a crowd."

"Yeah, right."

I watch him walk away. I've been practicing resisting him, really I have. I thought practice makes perfect. Shouldn't it be getting easier?

Ten minutes later, we've left Sheila with her nose in her book, and Jenn and Lark are trying to find a duck with a prize on the bottom.

I look up and see Jack scanning the crowd. The noise around me recedes, and he's all I can see. In my whole adult life, I've never felt like this before. Why now? Why this summer, when Jenn is here and things are so complicated?

I don't even realize I've lifted my hand, but when I look, I'm holding it in the air. Jack waves in answer and walks toward me, with Craig and Dirk beside him.

"Dr. Donovan! I saw you on TV." Mike Harris is one of my less tactful patients, and right now he looks like the cat that swallowed the canary. "I'm so happy that you've found a man that I don't care if you did go to Chez Pierre on the city's dime." Even in the blistering heat beneath layers of sunblock, I feel my face turn red.

Jack's coming up fast, and I just want to end this conversation. "Thanks. But we weren't there on city business."

"Oh, I know that. I'm just glad you finally found someone." He gives a little wave toward Jack who nods.

Thankfully, at that moment, somebody with a bullhorn announces that it's time for a little flag football. "Mike, I've got to run."

"Oh sure." He moves on into the crowd, and I hear him telling someone that his chiropractor is here with her boyfriend.

"What was that about?" Jack and I walk behind Jenn and Dirk toward the football area. I'm pretty sure that if we weren't behind them, they'd be holding hands.

"Oh, just more aftermath of Blair outing our relationship on TV. I hoped people had forgotten, but apparently our appearance here together is only going to fuel the flames."

Jack stops and turns me toward him. My breath catches for a minute as he looks me in the eye. "Listen. The way I see it, we have two choices. We can either let Blair ruin what has the potential to be a wonderful day or we can let it go. I know which one gets my vote."

I know he's right. I so enjoyed seeing Blair get her comeuppance at the coffee shop the other night. Why let her win today? And it does have the potential to be a wonderful day. Perfect, almost. "Okay. No more worrying from me." I glance at Jenn and Dirk, her hand firmly in his. "At least no more worrying about what people think about us."

Football is really not my sport, but I enjoy watching from the sidelines. With that in mind, I volunteer for the job of holding on to all the spare flags. So as people check in to play the game, they come to me for a flag.

"Could I have one of those?"

I turn to see Sheila standing beside me. The last person I would have expected to want to play football today. "Do you really think that's a good idea? I know it's just flag football, but sometimes it can be a little rough. I thought you were watching the singing contest." I see Lark looking at us from the huddle. She would kill me if I allowed the woman who is going to give birth to her child play football on one of the hottest days of the year.

"I'll be really careful." I can tell Sheila doesn't want to let this drop.

But I'm not going to drop it either. I soften my voice. "Sheila, I really don't think you should. Hasn't your doctor told you that you should refrain from certain activities?"

She takes a step back. "Oh yeah, I guess so. I just didn't think. . ." she trails off. "You're probably right. It might not be a good idea." Once again, I see Lark glancing in our direction.

Sheila shrugs and walks back toward the Shady Grove Idol crowd.

Within minutes Jenn makes the winning touchdown, and Jack and Dirk lift her to their shoulders amid cheers. When they reach me, they put her down.

She touches my shoulder to catch her balance. "Aunt Rachel, we're going to go sign up for the canoe race, okay?" The football game has left Jenn's face flushed. She looks so radiant. I can see from the admiring glances coming from Dirk that I'm not the only one who notices.

"That's fine. We'll meet you at the boat launch. Why don't you stop by the blanket first and get some water out of the cooler?"

They hurry off, laughing and arguing which of them is the better football player.

Jack waits for me as I finish getting all the returned flags back into their box. "So you let them go with no one on their tail. Are you finally becoming a fan of Dirk's?"

"Fan is a definite overstatement. But since you and my parents think he's a trustworthy guy, I figure I can at least let them go sign us up for the race." Right? They are in a very crowded public place after all.

I turn to see if I can still see them, and Jack takes my hand and tugs me back around. "No peeking. Once the baby chick has flown, you have to let it go."

Baby chick? If he only knew. I'm seized by a completely illogical desire to lead him over to a shade tree and tell him the whole sordid truth about my past and Jenn's parentage. He strikes me as a man who can take almost anything in stride. I think that strength is one of the things that draws me to him. He feels as steady as a rock yet as flexible as a river.

He pulls me a little closer, and I can see the concern in his eyes. "You okay?"

"Overheated, I think." The sun is surely baking my brain for me to be having such crazy thoughts.

"Let's go get you some water." He releases me but not my hand, and I follow him up the hill.

Chapter 27

As we walk up toward the contest, I recognize a patient's daughter onstage, belting out "God Bless America." Jack looks over at me. "Wow. She's got a great set of pipes."

"Rachel!"

I look down into my mother's face. "Mom! Dad! I didn't know y'all were here."

Dad motions for us to join them on their blanket.

"Actually, we were just going to get Rachel a drink."

Mom smiles and pulls a bottle of water from their cooler. "Have a seat."

I take the bottle from her, but inwardly I'm marveling at how much friendlier they are to me when Jack is around. Is that my imagination? Or do they like him better than me?

I try to think positively. Maybe he just serves as a buffer, and that's why it's easier with him around.

I sink down beside Mom and look up at the stage. "Think she'll win?"

She nods. "We think she's the best candidate for the national anthem at the rodeo. Hopefully the judges will agree with us."

"Who's judging?" I would never want that job. I can't

imagine having to dash anyone's hopes of being a singer, even if it's just for a small town event. I sure hope there isn't a Simon Cowell in one of the judge's seats today.

"I know Blair Winchester is one of them." Dad narrows his eyes. "She's probably going to show the less talented ones on one of her reality segments."

Obviously he still hasn't gotten completely over his anger from her accusations against Jack and me. I quietly congratulate myself for not making the obvious comparison between Blair and the famous *AI* judge. Well, at least not out loud.

"We're about to compete in the canoe race with Jennifer and Dirk if y'all want to come watch," Jack says.

Mom looks at Dad. "Oh, Alton, that sounds like fun."

He nods. "We'll be over to cheer you on."

When the girl finishes and the crowd breaks into wild applause, Jack and I head toward the boat dock. In the distance, I see Jenn and Dirk waiting for us, along with a crowd of other racers. "So you think it's okay for them to be holding hands?" I ask when we're still a good ways away.

Jack looks at me thoughtfully then down at our own entwined hands. "I think so. They seem like they're not going to push the boundaries."

I glance at them again. They really are good kids. "I think you're right."

"I never thought about it, but I guess these are the kinds of things parents have to talk over and decide." He shakes his head. "Every detail is important."

"Scary prospect, huh?"

"It is, but I still think I might be up to the challenge someday." He squeezes my hand. "With the right person."

Whoa. Have I lost my mind? I'm letting this wonderful, amazing man mentally plan a future with me. This man who has already told me that honesty means so much to him.

The race hasn't started yet, but my canoe is already sunk.

~

"Are we sure about this?" I ask Jack as I fasten my life jacket.

He shrugs. "Too late to be having doubts. We're already committed."

Why does everything seem to have a double meaning today? I glance at the four-man canoe. Two heats have already been completed, and we're in the third and final one. Guess there's no putting it off. "Who rides where?"

Dirk steps up. "I've been watching the other teams get in their canoes—the big guy needs to sit in the back." He grins at Jack. "That's you, boss."

Jack salutes, and we all laugh.

"And I'll take the front."

I look at Jenn. "I guess that leaves us in the middle."

"Okay." She double-checks her life jacket and steps in, climbing into the seat behind the front one.

Jack and I exchange an amused look at her obvious hurry to get the seat closest to Dirk.

Jack holds out his hand to help me in. "Ready?"

"As ready as I'll ever be."

After I'm settled in my seat, Jenn twists around. "Look. Up on the bank."

I follow her direction and see Lark, Craig, and my parents all waving. Beside them, Victoria and Adam, as well as Allie's mom and Katie and Miranda are waving, too.

"We're here to cheer you on, shugah," Victoria calls and pushes her sunglasses on top of her head.

Over the loudspeaker, a familiar voice announces that contestants can paddle around and warm up a little. The contest will begin shortly. Blair is pulling double duty today, having left her post as Shady Grove Idol judge to come over and be the announcer of the canoe race. I'm trying just to tune out her voice.

Jack climbs in and gets settled; then Dirk jumps in the front.

I twist in my seat to look at Jack. "Captain, do you have any instructions for your crew?"

He laughs. "Y'all have been in canoes as much as I have. But I've never raced one, so I'm not sure I have much of a strategy. How about we just row together in rhythm as hard as we can?"

"Sounds like a plan to me." Dirk seems to have finally lost some of his shyness. "I think our other plan should be to try not to tip over."

"Good idea." I definitely don't want to end up in the lake.

We paddle around for a little while with Jack directing us, until I think we have the hang of it. "This is not as comfortable as being in a saddle, but it's kind of fun."

"You took the words right out of my mouth," Jack says, just as Blair calls us over to the starting line.

She counts down with enthusiasm. "Five—four—three—two—one—go!"

We set off, rowing with all our might. Our competition is a team of volunteer firemen and a group of teachers from the elementary school.

"Go, Rachel! Go, Jenn!" I can hear our friends, and even my parents, screaming from the bank.

The volunteer firemen are a boat's length ahead of us.

"Y'all are doing great." Jack's voice is steady. "Let's try and get our oars in sync. Row hard and don't look behind us."

Jack starts calling out commands in rhythm, and our canoe

seems to fly over the water. I can hear the screams of the crowd as we catch up to the firemen.

"Just a little farther." Jack's voice guides us from the back of the boat.

Suddenly, we're at the bank. Jenn and Dirk cheer. Jack helps me climb out of the boat and gives me a big hug. A big hug that, despite the life jackets between us, still makes me a little shaky.

"That was so much fun." I high-five Dirk and Jenn. "Way to go team!" The firemen and elementary teachers yell congratulations, and we wave.

"One more race to go before victory is ours." Jack motions for us to gather around him. "Same strategy. I'll call out the commands. You guys row as hard as you can. Sound good?"

We all nod.

"Okay, let's do it." Jack puts out his hand, and one by one we put ours on top of his. "Row, row, row, on three. One—two—three..."

We all cheer and climb back into the boat. For the championship, we'll be rowing toward the crowd. This time we're racing the winners of the first two heats—a group of paramedics and the four Jones boys who are home from college for the summer.

"Ladies and gentlemen, it's time for the Shady Grove Annual Canoe Racing championship. It looks like all of our teams are ready." Blair's voice reverberates from the loudspeaker. "Five—four—three—two—one—go!"

We take off, using the same strategy as before. Jack is in the back, Dirk is in the front, and Jenn and I are in the middle.

Jack's voice guides us as we row.

Our competition is tougher this time, and we're practically neck and neck with both of the other boats.

"Ladies and gentlemen, this race looks tighter than ever," Blair drones on from the announcer's box, and I can't help but listen to her commentary. "It appears that the local paramedics might be the team to beat. They look like they're in pretty good shape. But don't count out the Jones boys. Their mom told me they're all weight lifters." She pauses.

"Keep rowing, slow and steady," Jack calls from behind me. "Just ignore the announcer."

"And the third team includes Shady Grove's newest power couple, chiropractor Dr. Rachel Donavan and rodeo hotshot Jack Westwood." Blair's voice cuts to my core. "If they can concentrate on the task at hand instead of each other, maybe they'll have a shot."

For a split second I quit rowing.

"Rach, just keep going. Don't let her get to you." Jack calls to me from the back of the canoe. "It's not worth it."

I glance at Jenn in front of me, the daughter I gave up. The daughter who will probably never forgive me if she finds out the truth. I feel Jack's gaze on me from behind. Jack, who loves me for my honesty and is determined to convince me that we have a future together.

And sitting there in the middle, it hits me. I've been desperately hanging on to that middle ground, as if I could have my secrets and still keep Jenn and Jack. But there never was any middle ground. If I'm going to have a relationship with this man, I will have to tell my deepest secrets and possibly ruin the lives of those I love best. What kind of dangerous game have I been playing?

"Come on, Aunt Rachel, you can do it." Jenn's prompting breaks my thoughts. I grip my oar and start rowing on Jack's command.

"Let's go, Rachel and Jenn! Go, Dirk and Jack!" The Pinkies

are cheering for us as we get closer to the bank.

Just as we're about to reach the finish, the Jones boys power ahead.

"Second place is nothing to sneeze at." My dad helps Dirk and then Jenn out of the canoe. He holds his hand out to me, and I grasp it.

"You're exactly right. That was a great job." Jack climbs out of the canoe and pulls me into a loose hug.

"I guess you just couldn't keep up with the Joneses," Adam teases us.

Victoria punches him. "I think he was hoping they'd beat you just so he could make that joke."

"You know how to hurt a man, Vicky," he says.

The chatter goes on, but I can't help but think about freezing up back there. I've got to put an end to this conflict inside me.

Chapter 28

Patriotic music blares as we make our way out of the crowd and start up the tiny trail. The orange sun casts long shadows ahead of us.

"It was nice of your parents to ask Jenn and Dirk to sit with them during the fireworks. I think they knew you could relax a little bit if you didn't have to keep a constant eye on her." Jack leads the way up the trail that he and Craig scouted out earlier.

"Yeah. I know my dad will be watching them like a hawk." I laugh. "No matter how romantic watching fireworks in the dark is, I have a feeling sitting with the Grands will take it down a notch."

"Lucky for us, we'll be the only ones on our blanket." Jack's voice is husky.

True. We will be the only ones on our blanket. Is it too late for me to go fetch Jenn and Dirk and drag them back to where we're sitting? Maybe throw in Mom and Dad for good measure? "Well, even though you and Craig found us that 'really cool' place up on the bluff, Lark, Craig, and Sheila will be right beside us, so it's not like we'll be completely alone."

Jack looks like Cocoa and Shadow do after I scold them. I almost feel sorry for him. But after my epiphany in the middle of the lake, I know I can't give him the relationship he wants. The relationship he deserves.

"Hey, guys. Great job out on the lake." Craig is standing beside our blanket. I immediately notice that their blanket, along with Lark and Sheila, is nowhere to be seen.

"What's going on?" I toss my bag down on our blanket and search Craig's strained face for an answer.

"Lark wanted me to wait until you got here to let you know that we're going to have to miss the fireworks. Sheila wasn't feeling well." He looks irritated. "Something about too much sun." He shakes his head, and his sour expression disappears. "And keeping Sheila healthy and happy is the most important thing right now."

I have a feeling he's quoting Lark but don't say so. "Well, I hope she feels better soon. Tell Lark I'll call her tomorrow."

Craig hurries off, and we sink down onto the blanket.

"He seems a little unsure about the whole Sheila situation. Did you tell them about the waitress the other night?"

I pull out a couple of bottles of water from the cooler and offer one to Jack. "I told Lark. She says it's probably just a misunderstanding."

"But you're not so sure?" Jack's steady gaze never leaves my face.

"I'm trying to give Sheila the benefit of the doubt. I just hope it all works out the way Lark wants it to." I take a sip from my own water bottle. "Having a child means everything to her right now."

Jack leans back on his elbows. "How about you? Do you think you want to have kids someday?"

I feel the blood rush to my face, but hopefully the impending darkness gives me some cover. Now would be the prime time to tell him the truth. But I just can't bring myself to ruin such a perfect day. "Maybe. I guess it just depends on what my future holds."

Jack nods. "I know exactly what you mean. A couple of years ago, I figured I'd live a bachelor's life forever. Run the ranch, work with up-and-coming cowboys." He looks at me intently. "But lately I've been thinking there may be more to life, you know?"

Boy, do I. Here I sit, lakeside on a sultry evening, about to watch the night sky light up with fireworks with a handsome man at my side. But it's not just his looks that make me yearn to be in his future. Jack is everything I've always hoped to find. Unfortunately, he's also everything I don't deserve. And although my mind knows this and has for weeks now been sensibly explaining to me why he can never be my "more to life," tonight my heart is tired of listening to reason.

So as I look into his eyes that are practically enveloping me with their warmth, I decide to put my fears aside. At least until after the fireworks are over. Because right now, in this moment, I know that he has a piece of my heart. I can't help but let myself enjoy it, even if it's just for a couple more hours.

The streetlights and stage lights go out, and the crowd *oohs*.

"Almost time." Jack sits up and pulls me closer to him. He takes my hand and raises it to his lips for a slow kiss. "Enjoy the fireworks, Rach."

As he lowers my hand, I'm left wondering if he means the literal fireworks in the sky or the ones that seem to be sparking between us. I try and relax against him, my hand still encased in his.

The music gets louder as the first fireworks erupt. Brilliant reds, whites, and blues begin showering over the lake. I glance over and admire Jack's profile, illuminated against the light.

How can I walk away from him? There's no way a guy like Jack will wait around forever while I try to get my life figured out. Some other girl will swoop in and scoop him up. I've seen it happen. And I can't tell him the truth until I'm ready to tell Jenn. *If* I'm ever ready to tell Jenn.

"Something wrong?" Jack catches me looking at him.

"No. Just enjoying the evening." I pull my gaze away from him and try to pay attention to the gorgeous fireworks. They must've had an extra large budget this year due to the centennial celebration, because I don't remember the fireworks ever being more incredible. I glance at Jack again. Or maybe it's just the company I'm keeping.

The first strains of the "William Tell Overture" float out of the speakers, and Jack leans in even closer.

"I think this must be the finale," he whispers, his lips brushing my ear.

I turn my face toward his and meet his eyes. As the fireworks flare above us, Jack leans in and gently kisses me. "Just this once," I murmur against his mouth.

"What?" he whispers and touches my lips with his once more.

"Nothing," I murmur. How many years can I live on the memory of this moment?

Jack pulls back and smiles. "I've wanted to do that for so long. And just so you know, it far exceeded my expectations."

Mine, too. The internal battle waging within me is fierce, my heart in total mutiny, my mind rolling over and playing dead. I am so desperately falling for this man. But the timing is all wrong.

Jack reaches over and takes my hand again. "Was that okay?" He looks concerned. "I hope I didn't overstep any boundaries."

"It was perfect." And it was. I put my head against his shoulder and congratulate my heart for winning tonight's battle. Unfortunately, I know the war is just beginning.

~

The next morning as I watch the familiar scenery fly by my car window, I psych myself up for talking to Jack. And try to decide the best way to do it. The possibilities—so many possibilities—are marching through my mind like little ants to a picnic. Okay, maybe ants don't really march, but in my mind they do. Yes, I know that's the same mind that went haywire last night, but in the clear light of day, reason is once again king.

I glance over at the empty seat beside me. I love going out to ride the horses with Jenn in the morning, but I also enjoy the days she sleeps in. For one thing, I get to ride Sweetie on those days, and while Lady is a wonderful horse, she's not my horse. But I guess I enjoy it most because, on the days I ride alone, I can just be me. I'm not the teacher trying to perfect Jenn's barrel-racing skills or the prison guard trying to keep her and Dirk from being alone. I'm just me.

I run my hand over the steering wheel as I turn onto the lane leading to the ranch. This morning I'm just me. . .with a mission.

My phone rings. I glance at the caller ID and flip it open. "Are you watching me again?" Oops. Joking is not a part of the mission. "I mean, good morning."

"Good morning." Jack's deep voice sends shivers down my spine even at six in the morning. Danger! Danger! Remember the mission.

"And no, I'm not watching you. I just know this is when you usually go out to ride."

I laugh. "I was kidding. I'm glad you called."

"Is Jenn with you this morning?"

"Nope. She slept in."

"In that case, would you like some company on your ride?"

"I'd love that."

"Want me to meet you over there?"

"Sounds good."

By the time I get Sweetie saddled, I hear Jack outside.

I climb up on the mare before I go out the barn door. Not my normal practice, but I think my heart needs the safety of me being out of reach when I see him. It would kind of ruin my plan if I throw myself in his arms. Although after last night's fireworks, that's incredibly tempting.

Jack is standing beside his black gelding, Lightning, when I ride out. He looks up, surprise etched on his face. He rubs his hand over his chin and adjusts his hat. "I take it you're ready to ride."

I smile. "If you are."

"Sure." He easily slips into the saddle and gives me a nod. "You lead the way."

I lay the reins against Sweetie's neck and turn toward the trails behind the barn. We ride in silence up the hill and into the edge of the woods. Then, by unspoken agreement, we break into a gallop down the forest road. When we get to the creek, I pull up. And he does the same beside me.

For a second we rest; then, I'm not sure what the imperceptible signal is or which of us even gives it, but we're off again down the creekside trail, the wind whipping my hair and making my face tingle.

When we get to the bluff, we pull up again, and he slides down from Lightning. Staying on the horse would be like remaining standing when a friend sits down. Awkward. I dismount and tie Sweetie's reins around a tree limb.

My knees are trembling as I walk over to the edge of the bluff.

"Are you scared of heights?" Apparently he notices.

I shake my head. Just of getting my heart broken. "I've just got a lot on my mind."

He adjusts his hat. "Wait. Before you say something that's going to ruin my good mood, look out there."

I lift my gaze and take in the valley below me. Lush treetops stretch out forever, and the sun, hidden from view, makes its presence known by casting myriad shadows and splashes of light on the bright green leaves. "It's beautiful."

"So are you."

He reaches up and brushes my hair away from my face. I take a step back. Whoa. Got to stay focused.

I think of the verse in Psalms I ran across when I was flipping over to Proverbs this morning. *I have chosen the way of truth. . . .* Since I'd been up most of the night trying to decide what to do about Jack, the words had a special significance to me. So I'm going to be truthful with Jack. As much as I can at this point.

"I need us just to be friends for a while," I blurt out.

He frowns and looks up at the sky. Is he beseeching God to deliver him from me? Asking why out of all the barns in the world, I had to wander into his? I don't blame him.

"Okay."

"Okay? You're okay with that?" Where's my giddy feeling of relief? Is that what this sick feeling in the pit of my stomach is? I don't think so.

He reaches toward my hand then lets his own fall back by his side. "I do have a question for you."

"What?"

"Do you want to just be friends because you're not interested in me"—he glances at the ground—"in another way?"

"No!"

He jerks his gaze up to meet mine, and I feel my face grow hot. That denial was possibly a little too vehement.

"So you just need some time?"

I nod, not really trusting myself to speak.

"Then you've got it. From now on, we'll just be friends for a while. Good friends, right?"

"Definitely."

He holds out his hand to shake mine.

I hesitate, and he frowns. "We're friends who can't shake hands?"

I choke out a laugh and slide my hand into his. "You make me sound crazy."

He shakes my hand firmly then releases it. "I think I may be the one who's crazy."

Chapter 29

I think I'm crazy."

Lark laughs and glances down the hallway toward Sheila's room. "You are not. Why would you say that?"

"It's been two weeks since I told Jack I just wanted to be friends. I thought that would fix everything, but I've never been more confused." I take a sip of my green tea.

"You've been spending a lot of time together, haven't you?"

I nod. "Lots of time. More than ever. Friend time."

"You tell him you just want to be friends. He agrees. And your problem is. . . ?"

"He treats me like a pal, a buddy, an old college roommate."

She grins. "I take it that's not really how you want to be treated."

"Yes. No." I rest my elbows on her table and put my face in my hands. "Lark, what am I doing? I came by to cheer you up." This time I'm the one who glances toward Sheila's room. "Let's talk about you."

She shakes her head. "No way. Your life is infinitely more exciting than mine right now. I'd much rather talk about you. Really."

"Well, no more about Jack. I have to think about something else."

"How's Jenn?"

I smile. "She babysat for Allie today and is staying over tonight. But she's doing really well. As a matter of fact, she hasn't mentioned her birth mother search in a while. I'm hoping that with the excitement of the rodeo coming up, it might just blow over."

Lark puts her hand on my arm. "Honey, you know you're not honor bound to tell her the truth. When you give a baby up for adoption, there's nothing wrong with not wanting that to come out."

I nod. "I've kind of come to peace with that. So as long as I'm just friends with—" I stop, remembering my earlier edict. "With you-know-who, I don't feel so bad."

"You could tell Jack and still not tell Jenn."

"No, I couldn't. I know it's not logical, but with her wanting to know, I just wouldn't feel right telling him and not her. If she ever found out I'd done that, she may feel so betrayed that she wouldn't have anything to do with me. I can't risk hurting her like that. Besides, if he knew the whole truth, there's a good chance he wouldn't want anything to do with me. This. . ." I hold out my hands. "This being friends thing is the best I can do."

"Whatever you think." I can hear the doubt in her voice. "But I don't know how long you're going to be happy like this."

"I'm just taking one day at a time." I push my empty mug back and stand.

"I'm glad today brought you by to see me. Will you stay for supper?"

I shake my head. "I came straight from work, so I haven't

even been home to let the dogs out."

"I hate for you to go home to an empty house."

I smile. "I've seen Jack almost every day since the Fourth. It won't hurt me to be alone a little bit. Besides, I just got my first shipment in from that Christian mystery book club I joined. I think I'll curl up with a good book tonight."

She hugs me and watches me walk out to my car. As I drive home, I plan out my evening. How long has it been since I just vegged out, as Jenn says? Too long.

The dogs are glad to see me. I have a doggie door, but several months ago a tree fell on my backyard fence, and I haven't had time to get it fixed, so for now the doggie door is sealed. Maybe I should call someone about that tonight. . . . No. Tonight is veg night.

After a shower, I slip into capris and a T-shirt then pad into the kitchen to forage up some supper. Cocoa and Shadow follow me. "Hey, girls, wanna help me clean out the fridge? You can eat what I don't."

Just as I touch the refrigerator door handle, the doorbell rings. I groan and head to the door. When I pass the mirror in the hallway, I groan louder. Riotous curls play around my face, which is bare of makeup. Please let this be a traveling evangelist or a Girl Scout selling cookies.

The doorbell peals again, and the dogs are in a perfect flurry of joy. I peek out the side curtain and open the door to Jack's upraised hand. He halts just before knocking on my forehead and offers a sheepish grin.

"Guess I shoulda called first, huh?"

"Um, that's okay." I step back for him to enter, and the dogs have a contest to see who can bark louder as they leap around him.

"Nice T-shirt."

I glance down at my shirt, which proclaims, "I ride Missouri fox trotters. If I wanted to bounce, I'd buy a trampoline." Since we both own gaited fox trotters, I guess it's appropriate. "Thanks. What's up?"

He squats down to pat the dogs and looks up at me. "I heard a news report that people need more spontaneity in their lives. So I thought we'd do something on the spur of the moment."

"Who are you kidding?" I give his hat a playful nudge. "You forgot to call. You are so busted, buster."

He readjusts his hat and stands with a rueful grin. "Okay. You caught me. I did hear that report a few days ago, but I forgot about it until just now. I was just thinkin' we could take the dogs to the lake and let them play awhile. I meant to call earlier and ask you, but I got busy, and, well, it seemed silly to call five minutes before I got here. So. Wanna go? Jenn can come, too."

"I'm sure Jenn would love to, but she's spending the night with Miranda."

"Well, how about it? I'll load the dogs." He scratches a dog with each hand, and they look up at him like he's their hero.

"I'm not ready."

"You look fine to me." He must be wearing blinders. Oh wait. I guess he wouldn't care what his old college roommate's hair looks like, so why should he care about mine? Still, I have a little self-respect.

"I have to do something with my hair and change clothes before I can be seen."

His dimples flash. "Wrong. I see you right now. You've got to outgrow this notion of invisibility, kiddo."

"You are so funny." I want to tell him I'm going to stay home and read a book, but I admit it, I'm weak. So sue me. "Go ahead and load the dogs while I get ready. I'll be out in five minutes."

Four minutes later, I exit the house, still in my capris and T-shirt but with my hair piled on my head and held by a giant clip. No makeup. What are a few freckles between friends?

"I am so impressed." Jack opens the truck door for me.

"All I did was put my hair up. I don't look that much better," I protest as I climb in.

"I wasn't talking about your looks, missy. I'm impressed because you got ready so fast." He shuts my door, walks around the truck, and gets in. He flashes me a mischievous grin as we head toward the lake.

So is he saying my looks don't impress him? I take a deep breath. That's a good thing. Friends. Buddies. Pals. Got to stay on the right page, Rach.

When we arrive at the lake, the dogs leap out of the backseat and head straight for the water. The summer sun is still fairly high, but the oppressive heat has lifted. Jack hands me one of the bright orange dummies the dogs are trained to retrieve. He takes the other, and we follow the dogs. We start with short throws, but in our bantering mood, we're soon seeing who can toss the dummy farther.

It's a foregone conclusion that Jack will win, but I keep trying. I want to keep trying forever. When I was a kid, I remember that sometimes a moment that seemed perfect to me would occur, and I'd think, *I wonder if I'll remember this moment when I get old. I want to, because I'm happier than I've ever been, right now.* That's how I feel. No matter what the future holds, right now, in this moment, I'm happy. And I'm thankful for that.

❧

"One thing about it," Victoria drawls, "after takin' care of Sheila, a baby will be a picnic." She carries her tray to our table, with Allie and me tagging along behind.

"Lark's running herself ragged, all right," Allie agrees as she pulls out a chair.

"I wonder how Craig's holding out." I'm still amazed that Lark missed our Pinky gathering.

Allie shakes her head. "Lark says even though it was his idea to adopt, he sure isn't crazy about the way things are going."

Vic sits down and takes a sip of her latte. "We need to keep praying for them."

"I know." I sit down next to Allie. "I haven't seen her since I stopped by her house a couple of weeks ago. When she called me this afternoon to say that she wouldn't be able to come tonight, she sounded so worn out. So I told her my news on the phone."

"Having a baby has been her dream for so long," Victoria says. "What if it doesn't happen?"

"Lark's stronger than we think," Allie says softly. "She'll lean on God to get her through whatever comes."

For a second, I wonder if my friends could say the same about me. Will I lean on God to get me through whatever comes? Or will I just keep trying to stand on my own?

"Speaking of news, what's your big announcement, Rach?"

"Yeah, spill. Was Mama Ruth right after all?" Allie grabs my hand and holds it up. "Where's the ring?"

"You're just hilarious." I stir my coffee to buy a little time. "I've told you both, Jack and I are just friends."

"We hear what you're saying, but we see what we're seeing." Allie daintily sips her latte and blots her lips with a napkin. "And from here, it doesn't look like 'just friends.'"

"Seems to me, shugah, like you're spending more time together than some married couples do." Victoria winks at me.

"She's right. Let's see"—Allie begins ticking off items on her fingers—"you ride horses together nearly every morning, you have the committee meetings every Tuesday night. I don't believe there's a decent eating place within a fifty-mile radius that the two of you haven't been to together. What am I forgetting?"

Victoria picks up the count on her own fingers. "Bowling? Fishing? Didn't you take Jenn and Dirk to a rodeo the other night?"

"Jenn needed to see for herself how the events were done. Our rodeo is in two weeks."

"Sounds logical," Victoria says, nodding exaggeratedly.

I blow out an exasperated breath. "Is there a problem with two people who are friends doing things together? We're all friends, and we do things together all the time."

Our gazes lock, and we burst out laughing, since this is the first time in over a month that we've actually sat down and talked. Now that I think of it, most of my spare time *has* been spent with Jack.

July has gone by in a haze of activities, punctuated by "committee meetings" and connected by office hours. But the highlights have all included a certain cowboy.

"So really, Jack's happy just being friends?" Allie presses.

"I don't know."

"Are you?" Victoria asks quietly.

I shrug and shift in my chair. "What choice do I have? For now, it's all there is. I can't really go forward with a relationship."

"Maybe you need to—" Allie starts.

But it's time for a subject change. "My news." I sigh. "Ron called the other day. It's official. I've been nominated for Shady Grove Citizen of the Year."

Vic frowns. "Well, shugah, I surely do sympathize with you. It must be an awful burden, having people think you're so wonderful, an' all."

"Be serious. You know how I hate to be in the public eye."

Allie pats me on the shoulder. "Congratulations, Rachel. You do so much for your patients and this town. It's about time someone recognized it. I'm proud of you."

Victoria shakes her head. "I'm proud of you, too, you goose. But I want *you* to be happy with yourself, too. You've got to let go of the past. You're carrying it around like a camel carrying an extra hump."

Allie spews coffee and fumbles for a napkin.

I laugh and reach around to check for humps, extra or not, on my back.

Vic says, "Well, you know what I mean."

Ever tactful Allie snatches me from the frying pan—"Did you invite Jack to go with you to the banquet?"—and throws me right into the fire, thank you very much.

"Well, of course she did," Victoria pronounces. "The girl is not dumb. She knows a good thing when she sees it. And he is definitely a good thing."

I sigh. I seem to be doing a lot of that lately. "Do you know how hard I've worked this last month to keep my relationship with Jack strictly friends? Then there's all that awful publicity we had with Blair. My patients are finally letting me treat them without asking for the latest development in my social life. I already told Jack about the banquet, and he knows I'm taking Jenn."

My friends look at me as if I've lost what little sense they thought I had.

"Rachel," Allie says, as if she's talking to a particularly stubborn child, "you can't let Blair intimidate you. I, of all people, know how hurtful her broadcasts can be. But look at me now. If I'd let her get to me, I wouldn't have the landscaping contract with the city, I wouldn't have Daniel—" Her voice cracks, and she falls silent, unable to continue.

"Allie's right," Vic chimes in. "Each time Blair walks on someone, she just gains power and steps higher. You've got to stand up to her. Take the bull by the horns. Or, in this case"—she grins—"the bull rider."

Allie and I groan.

But my friends do make sense. I've run from "What will people think?" since I was seventeen years old, leaving home to save face. "Okay, I'll ask him to go. But only as friends."

Vic shrugs. "That's a start."

Chapter 30

About half a mile from the Lazy W, it occurs to me that Jack may be busy, gone, or even—this thought is a shocker that doesn't bear considering—have a date already for tomorrow night. He answers my call on the first ring.

"Jack, is it too late for a friend to drop in?"

"Of course not. Is everything okay?"

"Things are fine. I just need to talk to you a minute."

His tone is guarded. "Good talk or bad?"

I pull into the driveway as he finishes the last question. He's standing on the porch watching me. I close my cell phone without answering and climb out of the car into the warm moonlit night. A night that's playing havoc with my heart, which is once again threatening mutiny.

The cowgirl always falls for the cowboy in the moonlight. It's a known fact. And seeing Jack striding down the porch steps toward me, all broad-shouldered and long-legged, with horses whinnying in the distance and crickets singing their hearts out, well, what's a cowgirl to do?

Get a grip, that's what. Jack meets me halfway across the drive and pulls me into a loose hug. I allow him to hold me for a minute. Because there's the moonlight and the crickets, and. . . and because it makes me feel incredibly peaceful, like all is right with the world.

"What's wrong?" he whispers against my hair.

I push back, and he releases me but slides his hand down to enfold mine.

I don't pull away as we walk up to his porch swing and sit down. "Nothing's wrong. I just need to ask you something."

He smiles. "Since when do you drive out here at bedtime to ask me something?" He squeezes my hand, and I stare down at our entwined fingers. What am I doing on a dark porch holding hands with this cowboy?

I gently tug my hand free. "Since I decided at the last minute that maybe I do need an escort for the Citizen of the Year banquet." I try so hard to sound casual, but I'm afraid that I just sound like I'm trying hard to sound casual. I push to my feet, lean out over the porch railing, and look up at the moon. "I thought you might want to go with me."

"You askin' me or the man in the moon?" Jack says from behind me where he's still sitting. There's a tone in his voice that I haven't heard before.

I turn around and rest my back against the railing, suddenly nervous. "I'm asking you."

"As a date? Or as friends?" His face is in the shadow now, but his clipped words are giving me a bad feeling in the pit of my stomach.

"As friends." Nothing has changed. So that's all I have to offer. Take it or leave it. Except, please take it.

"No."

"No?"

"I'm sorry, Rachel. I can't go with you to the banquet."

Anger, hot and sudden, flares through me. "Why not?" I

can see Allie and Victoria counting off all our excursions on their fingers. I can hear their voices, teasing me that Jack is just waiting for me to give him the all-clear sign. "You've gone everywhere else with me for the last month, but I need an escort to a public banquet where I'm the guest of honor and you can't go?"

As quickly as the anger comes, it's gone, and mortification takes its place. He didn't say he won't go. He said he can't go. He probably has another engagement, or he's expecting company, or he's allergic to banquets, or he has to wash his hair. . . . I'm sure there's a good reason.

He stands and crosses over to me, and the moonlight falls on his face. His features are set in hard lines tonight. The laughing, joking cowboy I know isn't anywhere to be seen. "You asked for us to just be friends for a while. And I agreed. But it's been awhile. And I can't do it anymore. I thought I could give you all the time you need. But I can't."

"Oh." My voices is as small as I feel. He *could* go. He *won't*.

He touches my shoulder, and I cross my arms in front of me. If I let him hold me again, I'll crumble.

He drops his hand as if he's touched a hot stove. "I love you, Rachel."

All sound ceases. The night sounds are no more. I stare at him, his brown eyes so dark, and the horror of what is happening dawns on me. "I. . .I. . .don't know what to say."

He utters a short laugh, void of mirth. "I didn't think you would." Then he nods slowly. "Let me know when you think of something."

He turns toward his front door, his boots tapping against the wooden porch as he walks away from me.

"Jack?"

He turns around, holding up his hand to silence me.

"Remember when I told you about Maggie? I said I reacted stupidly after she left?"

I nod.

"The truth is I found out later that she'd been engaged to some guy even while we were together. I followed her back to Boston and punched out her fiancé. I guess I thought he was the reason she wouldn't love me. A night in jail woke me up to the fact that you can't force love. Either it's there or it's not. I promised myself I'd never try again to make something be there that isn't there. And obviously, for you, it's not there."

"But I. . ." I what? I love you? If I say that, then I've opened the gate. The rest of the truth will come tumbling out. All my shame will be right out in the open, and he'll hate me anyway. Either way, I've lost him. "I. . ."

He opens the screen door and turns back to face me one more time. "Bye, Rach."

And just like that, he's gone.

~

"I still don't understand why I couldn't ask Dirk to go to the banquet with me." Jennifer spins around, admiring her white dress in the foyer mirror.

I lean forward and peer at my reflection. My extra-heavy makeup is hardly noticeable. "I told you, it's a girls' night out." *Besides, if I can't have a date, you're not about to have one either.*

"Miranda and Katie's dad will be there."

A smile plays across my lips. How quickly Daniel became "Miranda and Katie's dad." "He and Adam and Craig don't count."

"Just because you and Jack—"

I turn and raise an eyebrow in warning, and she shuts up.

She doesn't know what happened with Jack, but she's

definitely taken note of my puffy eyes and red nose today. And noticed that I didn't get up for our morning ride. I think she figured out right quick that I don't have a cold.

"So, are you okay?" she asks a little grudgingly. But still, for a fifteen-year-old, that's pretty considerate, I think.

"I will be." I hope. I cried so much last night the dogs finally got off the bed and went to sleep on the floor. Today I'm numb. Nothing. It's weird really. But I remember when I first moved back to Shady Grove, a widow we knew lost her home and all her possessions in a fire. The next day she seemed fine. Lark and I marveled at how quickly she'd found peace, but Lark's granny said, "Peace takes time, honey. Shock is what gets you through the first few days."

So I guess this is shock.

And if peace takes time, then I'm not about to get any, because time is a luxury I don't have. I have a banquet to attend, with or without Jack. And it looks like I'll be doing it without him. And everything else, as well. For the rest of my life.

I can't think of that or I'll never make it through an entire night of being on display. Jenn runs to her room to get her purse, finally giving me a turn at the mirror. I step back and examine my full-length appearance.

I love this dress. Bright red, flapper-style, with a handkerchief hem hanging around my knees. Completely decent, but it always makes me feel a little daring. It's not green, but I still think Jack would have liked it.

Groan.

It's going to be a long night.

"Jenn. Time to go," I call down the hallway.

"Okay—coming."

In a few minutes, she dances into the room, clutching her tiny cell phone purse. She twirls one more time for the mirror.

"This dress is so awesome—I love it. Thanks again for getting it for me, Aunt Rachel."

She does look so beautiful. I feel like the big bad wolf. Maybe I should have let her ask Dirk. "I'm sorry Dirk isn't going to see you in it."

She gives me an odd look then shrugs. "I'm ready whenever you are."

"I'm as ready as I'll ever be," I mutter and grab my keys.

When we walk in the Civic Center and my parents are the first people I see, I think maybe I should have spent a little more time mentally preparing. Oh, who am I kidding? It would take one of those twenty-four-hour prayer vigils to prepare me for what I'm going to face tonight.

"Rachel, congratulations." My mother shakes my hand. *Shakes my hand.* As if she were glad to make my acquaintance. Then she pulls Jenn into a warm embrace.

"Good going, girl." Dad's voice is gruff, but at least he pats me on the back. He hugs Jenn. "You look beautiful, kiddo." Then back to me. "Where's Jack?"

And so it begins. "Um, he's. . ."

"Doc!" Ron's voice causes me to turn. He and Alma are walking quickly toward me.

I throw my parents an apologetic look. "I'd better see what he wants."

"You go on ahead. We'll see you inside," Dad says.

Ron gives me a thumbs-up as he approaches. "You look great." He grasps my forearms and leans close. "Hope you've got a good speech ready, girl," he whispers and winks.

"Speech?" I shake my head and clutch my small red evening bag as I realize what he's saying. I won. And now I'm supposed to give a speech. The one they told all the nominees to prepare. The one I was going to write last night but completely forgot about as I drowned my dogs in tears. What am I going to do now? Waltz up to the podium, smile brightly, take the trophy, and...what? Run? Thanks a lot, Jack. Great timing.

"You're such a joker." Ron laughs heartily, and Alma joins in.

I try to laugh, my mind frantically racing. Really, seriously, what am I going to do?

Alma looks at me and then at Jenn. "Where's Jack?"

I'm going home. I *cannot* do this. I cannot deal with distant parents, an absent Jack, and a nonexistent speech all in one night. Wait a minute, is there a theme running through there somewhere? A theme that's running through my life? Like I said, I *cannot* do this.

"Yoo-hoo, Dr. Donovan," Mrs. Peabody, one of my oldest patients, hails me.

"I'm sorry, Alma, Ron. I have to speak to Mrs. Peabody."

Suddenly, I envision an evening of bouncing from one "Where's Jack?" to another like a pinball. Which will work, if I can time my exits and keep them oh so graceful.

"I'm going to hang out with the Grands," Jenn says.

I nod, and she walks over to join my parents as I greet my sweetest patient.

"Hi, Mrs. Peabody."

"Hi, sweetie." Her bony hands clutch mine, and she pats me on the cheek. "I'm so proud of you."

"Thank you for coming."

"I'm so glad Paul was able to bring me." She looks over her shoulder at a tall gangly boy standing awkwardly a few feet away. "I was just telling him how I came in to see you because of my neck and ended up getting rid of my heartburn. If anybody deserves Citizen of the Year, it's you."

I smile at her reasoning, my terror at not having a speech receding for a minute. "Thank you." I give her a quick squeeze and start to move on, but she grabs my arm and narrows her faded blue eyes at the milling crowd over my shoulder. "Is that cowboy with you tonight?"

"No, ma'am." At least she didn't ask me where he was.

"Oh good." Uh-oh. I've heard that gleeful tone in many a mother's voice just before. . . She turns and waves to the boy. "Paul! Come over here and meet my chiropractor."

This night just keeps getting better and better. All I need now is food poisoning from the filet mignon. Wait. That would be a step up. At least I'd get to leave.

Paul walks up to us, his Adam's apple bobbing. "Hello."

I shake hands with him, hiding my shock. Surely she can't be trying to fix me up with this high school boy.

"Paul's thirty. He's mature for his age."

Oh my. She is. And apparently I'm not very good at hiding my shock. At least he's not eighteen as I imagined when I first saw him. "That's nice. Much better than being immature for your age," I say to Paul. Where did that come from?

He smiles. "Grandma brags about you all the time."

I glance around the lobby. Surely somebody wants to know where Jack is.

Chapter 31

With perfect timing, Allie and her family walk in with Victoria, Dylan, and Adam. They wave, and I lift my hand gratefully. "Paul, it was nice meeting you. Mrs. Peabody, thanks again for coming. I see someone else I need to be sure and speak to."

And away I go. I'm getting to be an expert at leaving conversations. Hopefully without hurting any feelings.

As I stride across the lobby to Vic and Allie, I try to put a speech together. If I'd have been thinking, I could have asked Tammy to write an awe-inspiring acceptance speech for me. What's the use of having a speechwriter in the family if I don't make use of her?'

For a second, I envision me at the microphone. *You like me. You really like me.* No, that's already been done. *Four score. . .*

"Hey, girl, what's got you in a tizzy?" Victoria's familiar drawl brings me back to the present. Adam is standing beside her, resplendent in a suit and, judging from the tan lines, sporting a fresh haircut. She hugs me.

"I think Ron just told me that I won. And I have to give a speech," I whisper into her hair. "I don't have one. I'm going to look like an idiot."

"Come with me." She grasps my arm and tugs. Then grabs Allie's. "C'mon."

Allie looks up. "Where are we going?"

"We need a pregame huddle," Victoria says.

Allie nods as if that makes perfect sense.

Victoria leads us down a small corridor and around the corner. She opens a door and flips on the light. "Perfect."

I follow her into the tiny room. "A janitor's closet?"

"It works for our purposes."

Allie shakes her head. "I don't know if I even want to know."

Vic jerks her inside. "Insider info says Rach won, and she has to give a speech. But she doesn't have one."

Allie squeals and throws her arms around me. "Rach, you won! I knew you—"

I break away in desperation. "There's no time for celebrating now, Allie. Right now, I have to figure out something to say." My voice goes up an octave. "I was sure I wasn't going to win— I was up against a fireman, for Pete's sake! Who knew?"

Allie fishes in her purse and comes up with a bank deposit receipt and a pencil. "We can do this. What do you want to say?"

I think my throat is swelling shut. An allergic reaction to some cleaning chemical in the janitor's closet? Vic's perfume? I should be so lucky. This is good, old-fashioned, run-for-the-hills panic.

I try to think. " 'Thank you so much for this honor. But the truth is I'm a fraud. I don't deserve this award. I messed up my life totally, and I can't be honest with the people I love.' How's that?"

Victoria's eyes are huge. "Oookay, honey. Let's do it this way. You take a couple of deep breaths, calm down, and. . .shut up."

She looks at Allie. "Write this down. Thank you so much for honoring me with this award. There are many other people who work to make this town a close-knit community. I count it a privilege to work alongside these two wonderful, selfless nominees who are also up here tonight. Mayor Kingsley has labored diligently and done a great job on the centennial celebration. There are others too numerous to name who deserve mention. Thanks to all of you."

"Then you sit down to thundering applause," Allie declares as she writes the last word with a flourish.

I clutch my stomach. "I can't do this. Tell Ron I'm sick. Tell him I died. I cannot go out there." My voice rises with unmistakable hysteria.

"Rachel, don't make me slap you. Do you really want my handprint on your face when you get in front of those people? Get hold of yourself." Where did Vic's accent go?

Her stinging words hit me like a dash of cold water, and I nod.

"Remember, most of us came for the food anyway," she drawls.

I give a shaky laugh, but my stomach is back where it belongs, and I can breathe again. "Thanks, y'all. What would I do without you?"

Allie laughs. "Hide out in the janitor's closet until everyone leaves?"

They escort me back to the auditorium, and I stop by Mom and Dad's table. Jennifer is sitting by Mom. "Kiddo, you're my date. I need you to move up to the honoree's table with me." I brace myself for the inevitable repeat of "Where's Jack?" but all three of them exchange looks, so I'm guessing Jenn has told them what little she knows about the case of the missing cowboy.

She stands and follows me to the head table. When we finish eating and the plates are cleared, Ron stands and taps his water glass for attention.

He launches into a long, flowery speech. After the first five minutes, I relax a little. If I'd known his speech was going to go on so long, I wouldn't have worried so much about mine. People will applaud me for my brevity if for no other reason.

I glance down the table at the other two nominees. Gary Anderson, our fire chief, and his wife are seated on the other side of Jenn. Surely Ron's wrong. How could I have beaten someone who rescues people from burning buildings? Jane Matheny and her husband are next to them. The librarian organized a very successful reading program for local children.

Ron is working his way through Shady Grove's history, and he's just now to World War II. I zone out again and glance into the crowd. Daniel's brother-in-law, Carl, is sitting at the table with Daniel and Allie. He was in the war in Iraq—he should be up here instead of me. I'm such a fraud.

"And the nominees are. . ."

Ron calls out each of our names and motions us to stand. When he finishes, everyone applauds, and we sit again.

"Our Shady Grove Citizen of the Year is obviously beloved in our fair community." He fishes in his pocket and pulls out a few slips of paper. "Tonight I'd like to share just a few descriptions of this person from the nomination letters."

He flips through the papers. "Numerous people described this person as. . .completely selfless. . .available any hour of the day or night. . .sympathetic. . .caring. . .understanding. . .and generous."

Tears prick my eyes, and I stare down at the deposit slip speech clutched in my hand.

He looks up at the audience. "And finally. . .this Shady

Grove citizen has a heart filled to overflowing with love for others. Those of us who know her are blessed every day by her giving nature—to the community as a whole and to her fellow citizens as individuals." He glances down at me. "It's with great pride and pleasure that I introduce to you the Shady Grove Citizen of the Year, Dr. Rachel Donovan."

I stand on trembling legs and walk to the podium. The tears that have been threatening rush down my cheeks as I look out at the audience again. I hold the deposit slip up and laugh. "I can't see the words for the tears."

Everyone laughs and I relax. I don't have to worry what they think. They didn't vote for me because they think I'm perfect. They voted for me because I love them, and they know it. And that part of me isn't a fraud. "I love this town. And I love you all. Thank you so much for this honor."

I motion toward Jane and Gary, then to the whole audience. "When I look at y'all sitting here today, I see heroes. Heroes of courage"—I glance at Carl—"whether on the battlefield"—then my gaze falls on my patient who recently lost her husband—"or in a hospital waiting room." Allie gives me a thumbs-up, and I smile at her and Vic. "And I see determination to follow your dreams and help others make their dreams come true. And most of all I see your love for one another. When I look at you all, I'm proud to live in Shady Grove. Thank you."

I hug Ron and stumble back to my seat.

Vic and Allie were right. The applause really is thunderous.

Ron makes a few closing remarks, and soon I'm surrounded by well-wishers. When my friends gather around a few minutes later, I look over at Vic and Allie. "Where's Lark?"

Vic frowns and leans closer to me. "Sheila decided at the last minute that she didn't feel well. So they didn't get to come."

We share a look. When is Lark going to come to her senses?

An agency adoption might take longer, but this road she's walking is fraught with land mines.

I'm a fine one to talk. I look around for my own land mine. "Has anybody seen Jenn?"

"Maybe she's with your parents," Allie says. She turns to her girls. "Have y'all seen Jenn?"

Katie shakes her head, and Miranda shrugs. "I saw her earlier but not lately."

I spot Mom and Dad across the room, surrounded by their own group of well-wishers. She's not with them. As I watch them shake hands, I wonder if deep down they feel like I'm a hypocrite for accepting a Citizen of the Year Award. I sigh. If they do, they do. It's all I can manage to keep everyone else from finding out. I can't worry about the people who already know. "I'd better go check with Mom and Dad and find out if they've seen her."

When I reach them, they both hug me. What else can they do with the whole town watching? "I'm trying to find Jenn. Any ideas?"

"I saw her heading toward the front door when the ceremony first ended. She said she was going to get some fresh air."

Fresh air? Even at eight o'clock at night, it's still ninety degrees. How could that be better than the air-conditioning in here? Fear grabs me. Unless the company is better outside.

I make some lame excuse and hurry toward the door. People are leaving, but I don't see Jenn anywhere. I take off at a sprint for the parking lot. Why did I wear high heels? I'm a chiropractor. I know better.

Out in the parking lot, I take a deep breath. She's probably in the bathroom. Maybe she got some fresh air and came back. I turn and walk more slowly back up to the Civic Center. Everyone's right. I'm paranoid about her and Dirk.

I pull the door open then glance over toward the empty overflow parking lot around to the side. Berating myself silently, I walk over and look around the building. And there—standing right out in the open lot—is my beautiful Jenn, looking like a princess in her white dress. . .passionately kissing a toad in a cowboy hat.

"What are you doing?" I yell as I run toward them.

She spins around and almost trips. He catches her, then takes one look at my face and pulls his hands away from her elbows and steps back.

Her freckles stand out on her ashen face, and for a second, I think she might faint. "It's not what it looks like, Aunt Rachel."

I snort. "I'm not quite that out of touch. I know what it is."

"I called Dirk and begged him to come see me in my dress. Just for a second."

Unlike Jenn's, Dirk's face is bright red. "I didn't plan to—"

I hold up my hand. "Don't try to snow me, Dirk. I know exactly what you planned."

Jenn steps forward and touches my arm. "Honestly, the kiss. . ." Now her face reddens. "It just happened."

"Yeah, honey, that's how it usually works. It just happens. Let's go." I'm so upset I'm shaking, and I have to get to my car before I make a fool of myself—okay, a bigger fool of myself.

I turn back around to Dirk. "If you know what's good for you, you'll stay away from my. . .niece."

He just nods and walks away slowly to his truck, his shoulders slumped.

Jenn follows me to the car without speaking, but when she gets in, she uses plenty of force to close the door.

"Why did you have to humiliate me?" she says as soon as I start the motor.

I stop with my hand on the gearshift and gawk at her. "What did you want me to do, Jennifer? Step back into the shadows and let him take advantage of you?"

"For your information, I kissed him."

I pull out onto the road and try to process that. "He shouldn't have been there in the first place."

"I asked him to come."

"Behind my back?"

She shrugs and slumps down in the seat. "You wouldn't let him come. And I think I may be in love with him."

I put on my right blinker and turn toward my house, trying to pretend that I'm not terrified by her admission. "Love is never an excuse for deceit, Jenn. Not real love."

As I hear my own words, nausea rolls over me. We ride home in silence.

Chapter 32

"Bye, Mr. Johnson. Be sure and ice that back when you get home." I pat the elderly man as he leaves the adjusting room. Thursdays usually fly by, but in my present mood, I'm thankful to see the last patient of the day. I muster a smile as he thanks me for helping him feel better.

I bump into Norma outside the adjusting room. "Company in your office," Norma says and gives me an odd look. "Blah, blah, blah."

My heart thuds in my ears, and I struggle to take slow deep breaths. It has to be Jack. He's been as miserable as I am, and he wants to go back to being friends. Or he wants to talk about the somewhat caustic message I left on his voice mail Saturday night concerning Dirk. I probably should have slept on that impulse instead of calling as soon as we got home.

Either way, he's here.

Norma puts a hand on my arm. "Dr. Donovan? Did you hear me? I said is there anything I need to do before I leave for the day?"

Oh. That was the "blah, blah, blah." I really need to get a grip.

"No. Thanks, Norma. I have a few things to do here; then I'll lock up."

As soon as she's gone, I make a mad dash for my private bathroom, where I run a brush through my hair and apply a hasty coat of lip gloss. Not great, but I don't have time to do more. I rush to my office.

"Allie." Dreams of Jack crumble in a heap of dust. "Victoria. What are you doing here?"

"Nice to see you, too," Victoria says. "We have a problem."

She nods to Allie who picks up the story. "This morning was Lark's first trip to the doctor with Sheila. She was supposed to come to work after, but she never showed up. It wouldn't be such a big deal, but three of my crew had to go to Jonesboro to pick up some special seedlings, and I needed her to help me in the office. So I called her."

"Only Craig answered," Vic says in the same tone she'd say, "The sky is falling."

"And?" I'm still back at the beginning, trying to get over the disappointment that they're not Jack. I'm having a hard time following what they're saying. Didn't I just have this same zoning out experience with Norma? I force myself to focus on Allie.

"And. . .Craig works during the day, remember? He never takes off unless there's an emergency." If someone was standing outside the room, he would swear that Allie was talking to a child. She was trying so hard to be patient. "When I asked to speak to Lark, he said she didn't want to talk to anyone."

"Maybe Sheila is being Sheila again."

She shakes her head. "If it was just 'Sheila being Sheila,' Craig wouldn't be home from work in the middle of the day. Plus, he sounded terrible—I can tell he's worried sick about Lark. Something's happened."

"So"—I'm finally getting the picture. When did I get so self-absorbed that I would ignore a crisis involving one of my dearest friends?—"what are we going to do?"

Victoria snatches her cell phone out of her pocket and pushes a button. "Craig, hi. Is it okay if we come over and talk to Lark for a few minutes?"

"We'll be right there." She snaps her phone shut. "He says, please come."

~

Craig looks grim and worn out when he opens the door. He motions toward Sheila's room. "She's been cleaning that room ever since Sheila left."

Sheila left? Uh-oh. Poor Lark.

"She even wanted to burn the sheets, but I finally talked her out of that."

When we get to the doorway, Lark has her back to us, shoving the vacuum cleaner back and forth, her dark curls bouncing.

Vic walks in and taps her on the shoulder.

She whirls around like she's going to do a martial arts move then turns the machine off and releases the handle.

Her eyes are swollen and wild, but dry.

For a second, no one speaks.

"Did y'all come over to tell me how stupid I am? I knew you thought I was crazy for letting a total stranger move in. And you were right. Go ahead and say 'I told you so.' I'm the most gullible idiot on the planet." Lark hides her face in her hands, her anguish as tangible as a fifth presence in the small room.

"Lark, let's go sit down, and you can tell us what's going on." Vic gently takes her by the shoulders and steers her toward the kitchen.

Allie pulls a glass out of the cabinet, pours a glass of tea, and hands it to Lark, who takes a sip and draws a shaky breath.

"You know Sheila said she had a doctor's appointment this morning. I told her I wanted to go." She looks at Allie. "Even though I could tell she wasn't crazy about the idea, I figured if she saw I took off work for it, she'd have to let me go with her."

"Makes sense," Vic says.

"I wanted to see the ultrasound." Lark's voice trembles. "But she threw a fit when I pressed the issue." Tears fill her eyes. "Anyway, I insisted, and she got mad and started yelling. Then I got mad and told her that I had a stake in this, too. And if I couldn't see the ultrasound, she was going to have to move out."

She looks at the ceiling. "All those weeks of waiting on her hand and foot. Putting up with her tantrums and whims. I think it just pushed me over the edge."

"It's okay, honey." I touch her arm, and she looks at me. "More than likely she wouldn't have given you the baby anyway when it was time."

"That's just it." She shakes her head. "There never was a baby."

We all three draw in a collective horrified breath. I had doubted Sheila's sincerity in giving up her baby, but it never occurred to me to doubt the actual existence of a baby. Now Sheila's behavior at the Fourth of July flag football game makes perfect sense.

"It turns out she knew all along she wasn't pregnant. She never went to any doctors. It was all a lie that started as a way to force her boyfriend to marry her. If he didn't, she'd give up the 'baby' to a willing couple." She flinches. "Us. What an idiot I am."

"You're not an idiot. We all believed she was pregnant," Allie says quietly.

"But you didn't all take her into your homes and treat her

like a princess. No wonder she didn't want to leave even after she knew she couldn't get her boyfriend back. She had it made."

I shake my head. "Not really. Because she was living a lie. And that's no life at all."

Wham. Just like in the car with Jenn the other night. Another ton of bricks from my own words of wisdom falling right on top of my own head. Not exactly where I'd aimed them.

Lark is too lost in her distress to notice the sudden silence, but I can see that Allie and Victoria have raised their lovely eyebrows and are staring at me, having connected all the dots. I shrug. "Take it from me."

~

As we walk out of Lark's house, Vic looks over at Allie and me. "I hope they'll be able to get some sleep tonight. I feel so helpless. I can't even imagine the pain and disappointment they must be feeling."

Allie pulls her cell phone out of her purse. "No, but God can. And we're not helpless—we need to keep praying for His comfort to heal their heartache. And someday, in His own time, give them a baby."

I nod, too shaken by my own revelations to say much.

Allie puts her arm in mine. "It looked like you made a decision in there. Am I wrong?"

Tears well in my eyes at the sympathy in her voice. "You're not wrong. I have some things to take care of."

"We'll be praying for you, too, Rach," Vic says. "Is there anything else we can do?"

I shake my head.

She gives me a quick hug. "We've been kind of distracted by this worry with Lark." She looks over at Allie. "And by honeymoons."

"Yeah, but we're still praying for your happy ending, Rach," Allie says. "And believing it's going to happen."

"Thanks. I may drive a little slow on my way to pick up Jenn. I've got a phone call to make."

"Take your time. I'm calling the Pizza Den right now to order for the kids and Daniel. And I told Craig I'd put in an order for them, too."

After we say good night, I drive toward Allie's. On the way, I pull into my office driveway and park. I don't want to be driving during this call.

Tammy answers on the first ring. "Hey, Rach. How weird that you would call. Russ and I had the craziest idea."

I gulp, suddenly nervous. "Really? Me, too."

"You had a crazy idea, too?"

"Yes, but go ahead and tell me yours."

She laughs. "No, you go first."

I take a deep breath. I'd better, because I might chicken out otherwise. "I need to tell Jenn the truth."

The silence on the other end reminds me of those commercials about dropped calls. "Tammy, are you there?"

"Yes. I'm here. I'm just processing."

"So how do you feel about it, now that I really want to do it?"

"I think it will be a big burden off all of us, Rach. As anxious as she's been to know the truth, I've hated not telling her." She pauses. "*But*, Russ and I respect our original agreement and your privacy. We both understand that it's your decision, not ours, whether or not to tell her."

"I know. Y'all have been great about that."

"What made you decide you wanted to tell her?"

"So many things." I relax back against the car seat and stare at my small frame office building. It may not be the natural health clinic of my dreams, but it's not half bad. God has blessed me so much. Why do I have such a hard time trusting Him with my past?

"On some level, I've wanted to tell her since she showed up here that first night. I told myself that it was for her own protection that I didn't." Now it's my turn to pause. Some things are hard to admit. "But lately, more and more I've realized that it's shame. And pride. And those aren't good reasons for keeping a secret."

"Wow. I'm impressed by your wisdom, little sister."

"Oh yes, that's me, the wisest of them all. Not. I said something tonight that slapped me in the face with my own foolishness." I tell her briefly about Lark and Sheila. "I'd like to tell Jack, too, after Jenn knows. Even though I'm terrified of what he'll think."

"If he's half the man I think he is, he'll think he's incredibly blessed to have someone like you."

I laugh. "Okay, shut up before you make me cry. I've been doing that enough lately." I take a deep breath. "So I know y'all are coming in a couple of weeks to get Jenn. I guess you still want me to wait until you get here to tell her?"

"Actually, that's part of our crazy idea. You feel like having company this weekend? I went to the doctor this morning, and he gave me clearance to travel."

"You're kidding! Y'all could come this weekend?" I'd resigned myself to wait two weeks. The thought of just a couple more days. . .

"If I still feel okay in the morning, we'll leave then. Don't mention it to Jenn, though, just in case I decide I can't. I think this will be a good surprise."

"Me, too." And good surprises are something we could use a lot more of.

Chapter 33

Since Fridays are half days, I've got plenty of time to do some cooking and cleaning before Tammy gets here. *Perfect planning*, I congratulate myself as I pull up in front of my house and park. Allie's mom keeps the kids on Fridays, and Jenn usually sleeps in. She'll be well rested and ready to help me. If I can figure out a way to motivate her without giving away the surprise.

I bound up the steps, unbelievably lightened by the fact that I'm about to dump this burden of secrecy. Even if Tammy thinks we should wait until after the rodeo to tell her, one way or the other, I'll be out in the open with everything by the time the weekend is over. I prayed most of the night, read Proverbs this morning, and today I'm ready. Let the chips fall where they may. And please let them fall without hurting Jenn too much.

I push open the door and stop.

Jenn stands in front of the full-length mirror, braiding her hair in two braids. She's beautiful in the turquoise and rhinestone shirt and matching boots I wore when I was her age.

"Grandmom found it in her cedar chest and dropped it by awhile ago. I hope it's okay for me to wear it," she says to my reflection, her green eyes wide.

I swallow against the lump in my throat. "Definitely. But I should have bought you something new."

She grins. "This is a perfect fit. Besides, it's vintage. How much better can it be?"

"Vintage?" I say with mock dismay.

"Knock-knock."

Still looking in the mirror, I see Jack behind us, his expression guarded. He holds up a turquoise cowboy hat. "Mrs. Donovan sent this."

Armed with the knowledge that I'll be able to tell him the truth soon, I toss him a playful smile in the mirror. "Jenn's saying I'm vintage. I think that's just another way of saying I'm old. What do you think?"

He shakes his head and stares at us both, his mouth slightly open. "I think she looks enough like you to be your daughter."

His words strangle the air from my lungs. My mind races, frantic to erase them, to cover them somehow.

The buzzing in my ears blares as Jenn's gaze meets mine in the mirror.

I stare back, as if I'm encased in concrete, unable to break free.

Her eyes flare as she realizes the truth. "No way," she whimpers.

"Jenn. You weren't supposed to—"

She spins to face me. "How. . .how could you?"

I try to pull in a breath. I've had this nightmare so many times. Is it really happening? "I didn't—I was going to—"

She puts her hands to her ears. "I hate you!" she yells and runs toward her room. The door slams.

I'm still frozen, my ragged breath the only sound. No. This can't be the end. I have to make her understand.

"Rachel." Jack's hand touches my shoulder.

I jerk away and stumble down the hall to Jenn's room and slam my fist against the door. "Jenn! We have to talk." There has to be a way to fix this. With my ear to the door, I try again. "Honey, let me in."

I hear movement; then suddenly music blares. I jerk away from the pulsating rock music vibrating through my brain. She hates that music. She just wants to drown me out any way possible. I jiggle the doorknob, but it doesn't budge. "Please," I whisper, knowing she can't hear me. I stay there as the radio DJ announces the nonsensical title to the next song and the next. Every time there's a tiny pause in the broadcasting, I knock, but she ignores me.

Finally I give up and walk back to the living room.

Jack's standing where I left him, looking at the family pictures on my wall. He turns to me, his brow furrowed. "What's going on?" he yells over the music.

"Going on?" I croak. "Surely you've figured it out by now." I shake my head. "All this time, she's been trying to get me to help her find her birth mother, and I—"

"Birth mother?" he repeats dumbly. "She's adopted? But she looks. . ."

The realization dawns on him more slowly than it did Jennifer, but I see his eyes widen as the truth hits him. I turn away, unable to bear any more disgust and disappointment in the eyes of someone I love.

I'm not who he thought I was.

I'm not who Jenn thought I was.

All these years of being a big fraud has finally caught up with me. "Why don't you mind your own business?"

He laughs, but there's no humor in it. "I thought you were my business." I may not be looking at him, but the disgust is evident in his voice. "If I remember right, I told you all about my past on our first date. And I believed you were finally beginning to trust me. I must seem like a real idiot to you."

My chest tightens. "I'm sorry I hurt you. But look at it this way: You've paid me back. My relationship with Jenn will never be the same."

I can feel his breath hot on my neck, and when he speaks, he doesn't yell, in spite of the music. "Relationship?"

He doesn't say anything else, and for a few seconds I think he's gone.

Then, "Relationships are built on truth and trust."

I flinch.

"No wonder you couldn't say you loved me."

He's right. I was never the pure innocent girl he must have imagined I was. Not even back then. Not after that night. "Just leave me alone, Jack. You're better off, anyway."

Apparently he agrees, because the front door slams.

I turn and sink into my glider. The rock music pounds in my head, and I try to let it wipe out conscious thought. But I can't. I remember how I felt when, without discussing it with me, my parents decided to send me off to live with Tammy and Russ. And I'd done something horrible. How much more must Jenn feel betrayed by me? As the sunlight outside dims, I blink my swollen eyes, push to my feet, and walk down the hall. I bang on her door again. "Turn the music off so you can hear me," I shout.

Sudden fear clutches me. Would she do something crazy? I have to know she's okay. I sprint to the bathroom and grab a hair pin from the drawer. "Sorry, babe, I'm coming in." I stick the pin in, and the knob twists easily under my hand.

The music booms even louder, but the room is empty. I run over to the window where the curtains are flapping. For a second, I can't take it in. She's gone. Gone.

My legs turn to lead again as I realize whom she would have called. Is history repeating itself in spite of my efforts to the contrary? "Lord, please protect her. Help me find her quickly."

In the living room, I fumble in my purse until I find my cell phone and punch in Jack's number.

"Jenn's gone."

"What?"

"I finally unlocked her door and she's gone. Are you home?"

"No. I've just been driving around." His voice is husky. "Thinking. I'll come right over."

"No." I grab my keys from the hook. "I won't be here. I have to do something now. Do you have Dirk's phone number? I'm sure she's with him."

"We can only hope."

"Hope?" I snarl into the phone. Argh.

"I'll call him. Call you right back."

In seconds my phone rings. "He's not answering."

"Probably too busy seducing a hysterical girl."

His voice is soft. "Rachel—"

"Where would he take her?" I snap.

"Probably to the ranch."

"I'll be right there." I open my car door.

"Let me take you. You're in no shape to drive."

"I don't have time to wa—" His truck pulls into the drive-way behind my car. I slam the door and flip my cell shut. I also don't have time to waste arguing.

When I climb into his truck, he looks over at me. "It will be okay."

"That depends on how quickly we find them."

"Dirk—"

I hold up my hand. "If you're going to tell me again what

264

a fine, upstanding young man he is, I'm going to have to take my own car."

A muscle in his jaw jumps, but he keeps his lips clenched together.

We ride the rest of the way to his barn without speaking. Dirk's truck is parked right outside, and my stomach clenches. What will we find? Are we too late to stop Jenn from repeating my mistake?

As soon as I open my truck door, I can hear a male voice yelling. Jack is already running toward the barn, and I'm on his heels through the door. I stop in my tracks as I see Dirk inside the dirt-floored arena.

"Are you crazy?" he yells. "You can't do this."

Jenn, her hair flying wildly around her shoulders, looks down at him from inside the chute, astride a bull. The bright green shirt and red hair are incongruent with the brownness of the arena and the paleness of her face. The word *surreal* flashes through my mind. This can't be happening.

She glances up at me and lifts her chin.

Black spots dance in front of my eyes, and everything starts to fade. I blink and steady myself with my hand. "Jenn," I call shakily, "come on out and let's talk."

"I don't have anything to say to you," she yells, her voice hoarse from crying.

"I have plenty to say to you," I call back. "Please get off the bull."

Dirk climbs up on the chute gate in front. It can't open with him on it, surely. A movement near Jenn catches my eye. Jack has slipped around behind her.

Please, Lord, keep her safe.

Chapter 34

Jack's husky voice rings through the empty arena, but I can't tell whether he's talking to Jenn or the bull. I edge closer, and she answers him, so I guess he is talking to her. He continues to talk in low soothing tones as if the back of a bull is the perfect place for a long conversation.

Every muscle in my body is taut. I feel as tightly coiled as a lion ready to spring, yet as helpless as a mouse in a trap.

She looks over at me and nods, then reaches up toward Jack. A sigh of relief pushes from my lungs.

Dirk leans in to help Jack get her off the increasingly restless bull. Apparently, his foot catches the latch, because the chute gate he's standing on swings slowly open. He lets go of Jenn and teeters, then drops to the ground, trying to close the latch back.

The bull, sensing freedom, slams his massive body against the gate. Dirk loses his balance and stumbles backward.

Jennifer, still on the bull's back, screams.

I run toward them.

The bull throws his body sideways and meets no resistance. I reach the fence just as Jack snatches Jenn straight up in the air.

I sink to my knees. The bull rampages out from under her into the arena, snorting and bucking.

Jack stands on the back side of the chute with Jenn cradled in his arms.

Dirk, back on his feet, climbs the fence and jumps out of the arena. He starts toward them, but Jack waves him away. He carries Jenn as if she were a baby and sets her down on the bench behind me.

I clamber to my feet and sit next to her. I reach toward her, and sobbing, she clutches my hand. Tears gush as I stare down at our clasped hands. For a brief second, she's mine again. It's as if none of this awfulness ever happened.

"That was close," I say quietly, rubbing my trembling thumb across the back of her hand.

Jennifer stares up at me, her body shaking, her eyes clouded with fear and doubt. "I wanted you to pay," she whispers. "I thought it would serve you right if I got thrown off a bull."

I instinctively put my free hand over my heart. "It probably would have served me right, but I'm so thankful it didn't happen."

"How could you do this to me?"

"Jenn, things aren't always as they seem."

Her choked laugh is edged with sarcasm. "No kidding."

"There's no explaining why I did what I did. I guess that's why I put this off so long."

"Why didn't you tell me? Were you ashamed of me?"

I shake my head. "I was ashamed of me." My insides clench as I remember the day I handed her to Tammy. "I wanted you to be a phoenix, baby. Beauty rising from the ashes. And you are."

"Did you hate me because I was a mistake? Is that why you gave me up?"

I clasp her hand a little tighter, and she jerks it away as if she just realized we were touching.

"You were never a mistake. I loved you. More than life itself. That's why I gave you up."

"How could you have kept this from me all these years? Would...Mom—" She stumbles on the word. "Would they not let you tell me?"

I push her hair back from her face, and again she jerks away.

"No, I was the one who wouldn't let them tell you I was your birth mother. I said I didn't want you to know because I didn't want you to be embarrassed, but the truth is, if I couldn't be your mother, I, at least, wanted you to look up to me. Not to see me as someone who would do something so despicable." I pull in a shuddering breath and swipe at my face, slick with tears. "It was pride."

"My whole life has been a lie."

"You have two parents and an extended family who love you an incredible amount. That's not a lie."

"I loved you."

Her past tense stabs me. "Jenn, we were going to tell you this afternoon. Your mom and dad are probably at my house by now, actually. I called them yesterday, and they agreed to come today so we could tell you together."

Jenn stares at me as if I am a stranger and pushes to her feet. "It's too late now. I want to go home."

I follow her out of the barn then look around blindly for my car. Without speaking, Jack climbs in the crew cab truck and starts the motor. Suddenly, I remember I rode with him. Jenn gets in the backseat, and with great effort, I get in the front. My whole body is heavy with defeat. So this is what it's like when everything you fear will happen, does. I've lost them both.

I look over at Dirk, leaning on the fence, his head buried in his arms.

"What was he thinking?" I mutter.

Jack gives me a sharp glance. "He was thinking that a girl he really likes asked him to show her how he could ride a bull. But when he got the bull in the chute, she climbed down in there instead."

From the backseat, a quaking sob punctuates his words.

I try to fight back my own sobs, but I can't, so I turn to the window and bury my head in my arm.

"Rachel...," Jack says softly.

I shake my head. Nothing he can say will make me feel better, and if I feel any worse, I think I'll die. He must realize that, because he doesn't speak again.

When we get to my house, I get out, shut my door, and open Jenn's. She lets me help her down but pulls away from me when I try to put my arm around her. I mumble, "Thanks," in Jack's direction.

"Take care," he says softly and drives out of my life.

"I thought you said Mom and Dad were going to be here," Jenn says as if everything I say and do might be a lie.

"They should be here any minute."

"I'll be in my room." She scuffs down the hall. "Packing."

I should try to start something for supper. The game plan had been I'd have a nice supper ready, and as soon as they got here, we'd eat and then tell Jenn the truth together. I walk in the kitchen and open the pantry door. The labels blur together. I snag my little footstool and step up on it to stretch to the top shelf. Behind a twenty-pound bag of Jasmine rice, my fingers find what I'm looking for. I clutch the plastic and pull it toward me.

I barely look up when Russ and Tammy's headlights illuminate the dim living room. In a minute, she pushes open the screen door and flips on the light. "Rachel," she gasps.

I look down at my lap and the floor around me littered with candy wrappers. "I needed chocolate," I moan.

"Oh my goodness! She found out, didn't she?"

I nod, miserable in every way.

Tammy gives me a quick hug, and she and Russ hurry down the hall to Jenn's room. She apparently lets them in, and they disappear inside. I sit in the quiet house listening to the rise and fall of their voices.

I've never felt so alone.

Jenn will be okay. She may never forgive me, but she'll be okay. She has parents who love her, and someday she'll have a family and children of her own. But I'll never move past the mistake I made as a teenager.

Even in my sugar-clouded mind, I can see that I chose my own reality. Is this what I want? To live out my life and end up a bitter old woman with no one?

I jump up and hurry down the hall to the bathroom. After I wash my face and scrub my teeth vigorously, I put on a light touch of makeup, enough to cover my swollen eyes a little, maybe. I raise my hand and tap on Jenn's door. "Tammy?"

Tammy opens the door and smiles at me. "We were about to come out."

Behind her I can see Jenn sitting on the bed next to her dad, her head resting on his shoulder. She keeps her gaze to the floor.

"I'm actually going to run out for a little bit, okay? I've got some things I need to take care of."

She hugs me again. "Just give her a little time. She'll remember that Aunt Rachel's the best," she whispers against my ear.

Tears edge my eyes again, and I nod even though I don't believe it. "I'll be back in a while."

"Russ is going to go get us a pizza. We'll save you some."

Again I nod. "Thanks."

In my car, I sit in the driver's seat, unsure what I'm going to do. After a few minutes, I start the motor and drive mindlessly for a while, watching details carefully but not going anywhere. Finally, I turn down the lane toward Mom and Dad's. And Jack's. I pass his road, though, and head on toward my childhood home.

Sitting in the dark eating chocolate may not be a therapy I'd recommend to my patients, but as I sat there, I realized some hard truths. One is that somehow emotionally I ended up being frozen in time that Christmas Eve morning I told my parents I was pregnant.

I pull up into their driveway and kill the motor and my headlights.

I stare up at the dimly lit house. I left a large part of my heart here that day.

And as scary as the prospect is, I'm ready to reclaim it.

~

"Hey, baby girl. What are you doing here?"

I jump, startled by my dad's use of my childhood nickname almost as much as I am by his presence in the front porch swing. "Daddy! What are you doing out here?"

"I was just sittin' and studyin' a little until it got too dark to see." He holds up his well-worn black leather Bible. "Your mama's gone into town for her scrapbook night, so I wasn't in any hurry to get back in the house." He starts to stand. "But we can go on in if you want."

"No, we can just sit out here." I slide into the patio chair and pretend I don't see him pat the swing beside him.

A chirruping fills the silence.

"Crickets?"

"Tree frogs."

"I never could keep those straight." I stare out at the green flashes lighting up the yard. "Y'all have so many lightning bugs. I remember Tammy and me catching jars full of those."

He nods. "She'd forget and leave hers until they died. Then she'd cry. But you were so careful. You always made sure you let them out after you used their light a little."

I remember that. "I never wanted to take a chance that I might forget and be sorry."

"I think that made it a lot harder to accept the news when you told us you were expecting."

I jerk my eyes up to meet his, shocked that he brought up a subject that has been taboo for fifteen years.

His eyes, so like mine and Jenn's, have crow's-feet I've never noticed. "That is what you came to talk about, isn't it?"

I shrug then nod. "Mostly."

"I knew you would eventually. Or I hoped you would."

"What made it harder to accept?"

"You were always our easy child. The steady one. Level-headed. Careful. We were stunned beyond a parent's normal shock at that kind of news."

I hate to admit that I felt sort of the same way. Like what I did was worse because I was so not the type to do it.

"Not that I'm making excuses for that day. We've talked a million times about how we wished we'd handled it differently. But sometimes you don't get another chance."

I think of Jennifer's angry, hurt-filled expression today. Tears prick my eyes. Another surprise. I thought I was all cried out. "You kicked me out. On Christmas Eve."

"I know it seems that way to you, but at the time we just wanted to get you away quickly so that when you came back home. . .after, there'd be no rumors."

"You planned for me to come back home?"

He frowns. "We asked you to come back home with us after the baby was born. Don't you remember?"

I start to deny it, but then I stop. "That was just so that I'd be out of Russ and Tammy's way and they could get on with their new life with the baby."

He chokes a little and coughs. "It was because we missed you and wanted you here."

I know that's how he remembers it, because my dad would never lie, but I have a feeling his memory is a little skewed.

I guess mine could be, too.

Maybe reality is somewhere in the middle.

"We saved your presents for years."

I put my hand to my mouth. I've never admitted to a soul how hurt I was that my parents put me in a car on Christmas Eve and never offered me one gift from under the tree. For the first few years, I privately wondered what they did with them. I pictured a big bonfire. Or maybe an act as simple as returning them to the store. Finally I put them out of my mind. I thought.

"Why didn't you just give them to me in Georgia?"

"We had some silly idea that when you came home, we'd celebrate Christmas and pretend the whole thing never happened."

As the queen of pretend-it-never-happened, I can relate even though I don't want to. "Yeah. I tried that. Pretending. It blew up in my face today."

Concern etches deep lines on his forehead. "Jennifer found out?" He looks over my shoulder as if she might be lurking in the dark. "Where is she?"

"Tammy and Russ are with her. I called last night and asked them to come so we could tell her together, but this afternoon

Jack made a comment about us looking alike, and Jennifer put two and two together."

He reaches over and pats my hand, a little awkwardly, but the feeling is there. "I'm sorry."

"She hates me."

"Nothing hurts worse than that, I don't think." His voice is filled with pain.

"I never hated you, Daddy. Or Mama, either."

"It sure felt like it for a lot of years."

"I thought y'all hated me."

"That's just another way we failed you. Not putting aside our pride enough to make sure you knew otherwise."

"I should have come to talk to you about it sooner."

"We thought when you moved home that things would straighten out in no time."

"They should have," I say softly and lean my head back against the chair. "I've been an idiot."

"We all have."

I laugh a little, and a permanent tightness in my chest loosens. "Mama might not like you speaking for her on that."

He chuckles. "It sure was nice of you to invite her to go to the concert with you. You'll never know how much it meant to her."

"I had fun."

"So did she. She talked about it for weeks after."

"Maybe we can do more together."

He nods. "Maybe we all can."

I reach over and squeeze his hand. "Count on it."

"Don't give up on Jennifer, Rachel. She loves you, and if you just keep showing her you love her, she'll come around. And I think it'll be sooner than you think."

I push to my feet. "From your lips to God's ears."

"I really will be praying about it, honey."

"Thank you. I'd better be getting back home."

He stands and pulls me into a hug, then drops a kiss on my forehead. "Love you."

"I love you, too, Daddy."

He walks me out to the car. "Don't be a stranger."

"I won't."

"You're welcome to bring our neighbor over with you anytime."

I shake my head, trying to ignore the pain stabbing through me. "You and Mama are going to have to give up on that dream. We had a parting of the ways today, too."

"Partings can be mended."

I slide into the driver's seat. "You may be a tad bit overly optimistic."

He shakes his head. "After what happened here tonight? I don't think so."

"We'll see." I start the motor and put the car in reverse.

He stays where he is until I get turned around and head out. In my rearview mirror, I watch him walk back up on the porch.

As I pull out of my parents' driveway, I roll my windows down and slow to a crawl. The stars out here are so big. A gentle breeze across my face matches the peace I feel inside. But when I near the turnoff to Jack's ranch, a wave of longing broadsides me.

Regardless of what Daddy said, some fences can't be mended.

Chapter 35

I waited too late to figure out my true feelings for Jack. With today's fiasco fresh on his mind, I doubt he's in any mood to listen. And now that he knows the truth about what happened all those years ago, I'm sure he never will be. After tomorrow night, the rodeo will be over and he'll again become someone I just see around town occasionally.

I push the gas pedal down, and the wind whips through my hair as I regain normal speed.

Maybe losing Jack won't matter so much if I can patch things up with Mama and Daddy and possibly Jenn.

Yeah, right.

I thought I was done lying to myself, but apparently not.

~

When I walk into my house, the smell of baking greets me. I sniff. Chocolate chips. Cinnamon definitely. Maybe banana? In the kitchen, Tammy, in my Takeout Is for Wimps apron, is pulling a tray of cookies from the oven. She slides in a loaf pan with the other hand and turns back to a mixing bowl.

"Where did you find all this sugar?"

She smiles at me. "Hey, girl. I had Russ pick some up when he ran out to get pizza." She comes over and enfolds me in a hug then nods toward a pizza box on the end of the bar. "We saved you a couple of pieces, by the way."

"Thanks. Where are Russ and Jenn?"

"They went on to bed. It's been a long day for everybody."

"I'll say." I sink onto a stool, snag a paper plate from the dispenser, and plop a slice onto it. Cold pizza doesn't sound wonderful, but I'm too tired to heat it up.

Tammy frowns and shakes her head, then snatches the plate from my hand and sticks it in the microwave for a few seconds. When she sets it back in front of me, the cheese is soft and inviting.

"Thanks again," I murmur then reach out and tug on the apron, stretched tight over her round tummy. "So this is the little guy, huh? Very cool."

She puts her hand to the bulge and smiles. "Yes, it is very cool."

"How did your doctor visit go this morning?" I take a bite of pizza. It's so much easier to ask about things that have nothing to do with what happened in Shady Grove today.

I can see that Tammy is on to me, but she answers the question. "Everything looks perfect. She gave me the clearance to travel." She raises an eyebrow. "As long as I rest up a few days before I make the trip home. Hope that's okay."

"Like there was ever any doubt. I'm thrilled to have you here. But Jenn seemed ready to get home."

"That's the joy of being a teenager, sis. You can change your mind quicker than you change your clothes."

"She doesn't mind staying?"

"She wants us to see her barrel race, and she can't wait for us to meet her cowboy. And your cowboy for that matter. She thinks Jack is awesome."

"In the first place, he isn't my cowboy. Not after today. And in the second place, she can't stand me, so why would she care?"

Tammy scoots a stool over and sits down beside me. "One of the many wonders of Jenn is her ability to take things in stride. That's one reason I was so stunned she ran away."

My dad's earlier words rush back at me.

"She's absorbing this new information and processing it faster than I possibly could. By tomorrow I think she'll be full of questions for you."

"What should I tell her about Brett?" That question has bothered me all night.

Tammy shakes her head. "She asked me about him, and I told her a little. She said maybe someday when she's older, she'd like to contact him. But no time soon."

"That's a relief. Thanks for handling it. I'll answer whatever questions she has. As long as she's willing to talk to me, I'll be happy."

"She loves you, Rachel. That's never going to change."

I shake my head. "I always thought I'm the queen of thinking positively, but you and Daddy have got me beat with your overly optimistic views. She said she hated me, and I'm pretty sure she meant it."

Tammy frowns. "Daddy? Is that where you've been?"

I get up and snag us both a couple of cookies and tell her about my visit to the ranch.

"Mama wasn't there?"

I shake my head. "It's her scrapbook club night. I forgot."

"We'll have to call her when we get up in the morning and tell her Russ and I are here. Otherwise she might get her feelings hurt."

"I'll let you call her. She won't get mad at you."

"Ha. You're living in a dream world," Tammy says as we stand to clean off the counter.

"Not me." I shake my head and wipe the dishcloth across the shiny surface. I think of Jenn hating me. Of Jack leaving me. No dream world for me anymore. Just painful reality.

~

Just as I open my eyes to greet the day, the doorbell rings. The dogs bound down the hall barking, and I grab a robe and chase after them. "You're going to wake the whole house up," I hiss, but they just bark louder.

I squint at the kitchen clock on my way through. "Seven o'clock? Who comes to the door at seven o'clock on Saturday morning? It's too early for visitors." Especially since Tammy and I sat up and talked until the wee hours.

I peek out the curtain and yank the door open. "Daddy? What's wrong?"

He ducks his head and runs his hand up the back of his neck. "We've got a problem."

I step back. "Come in and tell me."

He walks into the foyer and shifts from foot to foot.

"You're making me nervous. What's wrong?"

"Daddy!" Tammy comes around the corner, wrapped in a white terrycloth robe, and throws her arms around his neck. "It's so good to see you!"

He pulls her into a tight hug. "I see you brought my grand-boy with you."

"We don't know that it's a boy." She pushes back to look at him. "What are you doing here so early?"

"You got any coffee?" he asks me.

Tammy and I exchange a quizzical look, and I motion them to follow me into the kitchen.

They sit at the bar while I fumble with the filters. "Quit stalling, Daddy."

"I was asleep in my chair when your mama got home from her meeting last night. So I just stumbled on to bed and never mentioned you coming out." He runs his hand along the wooden trim on the edge of the bar. "But this morning, when she was fixing coffee, I told her about it."

"And?" My heart is doing flip-flops. Was he wrong? Was she happier not having me in their lives?

"She's madder than a wet hen."

"That you and me made up?"

He frowns. "That she wasn't there. That you didn't come see her. I tried to tell her that you didn't realize I was going to be there by myself, but she's convinced that you blame her for what happened all those years ago, so you only wanted to reconcile with me."

"Did you tell her that's not true?"

"While I was trying to explain, I mentioned that Tammy and Russ are here. Oh boy." He shakes his head. "She blew a gasket. Said neither of our girls care about her. That no one even knows she's alive. She started crying."

"What did you do?" Tammy says softly, her eyes wide.

"I told her not to be silly and to give me some coffee." He flinches at the memory. "She dumped the coffee in the sink and poured the whole bag of ground coffee in the trash and on the floor so I couldn't fix anymore."

A laugh pushes out of me involuntarily as I envision the scene. I put my hand over my mouth. "I'm sorry. I know it's not funny."

"What are we going to do?" Tammy asks.

"First thing we're going to do," Daddy says decisively, "is have some coffee."

I jump up and pour us all cups. "Tammy and I will go out to the ranch and talk to Mama." I look over at Daddy. "You stay here and keep Russ company. Talk to Jenn about the rodeo tonight and try to distract her from hating me."

"You want me to just sit here this morning?" He looks around my house in dismay. I think he's only been inside it once or twice. To my dad, living in town is about as bad as it gets. "In the house?"

"A limb fell on the back corner of my privacy fence last storm we had. I haven't had time to get it off and fix the fence."

His eyes light up and he rubs his hands together. "I'll rustle us up some breakfast; then we'll take care of that for you. You girls run along."

"We have to get showers first," Tammy squeaks, looking down at her robe.

"Oh yeah. Well hurry. I've never seen your mama in such a state."

Ever obedient, less than an hour later, we're pulling into our parents' driveway. I look over at Tammy. "We're not going to mention seeing Daddy, right?"

"Right."

We ring the doorbell and wait. And wait. Finally, Tammy twists the knob. "Hello the house."

"Hello the house?" I make a face at her.

"That's what they say in movies." She whispers.

"What movies do you watch?"

"Never mind. Mama!"

No answer. We split up and go through the whole house then meet back in the kitchen. My nerves are taut.

Tammy holds her hands like Vanna White revealing a vowel. "She's not here."

"Nothing like stating the obvious," I snap. "I'm sorry." Looking at the coffee grounds splashed everywhere, the scene doesn't seem as funny as it did when Daddy was telling it. "I'm just worried."

"I know." She motions toward the door that leads from the kitchen outside. "Do you think she's out at the barn?"

"Maybe. I would be." I hurry to the door, and we practically run down the path to the barn. Halfway down I remember that Tammy is pregnant. I screech to a stop. "You don't need to be running."

"I'm not running. Walking is good for me. Come on." She grabs my shirt and tugs me toward the barn.

I look at Tammy. "Are you going to 'hello' the barn?"

She hits me on the shoulder. "Mama?" she calls.

I glance over at the stalls. "Lady's gone."

"Mama's horse."

I nod. "We should be thankful she's not on a bull, I guess. The women in our family are a little unpredictable."

"I noticed." Tammy looks over at me. "You'll have to go after her. I can walk, but I can't ride a horse. Not when I'm not used to it."

I hurry to the tack room to grab Sweetie's saddle when I hear voices outside in the barn.

"Everything happened so suddenly," Tammy is saying.

Mama brushes past me with her saddle in her hand. She tosses it in the tack room with barely a backward glance.

Whoa. I'm guessing her ride didn't work off the anger.

"I didn't expect your sister to tell me"—she shoots me a glare—"but nowhere during that eight-hour drive did you have time to call your mother and say, 'We're coming home for a visit'?"

Tammy steps toward her. "I was just so busy thinking and praying about Jenn."

Mama's face softens. "How is Jenn?"

"She's doing better," Tammy says. "It was a shock, but she'll be okay."

"That's good."

Tammy touches Mama on the shoulder. "I'm really sorry for not calling you."

Mama stares at her for a minute; then her eyes fall to Tammy's abdomen, and her eyes grow moist. "That's okay. How are you?"

"The doctor says everything is fine." She throws her arms around Mama's neck just like she did Daddy's earlier. And is pulled into a warm embrace.

I'm still standing in the tack room door like Ebenezer Scrooge watching a happy family celebration through the Cratchits' window. *Except that he was with the Ghost of Christmas Present and I'm with the Ghost of Christmas Past,* I think inanely.

When Tammy and Mama finally break apart, I step forward. Are those chains I hear rattling? "Mama, I'm sorry."

She spins around and looks at me as if she's already forgotten I'm here, and my heart physically hurts.

"Rachel."

Tammy gives me a "Hang in there" look and says, "I'm going to go up to the house and. . ." Her eyes narrow as she obviously tries to think of an excuse to leave us. "And. . .let y'all talk."

Before either of us can protest, she spins around and rushes out the barn door.

Mama and I look at each other, and she grabs a brush and heads outside. I snag the other brush and a curry comb and follow her out to where Lady is tied.

I walk to the opposite side of the Palomino mare and start brushing her. "She's really lathered up. I guess you rode hard."

"Humph." She keeps brushing in long, even strokes.

"I thought you'd both be home last night. I came to see you both."

She gives me the look she used to give me when I'd taken a cookie without asking. "You didn't know it was my scrappin' night?"

"I forgot."

"And it would have killed you to stay a few minutes later and wait for me?"

"No. I. . ." I rest my forehead against a dry spot on Lady's shoulder. "I should have."

"Humph." Brush, brush, brush.

I take a couple of steps around the front of the horse, brushing around her face so I can see Mama. "I'm here now."

She scoots toward Lady's flank, refusing to look at me. "We both know why you waited until I was gone. You've blamed me all these years."

"Blamed you? If anything I blamed Daddy. He's the one who made me pack my stuff and carted me off to Georgia without even letting me tell you bye."

"You know what I mean. Blamed me for you getting pregnant to begin with. And we both know it *was* my fault."

I frown and let the brush fall down by my side. "What in the world are you talking about? How could it be your fault?"

"I was gone off to take care of Tammy." She glances up toward the house. "She was a grown woman, I know, but losing that baby almost killed her."

"You can't watch a kid every second, Mama. I was responsible for my own actions that night."

She shakes her head, and I get a brief glimpse of her eyes, filled with tears. "You were always responsible. Almost too responsible. Tammy needed me. But you never seemed to. So

I didn't think about you getting into trouble. When I think about you having to go through that. . ."

"I didn't *have* to go through it." Has she thought all these years that Brett forced me? "I made a terrible choice, but it was my choice."

She draws in a breath through her nose and looks toward the sky. "I'm not talking about that night. I mean after. You kept that secret all by yourself then went off and never came back. And you just a baby yourself. I knew I was to blame, but there was no way of undoing it."

I reach over and take the brush from her hand. "Let's sit for a minute and talk."

"No." Her breath is coming in gasping sobs. "I don't want your pity."

"My pity?" How could two grown women be on such totally different wavelengths? "Come sit down." I check to be sure Lady is secure then pull Mama over to the wooden swing right outside the barn.

She sits but still won't look at me. "I'm not sure this is ever going to work—you and me."

Defeat seeps into my heart. If my own mother can say that, maybe she's right.

"Too much water under the bridge," she mutters.

Bridge. The word slaps me in the face. "That's not acceptable."

"What?" She looks at me. Finally. Even though she's looking at me as if I'm crazy.

"That's not acceptable. For it not to work out for you and me."

She chuckles, sort of a sick frog chuckle, but a chuckle nonetheless. "Not acceptable?"

"You're my mother. We're family. And I love you. Do you love me?"

Her eyes fill with deep horror. "How can you ask me that? I love you more than life itself."

I think of yesterday when I used those same words to Jenn. And how much I meant them. "You do?" My voice squeaks.

"Of course I do."

Wow. I never knew.

"Let's take this in small steps, Mama. We can make this bridge strong."

"What bridge?"

I reach over and take her hand. She lets me.

"Never mind. Just trust me. We love each other, so we've got a foundation. The rest of it we can build as we go along."

"Okay."

"We've had so many misunderstandings. Maybe if we just ask each other a question now and then. . ." I just don't know how much more drama I can take all at once.

"Did you set out to just sleep with a boy because you were mad at me for being gone on your birthday?"

Okay, that's a question. Not the one I was expecting, but a question. She starts to pull her hand from mine.

I hold on. "No! I had a huge crush on Brett all summer. All the girls did. Whenever he walked by, they'd bump against each other and giggle to get his attention, but I just stood by the gate or made a point to go up to the concession stand when he was up there getting something. One night I even bought a soda and got up the nerve to offer it to him. He tossed me the bandanna he had in his hand and took the drink but didn't even glance at me."

"That's that old blue handkerchief in your box of trophies?"

I nod. "But he never really noticed me at all until that night of my birthday. Then he turned his blinding smile on me, and I finally had him all to myself. The next thing I knew, I was in the dressing room of his horse trailer. And by the time I realized it wasn't what I wanted, it was too late."

She covers her face and starts to cry again.

I put my arm around her. "I'm sorry, Mama. I'm sorry I did it. And I'm sorry we lost all these years."

She nods. "I should have been here."

"Even if you had been, it probably still would have happened."

"I'm thankful for Jenn—don't get me wrong. But in all the years since, it's ended up feeling like we traded our baby girl for a granddaughter."

"You didn't, Mama." I reach over and hug her lightly then stand. "Let's get poor Lady finished and go up to the house. Our family has a rodeo to go to tonight."

"Are you riding?"

"No, I didn't register." I might still could, but after all these years, I think I'm chicken. "It'll be up to Jenn to uphold our barrel-racing reputation tonight."

We walk slowly up to the house. Tammy is waiting in the door. She reaches toward us, and the three of us hug briefly. Mama quickly pulls away and hurries into the kitchen. We've come a long way, but there are still links to add to our bridge. As Lark's granny used to say, "Shady Grove wasn't built in a day."

My phone rings. I glance down at it. Lark. I haven't talked to her since Jack made his comment to Jenn yesterday at my house. I should have checked on her. "Tammy, I have to take this call."

"That's fine. I'll go help Mama. . .do whatever she's doing." She smiles and steps inside.

I sit down on the white chair on the tiny back porch. "Hello?"

"Rachel? Rachel?"

I hold the phone away from my ear a little. "Lark, you don't have to yell. I can hear you. What's wrong?"

She laughs. Or cries. I'm not sure. But I think laughs. I hope laughs. "Nothing's wrong." I hear a deep voice rumbling in the background. "Oh yeah. Craig says to tell you we won't be able to come to the rodeo tonight."

"You're kidding! Why not?"

"We're out of town."

"Out of town?"

"Well, on our way out of town. The children's home representative called us this morning."

"They want to meet with you again?"

"Sort of. They want us to come get our baby."

"What?" I thought I was all out of tears, but I'm apparently a tear machine, because they're pouring down my face. "Lark, I don't believe it."

"I don't believe it, either. It's a girl! She's a girl." She's laughing and crying at the same time. "What an idiot I am. I knew we were on the list. But I rushed ahead."

"You're not the first person to do that, honey. Look at Sarah in the Old Testament."

"Oh yeah, and look how that turned out."

"Well, thankfully you didn't end up in that mess. So, can you tell me about the baby?"

"She's fourteen days old. They have a policy that you can't get them before then. And the lady called and asked if we wanted to pick her up Monday, but we talked her into letting us come today."

"I don't blame you."

Craig's voice rumbles again. "Oh yeah. I'll call you later and tell you her name. We haven't decided yet."

"Name her after me."

She laughs. "I just got off the phone with Vic and then Allie, and they both said the same thing."

"Looks like you've got your work cut out for you figuring that one out."

"We have a two-hour trip to discuss it."

"Lark, I'm so happy for you."

"Your happy ending will come, Rach."

I laugh. "You and Allie! Y'all don't have to say that. I'm happy with my life." Or I was until it blew up in my face twenty-four hours ago. But making up with Daddy and Mama was almost worth it. Almost.

"Um-hum. Whatever you say."

"I love you guys!"

"We love you, too, honey. I'll call you tonight when we get home with her. Y'all pray for us."

"Definitely."

I flip the phone closed and bow my head. Some prayers can't wait. Just as I say, "Amen," Tammy pecks on the glass.

"You okay?" she mouths.

I nod.

I am.

Or at least I will be.

~

When we get home, Daddy and Russ show us the new fence they built. While Tammy is still out admiring it, I walk into the kitchen and come face-to-face with Jenn for the first time since Jack brought us home from the ranch yesterday.

She looks at me, and I see something in her eyes that startles me. Something that's not hate. It might not be love, but it's at least. . .curiosity.

"Jenn?"

"This is kind of weird, isn't it?"

I nod. "Kind of. Do you want to talk about it?"

"After the rodeo's over, okay?"

I sink onto a bar stool and try to look casual instead of letting her see that my legs are weak with relief. "Sounds good."

~

"Daddy's bringing Sweetie, so all we have to do is show up, right?" Tammy follows me out to the car.

"Right. Actually, I'll be back before it's time to go. I'm just running out to the arena to take care of something."

"Rodeo business?" She reaches up to adjust the collar of my bright green Western shirt.

"No. Knowing Jack, he'll have that all under control. I've got some personal business to take care of." I wink at her. "Mister-Cowboy-in-Control is in for a surprise tonight."

She laughs. "It's good to have my little sister back in the game."

I give her a quick hug. "Say a prayer for me."

"You got it."

When I get to the Shady Grove Rodeo Arena, I pop my CD out of the car player and slide it into a plastic case.

Stock trailers are everywhere, but only a few early birds are milling around the arena. I know one bird who's always early—so keeping an eye out for Jack, I walk around to the announcer's stand. So far, so good. I slip up the stairs and tap on the door.

"Come in if your nose is clean," a voice yells.

I push the door open. "There isn't going to be an inspection, is there?"

Slim Bewell swivels around and lays his half-eaten sandwich on the table. "Rachel Donovan, as I live and breathe." He jumps to his feet, amazingly agile in spite of his three hundred–plus pounds. "You're a sight for sore eyes."

I shake his hand. "Good to see you, too, Slim."

He steps back and looks at me over his bulbous nose. "Not that I'm complainin', but what are you doing here so early? Committee business?"

"I need a favor."

"Anything for you, doll. Name it."

I hold up my CD. "I need you to play a song dedication for me during the rodeo."

"Oh. Can't do that." He shakes his head, his puffy, purple-veined cheeks jiggling. "Shoot me another one, honey."

"Are you kidding?"

"No, I'm sure not kidding."

I put my hands on my hips. "You can't play a song for someone?"

He puts his huge fists on his own ample hips. "Only way you get to pick a song is if you're ridin' in one of the events." He fixes his rheumy gaze on me. "You ridin' in an event?"

I force myself not to back down from his stare. Considering that the old rodeo announcer has tried to talk me into entering the barrel-racing event every year since I moved back to Shady Grove, I have a right to be suspicious.

"You ridin' in an event?" he repeats.

If I don't, my grand plan is shot. If I do. . .actually, if I do, it might be fun. Deep down, I've always known that I quit barrel racing as punishment for what I did with Brett. But how long do I have to pay for one sin? A sin I've already been forgiven of? "Is it too late to register?"

Slim's gap-toothed smile lights up his face. "Nope."

I make a split-second decision. "Then sign me up for the senior barrel racing." I slide my CD across the table and explain to him exactly what I want to do.

Chapter 36

"I'm more nervous than I used to be when I was in the Miss Shady Grove Rodeo contest." Tammy puts her hand to the bump that is my future niece or nephew. "I think the baby is playing with butterflies."

I hate to say it, but I'm nervous, too. For Jenn. And for me. And I don't mean the barrel racing, as far as I'm concerned. I have way more riding on tonight than a trophy.

Although a trophy would be nice.

Seeing Jack would be even nicer, but so far he's eluded me. Not on purpose, I hope. But I have to face the fact that it's a real possibility.

Russ, sitting on the other side of Tammy on the arena bleachers, pats her stomach, something that I've always seen dads do, but it's a little disconcerting anyway. "Maybe you should consider swallowing a net. He'd probably be able to catch them all."

She hits him. "*She's* not going to be a professional ball player, so give it up."

He holds his hands out, palms up, and gives me a wide-eyed look. "Who said anything about ball? We were talking about butterflies. Right, Rachel?"

I grin. "Leave me out of this."

"Is this a private party, or can anyone join?" Daddy says as he walks up the bleacher seats arm in arm with Mama. I'm glad to see they called a truce in the coffee war. To my surprise, I'm glad to see them. Period.

Mama hugs Tammy, and then with almost no hesitation, she pulls me into a hug. Daddy follows suit. I return their embraces warmly and send up another prayer of thanksgiving. Whatever happens tonight, I'm grateful for the fences that God has helped me to mend.

Victoria, Adam, Daniel, Allie, and Dylan and the girls walk up while we're watching the goat tying. I'm grateful for the distraction.

"We're not too late, are we?" Victoria asks. She rolls her eyes at Adam. "Somebody was in the middle of a tense video game and we had to wait."

He grins. "You didn't have to wait, Vicky. You could have called Daddy's limo driver and had him pick you up."

They tromp up the bleachers. Allie and Vic sit right behind me.

"Isn't it exciting about Lark?" Allie whispers where only the three of us can hear.

I nod. "I'm just thankful she never took her name off the adoption agency list. God had a plan all along."

"That seems to be the Pinky theme." Allie looks over at Vic. "For all of us."

Slim's voice rings out over the loudspeaker. "That's the end of the goat tying, ladies and gents. Let's give all our contestants a big hand."

I clap along with everyone else, even though I did keep thinking "poor little fella" every time a goat would play dead.

"Coming up next is our junior barrel-racing event."

Tammy grabs my hand and squeezes.

I lean over toward her. "She's going to do great. You'll be amazed at how good she is."

"It's in her genes." She laughs. I search her face for one bit of uneasiness and can't find it.

I feel a hand reach for mine on the other side. I turn my head, and Mama's smiling. "She's had a good teacher, too."

I give her hand a squeeze. "Thanks." Mama and I are a lot alike, and I know we'll still have our clashes, but today that bridge between us is looking like a ten-lane superhighway made from solid steel and concrete, with an amazing support structure underneath. I glance heavenward.

Thank You, Lord. You're an amazing bridge builder.

Finally we relax, as one contestant after another rides. Most have mediocre times, with a few who stand out as extra fast and a couple who knock the barrels down. When the announcer says, "And our last contestant is. . .Jennifer Wells riding Sweetie," Daddy and Russ both thrust their fists into the air and whoop.

From down near the arena, someone yells, "Go, Jenn!"

I lean forward and see Dirk standing against the fence, watching intently.

"Is that her cowboy?" Tammy whispers.

I nod.

Jenn gets ready just like we've practiced; then when "Life Is a Highway" blares out of the speakers, she turns Sweetie to face the barrels. Tammy, Mama, and I clasp hands again.

At the signal, she nudges the horse into a run. Together they work as a team, rounding the barrels as fast as they can without knocking one over. When they clear the last one, Jenn leans forward in the saddle, urging Sweetie to give it all she has until they clear the laser time recorder.

"Whoo-hoo!" I stand and yell, raising my hands in the air. I look down the row, and we're all on our feet. Behind me, I hear my friends hollering and clapping.

Down below us, Dirk is yelling and clapping, too.

In seconds, Slim calls out Jennifer's time, and I know she's won.

"Excuse me a minute," I say to the group around me.

I navigate my way down through the crowd to the fence just as Dirk starts to walk up toward the gate.

"Dirk."

He spins around, and his eyes flare. "I'm not—"

"I'm sorry."

He looks puzzled.

"I've treated you terribly. . .all summer really, and I was hoping you might could forgive me."

I see suspicion in his eyes, and when I think of how crazy I acted in the parking lot at the Citizen of the Year banquet, I don't blame him.

I hold my hands up. "No tricks. Just me being really sorry."

"It's okay." He takes a couple of steps backward like a nervous pup. "Forget it."

I smile. "I hope we can forget it someday." But while it's still fresh on our minds. . . "I do expect you to always treat Jenn with the utmost respect, though."

He gulps and nods. "Yes, ma'am."

"You going up to the gate to see her now?"

"Well, I. . .I. . .she. . ." His eyes plead with me to retract the question.

"Give her a hug for me, too. And tell her I said congratulations."

"All right!" He smiles.

I return his smile. "Just so we're straight, that's two hugs."

295

I hold up two fingers. "One from you. And one from me. Then I expect y'all to come right back up here to the stands where we're sitting. Okay?"

"Yes, ma'am." He turns and jogs toward the gate area, apparently eager to go before I change my mind.

While they're preparing for the next event, I glance through the fence across the empty arena. My breath catches in my throat. Jack. And he's staring straight at me.

I raise my hand in a weak wave.

He tips his hat.

And turns and disappears into the crowd.

～

Astride Sweetie, I wait for them to call my name. I can only think of one thing. Jack is out there somewhere. He'll be watching. And listening. Hopefully listening, for sure. And when it's over, he'll have no more doubts about me not wanting people to know my feelings. My gut clenches. All of Shady Grove will know. Blair will probably put it on her show for those few unfortunate souls who chose to do something else tonight.

"Our last contestant has a song request," Slim's voice begins over the loudspeaker. "And I'd say it's a pretty important dedication for a pretty important person. Because I've been trying for years to get this gal back in the rodeo arena." I cringe. I didn't expect him to tell a story. "And when she found out she couldn't request a song without entering, she said, 'Slim, sign me up. And dedicate this song to my rodeo cowboy.'"

Not an exact quote, but close enough. My face burns, but I'm not sorry I did this.

He rustles a paper around loudly. "Hmm...it doesn't say his name. But I'm pretty sure he knows who he is." The audience yells and claps. As the cheering dies down, he chuckles. "And I'm pretty sure you all do, too. So without further ado, I give you our Shady Grove Citizen of the Year competing in the senior barrels—Dr. Rachel Donovan, riding Sweetie."

The Beatles belt out "She Loves You" over the speakers, and everything seems to go into slow motion. I turn around to face the barrels. For a split second my gaze goes to the place I saw Jack earlier.

And there he is.

I squeeze my eyes shut. Got to concentrate on the task at hand. If I make a fool of myself, some dedication this will be.

The signal sounds. The song and the crowd fade to a distant roar as Sweetie and I repeat the routine she did earlier with Jenn. The wind whips my hair, and in seconds, it's all over.

My heart pounds in rhythm with Sweetie's hooves as we trot out of the gate. I slide off and pat her neck. "Good girl. Win or lose, we did a good job."

"You sure did."

I swing around to face Jack. "Thanks."

His brows draw together. " 'She Loves You'?"

I look up into his unreadable face and give a shaky laugh. "Yeah, yeah, yeah."

He pulls me into his arms, and I go willingly. Finally, I'm free. Free to be where I belong.

"I'm sorry," I murmur to his shoulder.

"I know," he whispers.

Slim's voice says, "And the winner is Rachel Donovan. C'mon up and get your trophy, kiddo."

I push back and look at Jack. He has a million things to do tonight. And Slim is going to keep announcing my name until I go pick up my trophy. "Meet me at my dad's barn at midnight, okay?"

He nods. And I jump on Sweetie and go to face the cheering crowd. I couldn't help but notice he didn't say he loved me, too. Was my grandstand show of love too late?

~

When I pull into the barn lot a few minutes before midnight, I see Jack on Lightning, Sweetie saddled beside him.

My feet crunch loudly on the path as I walk to where they are.

"You up for a ride?" he says.

I nod and mount Sweetie without speaking and try to swallow away the lump in my throat.

"Let's go," he says and takes off down the trail.

I follow, my mind whirring. I have so much still to tell him. Is he going to let me explain? Or is he going to tell me that after he found out about Jenn, he's not interested? My heart aches at the thought, and for a second, I want to turn the horse back to the barn.

But I lean forward and gallop to keep up with him. If there's one thing I've learned in the weeks since my past came to live with me, it's that avoiding the truth doesn't make life any easier. I refuse to live with evasions and lies anymore. I have to know the truth.

We come to the break in the trees by the creek bank. "Whoa." He pulls back on Lightning's reins, and I do the same with Sweetie. We both slide to the ground.

I stare at the moonlight dappling the water; then I look up at Jack walking toward me. Whatever happens, I've got to tell him the whole truth about the past. Now. Before I lose my nerve. "Brett Meeks is Jennifer's biological father."

He nods and puts his arms around me. "I know."

"You know?" My voice squeaks. "How?"

"I was there that night. Brett wasn't only a jerk, he was a braggart." He pauses. "I shut him up with a black eye and a bloody nose."

I stand there in his arms, listening to the steady beat of his heart against my ear, and try to process what he just said. "You've known all along?" I whisper.

"Not about Jennifer. I never even thought of that. Obviously. But about that night, yeah."

I push away and look into his eyes. "And you still called me the next month and asked me to go to the fair?"

"I was crazy about you. And I knew how Brett was." He runs his hand over his five o'clock shadow. "I was furious with myself for not trying to warn you. But I didn't think you'd believe me."

"I wouldn't have." I reach up and touch his face. "Thank you for knowing what I did and calling me anyway. Why didn't you tell me anything about this these last few months?"

A small grin plays across his lips. "You avoided me ever since I moved back. I figured it was because you thought I knew what happened that night. I wasn't about to jeopardize our newfound relationship by confirming your fears."

I nod. That makes sense.

"And I thought when you were ready, you'd trust me enough to tell me."

"Part of not telling you had nothing to do with you. I couldn't tell you without telling Jenn first, and I was really having a hard time bringing myself to do that. But I was going to tell you the whole truth this weekend. I called and asked Tammy and Russ to come so I could tell Jenn then tell you." I grimace. "But the timing went a little haywire."

"That's good to know." He pulls me to him again, and my heart pounds. "Rachel, it's my turn to tell you something."

Oh no. "What?" I'm barely breathing. He's married? He has four kids? He's an escaped convict? How many more revelations can we stand?

"I love you."

Oh. That one wasn't hard to take at all. "I love you, too."

"I'm going to kiss you, if that's okay."

I laugh. "That's more than okay."

And it is.

Epilogue

I told you that God had a happy ending for you, too." Allie zips up my dress.

"I know. It's hard to believe." I look around the room at the hustle and bustle.

Mama Ruth bursts in the door of the church nursery. "Is everyone almost ready?" She deftly snatches baby Valerie up just as the little girl reaches for her mama's bouquet.

"Sorry," Lark says and holds out her hands. "Come to Mommy, honey. You'll have your own flowers in a minute."

The one-year-old leaps into her mother's arms with a cry of delight, and Lark kisses her pudgy cheek. I remember how we laughed when we found out that Lark had taken the first letters of each of our names and come up with a name she and Craig both loved for their little girl.

Jennifer runs over to me and twirls around. "Aunt Rachel! How do I look?"

Tears threaten my makeup. Happy tears. "Honey, you'll turn that cowboy's head so fast, it'll spin."

"Yeah, right. He may have forgotten me. I haven't seen him since Christmas."

Tammy looks up from the corner where she's feeding little Russ Jr. once more before handing him over to his daddy for the ceremony. "And you haven't exactly sat at home pining after him either."

"Good for you, Jennifer." My mom gives Jenn a thumbs-up as she covers her face with her other hand while Mama Ruth sprays her hair. "You need to keep your options open."

Mama Ruth sets down the hairspray and claps her hands. "Five minutes, ladies. Do what you need to do, and let's get this show on the road."

She looks at Victoria who is clutching her bouquet. "You need to be taking notes, honey. I have a feeling you're next."

Victoria's mouth drops open, and the color of her face just about matches the red roses in her hands.

"I do declare, shugah. I don't think I've ever seen you speechless before," Lark says.

Victoria blushes. "Some things are just too ridiculous to consider."

Mama Ruth looks at the rest of us and clucks her tongue. "Denial is normal at first."

I burst out laughing along with the others. "Better be careful, Vic. I'm living proof she's never wrong."

My mother walks over and bends down to give me a hug and kiss. "We're living proof that anything's possible, too, aren't we, honey?"

I nod and hold on to her for a minute.

"I'm so proud of you," she whispers and drops an envelope in my lap. "See you soon." She hurries from the room.

I stare at the envelope. She's proud. Of me. God is so good.

Curious, I open the envelope and pull out a note.

To our dear daughter, on your wedding day,
Our gift to you—a deed in your name for the creek-
front property that joins your husband's land. May you
live your dream of having a natural health clinic. We love
you, honey.

Daddy and Mama

Tears prick my eyes. I'm thrilled to have the land, of course, but the best gift they've given me is the chance to live my dream of having parents who love me and are proud of me.

A few minutes later as I watch the last bridesmaid walk down the aisle, I hook my arm in Daddy's. "Mama gave me the envelope. Thanks."

He nods, his eyes moist. "Ready to do this, baby girl?" His voice is husky.

"I can't wait."

The opening strains of "The Wedding March" play, and Daddy guides me through the doorway. I look down the aisle.

And there's Jack, his eyes shining with love and expectation.

My beloved cowboy. And the beginning of my own happy ending.

Dear Reader,

On rare occasions I will write a book that surprises me. When I was working on *Along Came a Cowboy*, I kept hitting roadblocks. After months of unexplained struggling with a story that I loved, I finally saw that my own adolescent mistakes, though totally different from Rachel's, were staring me in the face. My unwillingness to let them go was stopping me from exploring Rachel's hurt and regret to the depth it needed exploring. After all these years of knowing about God's forgiveness—and certainly understanding it on an intellectual level—I hadn't truly grasped it. The scene in the barn when Rachel comes to an astoundingly simple realization about forgiveness was straight from my heart.

I'll always be thankful that God gave me this particular story to tell and that He allowed me to heal during the writing of it. And I'm also ever grateful that He gave me the opportunity to share it with you.

Blessings,
Christine Lynxwiler